RETURN
TICKET

Jon Doust lives in Menang Boodja, Kincannup, better known as Albany, named by men who hardly knew the place after a man who never saw the place. Jon never thought he would amount to much and finds it hard to believe he is still alive.

Return Ticket is the third book in Jon's trilogy, One Boy's Journey to Man. The first was *Boy on a Wire,* which was longlisted for the Miles Franklin Literary Award, followed by *To the Highlands. Return Ticket* is entirely a work of fiction, and any resemblance to real people living or dead is coincidental.

JON DOUST

RETURN TICKET

FREMANTLE PRESS

JON DOUST

RETURN
TICKET

FREMANTLE PRESS

For Betty, Hannah and Grietje

Kincannup 2018

1

The sink before me was not a trough, or a restaurant pit, it was a standard, domestic double sink. Before I started, I stacked items in their washing order. First the dinner plates, then the side plates on top. In a separate stack, dessert bowls, salad bowls and cups and glasses. All the cutlery I placed in a saucepan. Once the water was hot and soapy, I dropped in the cutlery made of fine steel, a set left to us by a Dutch friend. She died of a vigorous and nasty cancer and my wife lay beside her and wrapped her in love to keep her warm as she died. You can't wash those items and not remember. The silverware my mother bought to celebrate her marriage to a man who saved her sanity and her life, and who gave her all the things denied her in her own family. The plates given to us by my father: I never thought you two would last, to be honest, he said, as he handed my wife the box of fine china.

It wasn't you we were worried about, my dear, he told her, it was him. Until you came along, Jack was a hopeless case.

I left the cutlery to soak and only washed items with a soft cloth. The silver came to us with scratches and I decided they would be the last. The fine steel came unscratched because our Dutch friend was a meticulous woman who cared for all things.

When my mother died, she left us her silverware and I particularly enjoy caring for those shining items. She had clearly used harsh scrubbers, but in my house they are banned.

Back in the early 1970s, in Eliat, an Israeli city on the Red Sea, just around the bay from Jordan's Aqaba, I washed pans, trays and tabletops for an Israeli baker. He was a harsh and insulting man and never missed an opportunity to shout at me and the Bedouin labour force.

Fuck, man, he'd yell. I want bread pans. Why the fuck you don't finish?

Ken. Ani nudnik. Slicha.

My Hebrew was not fluent but I learnt enough to get by and I needed this phrase to cope with the schmuck. Loosely translated it meant: Yes. I am stupid. Excuse me.

The Bedouins laughed. The baker never did. And this fascinated me, because it had come to me that hardcore Israelis did not have a Jewish sense of humour, that willingness displayed by Woody Allen, Lenny Bruce, George Burns, to laugh at themselves, to laugh in the face of an institution, a cruel system, anything or anyone tormenting them.

The Bedouins did all the heavy lifting, and I washed, swept and wiped. We started work at eleven o'clock at night and finished around eight in the morning. The Bedouins shared their food, smiles and hot, sweet tea. There are times when, crouched over a steaming sink, I think of them, remember their hospitality, their goodwill and generosity, and I wonder why I never met them on a kibbutz, even as visitors. It seemed to me there was something about their spirit that was not unlike that of the kibbutznik. The Bedouins were Muslims, of course, and the kibbutzniks, although predominantly Jewish, were not religious, but secular, and welcoming.

I am never reckless with dishes. I am careful, cautious, considerate, and I enter a kind of trance. When I am there, over the sink, with my naked hands in the steamy water, each item is precious. It is not simply a fork, knife, plate or spoon. It is much more, each item the keeper of memories. If not cleaned with respect and care, the memories remain trapped, not released. I'm like that with places too, they all hold memories, histories, a collective memory and whenever I go anywhere, I want to know the past of the place, how it got to be what it is. It was one of the few interests I had in common with my father, a love of history. It was the only subject I passed in my final year of high school, and although he was disappointed the other five didn't make it, I knew if he had chosen one for me to pass, it would have been history.

I hear no-one else in the room. There are no sounds, no music, just the swish of the dish and the plop of the crock in the rinsing sink. Some days, I am back on Kibbutz Gavrot, wearing nothing but Speedos, rubber gloves and a rubber apron. As the dishes arrive over the kitchen counter, I pull them into the huge tubs and nothing escapes my vigour. If on a night my co-worker volunteer didn't arrive, then I took every one of the four hundred and fifty plates and knives and forks and spoons and not one was returned by the stacker behind me. Cleaner than whistles. One night, about halfway through, I looked up to see a small crowd gathered in awe of my speed, my dexterity, my love. Yes, love. Because even as a boy, when my father put our names on the kitchen noticeboard letting us know who washed, who dried, and who brought in the firewood, even then I loved and craved the steamy hot water and the rhythm of the wash. One night I was desperate to wash and my older brother was listed but I kicked up such a fuss they led me to the sink, splashed rinsing water on my face and left me alone until the tears dried and the dish rack was full.

Before items go in the drying rack, I hold them fast and drop them faster to release excess water. Perhaps I wash the dishes the way I do because it suggests a way I might have lived – ordered, structured, careful and meditative. As I have aged I've realised my life has been bereft of rituals and so this caressing of dish and plate and knife, spoon and fork, has become one.

2

Almost fifty years ago, I climbed on board the *Fairstar*, in Fremantle. The Jack Muir of 1972 had only recently left a family business and a secure future. There was something brewing in him then and some of it still brews today, and still much of that earlier version remains a mystery and I often think of him in the third person, someone I once knew, almost knew, knew well enough to challenge, to question.

Young Jack broke from his family, told them to leave him alone, not to try and contact him, that he might be gone years.

Not to worry, he said, it's not about you, it's me.

But it was, he thought, about them, and their culture, their town, their lack, its lack. It seemed to him that everyone he knew was unfinished, incomplete, and he wanted completion. He had begun to turn away from everything he had ever learnt, everyone he knew, or had ever known.

There's something going on out there, he said, and I have to find out about it and work out how I fit in.

Looking back through his journals, I read the writing of an arrogant, self-absorbed young man, very much of his time. He was also adventurous and random, and this makes him interesting, worthy of my attention and, of course, whoever he was, he was someone who had a dramatic impact on my life.

The first port of call for that ship was Durban, South Africa, ten days away from Fremantle. My immediate intentions were unclear to me, but although my ticket destination was Southampton, England, I never made it.

South Africa 1972

Durban

All Muir's new friends onboard the *Fairstar* were getting off in Durban, some to stay, some to catch a bus to Cape Town where they would rejoin the ship.

You'll dig Durban, said Dave, the South African hippie surfer. We grow the best marijuana in the world – Durban Poison.

They were huddled under a lifeboat on the upper deck, sucking and passing, sucking and passing. It was Jack's first suck and pass, and a long way from his last. It was the beginning of an odd journey, given he had only recently become a vegan and had sworn off casual sex and alcohol.

I never smoked before I got on this ship, said Muir.

Shit, man. This stuff we're smoking now, it's shit. Wait till you get your lips around Durban *dagga*.

Muir had two official cabin mates – one a South African homosexual, the other a drunk Queenslander who they had to put to bed more than once – and one unofficial, a stowaway they kept alive with food smuggled out of the dining room.

Durban is an ugly town, said Peter, Jack's cabin mate. It's not fun being a homo in South Africa. I'm not sure why I'm going home.

Muir stood on deck as the tugboat led the ship through the entrance to its berth. He was excited, wide-eyed and intrigued by the movement on the waterfront – black men everywhere, walking, carrying, loading, unloading. It was his first disembark, following his first embark in Fremantle. He was not sure he would do it again.

Onshore, the world turned hot, humid and nasty, and as Muir walked away from the port terminal he watched Peter yelling at a black man in a language he had never heard before.

The further Muir walked into the city, the nastier it seemed, from the signs designating seating permissions by colour, to the permanent snarls on the faces of authority, and the smells that dominated. Durban carried a stench of decay, of rotting matter, nothing like the sweet wafts from the Genoralup bush, full of eucalyptus, hakea, sheoak and banksia. It reminded him of the dead animals he happened on occasionally at home. When he opened the apartment window on his first morning, the stench rolled in and drove him out. Outside, his nose got used to it, but the street filth clung to his skin and as he walked the city streets it seeped into the soles of his feet and entered the pores of soft flesh around his nose and cheeks.

The ocean saved him.

Early every morning, he ran from the apartment to surf and look out across the Indian Ocean to where he thought Perth might be, to wonder why he left one place he didn't like for another he liked even less.

Berea

On the ship, Muir had met a drug dealer called Parsons. He seemed a reasonable sort of chap and so they hung out together, even shared their Durban apartment with two hippies. Following a street-side incident, and the slow-dawning realisation that the hippies were unable to wash dishes, sweep floors, or speak plain English, Parsons and Muir decided to leave them to the flat and rent a room in a house once owned by an Indian, up high in Berea, a leafy suburb out of Durban. The Indian had been an important businessman and, at that time, Indian businesspeople and their families dominated the street. They were driven out when the ruling skin colour wanted the view back over Durban. The new owner of the house was a German with a strong accent and several unhealthy relationships – with alcohol, his Alsatians and his girlfriend. They didn't know any of this, of course, when Parsons made the deal with the German over the phone.

He sounded Portuguese, said Parsons.

What did he say his name was? asked Jack.

Sounded like Storm Tartan.

Every day Muir would rise early, feed the dogs, wash the dishes from the night before, eat a bowl of muesli, hitchhike into Durban, swim at the main beach, bodysurf, buy a hot Horlicks and hitchhike back to Berea. Most lifts were with English-speaking South Africans, an occasional Afrikaner and a few Indians. Muir had known that people were separated by colour in South Africa but, having once lived in Papua New

Guinea as a colourblind innocent, he found the rules confusing and in his first week was asked to move on by a fat policeman.

I'm sorry? he said. You want me to what?

To move away, said the fat policeman.

But I'm having a chat with this man. If I move away, I won't be able to hear what he says.

The young Zulu was unable to suppress a smile and the fat policeman unable to suppress his rising anger. The three of them stood in the centre of Durban, on the edge of the pavement, not far from the rickshaw stand with its wild and extroverted drivers. Muir thought about calling them to join in the discussion, wondering how the policeman would deal with an impi of Zulus yelling in his face.

In South Africa, said the fat cop, the only time white people talk to black people in the street is to tell them to do something and, if you refuse to move, I will have to take action against your person.

Against my person? Which person is that?

The Zulu laughed so hard he bent over and held his face, but he also knew the danger and had begun walking away from the two men, one fat with a pistol on his hip and one wiry, packing a small pocketknife hidden in a pocket.

All right, said Muir.

He thought about looking back for his new Zulu friend but noticed the fat man following him and decided to hitch back to Berea.

In Berea, he walked into the kitchen and an argument between Sturmgarten, the German, and his girlfriend, who Muir believed was Belgian. He made his way through the dogs and insults to the sink, and set about arranging items to be washed the next day.

Don't you come to me with Hitler, said Sturmgarten, what about King Leopold in the Congo?

The mention of Hitler caught Muir by surprise and he turned to watch the woman. She was slim, dull in the eyes, yet her lips were set and determined. He worried about her safety under the massive frame and lard-laden body of the German.

Leopold was a colonialist, she said, like the English and the Dutch, but he was not a mass exterminator.

Sturmgarten rose from his chair, walked around the kitchen the long way, the other side of the sink, opened the fridge door, took another bottle of lager, turned, clipped the side of his girlfriend's head, then walked all the way back and sat down. She did not flinch.

Are you all right? asked Muir.

No, but he has done this before and I know how to be with him.

Late that night, Muir and Parsons arrived back at the house stoned and drunk, and Sturmgarten pulled a pistol and shot at them. They were attempting to enter the house from the upstairs balcony. This meant climbing a tree and making enough noise to wake the sleeping slug.

A light appeared from an upstairs room as the door to the veranda opened. The German slug stood there, silent. There was a red flash and the *pop pop* of his pistol.

It's us, you *dummkopf*! yelled Parsons.

More shots.

I'm hit! said Parsons.

The shirt on Muir's arm ripped and his flesh stung.

The crazed Nazi was mad, pissed, firing wildly and hitting them, trying to kill them.

Herr Sturmgarten! yelled Muir.

Sturmgarten dropped his arm.

Vot are you going? he asked. Vy you do dis to me?

You have locked us out of the house.

But I don't lock you.

Lucky the bastard can't shoot, said Parsons, he only grazed my leg.

The next day the undercover drug squad detective, who lived in the cottage next door, walked in on them in the back garden. Parsons had taken his first hit from the bong and passed it to Muir. There was movement through the bushes; Muir dropped the bong and forced it into foliage behind him. A man in a white safari suit appeared.

Is that marijuana? he asked.

What is? said Muir.

Don't be sassy with me, my friend, or I will have you arrested and we can lose the key. That thing you put behind the rose bushes, it was a bong. Let me introduce myself. Piet Duplessis from the Durban Drug Squad. If you cooperate, you can stay here, but if you don't, we can try some things they never heard of in Geneva. First, where did you get the drugs?

Duplessis was an ugly man with an ugly mouth and a voice that arrived deep, coarse, with accompanying foul stench. In the Berea tropical garden surrounding the house, the man's breath was an abomination. When he moved closer, Muir and Parsons stepped back.

I'll give you until the end of the week, Duplessis said. If you don't give me names, our next talk will be down in the central station. We don't want this country to become a drug Mecca.

The day after the bong in the garden, Muir and Parsons packed their bags and hitched a lift to Johannesburg.

Johannesburg

He was a hard man, Parsons, a drug dealer and an ex-inmate of Pentridge Prison. It showed on his face, in his walk, his talk, even the way he cleaned his teeth. When he stood at the basin, it was never for long, and always with looks to either side, as though expecting to be attacked from behind. He had good reason. Once, in the middle of a drug deal in outer Sydney, a car drove past, a man leant out and shot Parsons in the hip. He had proof of the shooting – a circular dent in his thigh.

Is that why you limp? Muir asked him.

No, it's because my mother always carried me on that side. Of course it is, you wanker.

Then Parsons had got caught up in a deal between rival dealers and Sydney cops. He was deemed expendable and turned in. Lucky for him, one of his cousins robbed a bank around the same time and handed him enough cash to flee.

Muir had never met such people. He was the product of a nice middle-class family and sent to an expensive private school. Many in his home town had thought he was destined for success, even though a large proportion of the available evidence suggested the opposite. That he had got off the *Fairstar* in South Africa and fallen in with hippies and drug dealers was evidence enough; even so, along the way, he learnt he was a good listener and he wanted to hear Parsons' story. He also needed a friend. Parsons wasn't really a friend, because Muir didn't trust him, he was more an acquaintance, someone he had met on the ship, a man he needed to help pay the rent in their Hillbrow flat – one room with attached kitchen and bathroom. It was on the second floor of a five-storey, run-down building on the slummy side of the suburb. It had electricity, a stove, running water, no furniture, no fridge. They slept in their sleeping bags on the floor and kept the window shut to close out the noise of traffic, angry voices and the heavy smells of a huge city that made Muir think Perth was a village. Up the hill was the hip Hillbrow, full of sleazy apartment blocks, nightclubs, bars, drugs and decay.

Over the road was a shop run by an Indian man and his family. Each day after he woke, with the first rumbles of hunger, Muir walked downstairs to the fruit and vegetable shop, yelled good morning at Suresh, the Indian shopkeeper, and bought mealies, sweet corn. Suresh was a good and fair retailer and Muir continued to treat him with respect and pay whatever he asked because he liked him and secretly hoped he had a sister who would one day appear behind the counter and surprise him with her beauty.

One day in Johannesburg, Parsons came home with a small machine he used to compress marijuana, which he packed into cheap clothing and mailed back to Sydney. Another day he came home with a tiny bag of tiny pills. They took one each and ran up the hill and through the streets of hip Hillbrow until they came to the dead body in the shop alcove. They stopped. Parsons prodded. The body seemed to move and they ran on. Nothing makes sense, thought Muir. Later, Parsons told him they had taken LSD and Muir wondered where the psychedelic colours were, the monsters, the freaking out. There was none of it, just an inability to sleep for the next three days.

Then they met Etienne.

Muir was short of money and when someone stopped him in the street and handed him a flier that offered work as an extra in an Afrikaner movie, he took up the offer, auditioned, was told he would be perfect if he cut off his beard, which he did, and found himself on set at a pretend rugby match. The extra sitting next to him was a large-boned man with woolly hair and a wild beard. On set, Etienne spoke in the language that felt like someone pouring stones in Muir's ears.

Some of my friends are having a bushfire party this weekend, he said. You like to come along?

Bushfire party? said Muir. That doesn't sound good to an Australian.

We light a big fire with roots and branches. We do it in a clear space and then we drink and smoke.

Etienne picked up Muir and Parsons from their flat, drove out of the city, kept on driving, past industrial areas, houses, vacant land, shanty towns, farmland, along a track into the bush and eventually stopped in a clearing with a raging fire at its centre.

We're here, he said. Let's light up.

The fire was huge, fed by roots and logs. People seemed to come out of nowhere, arrange themselves around the fire, light joints and pass them on. Much giggling. Someone arrived with a cake tin, opened the lid, offered, and handed on. When it made its way around the circle to Muir, he peered inside and took what looked like a chocolate biscuit. It was tasty, sweet and he wanted more before he finished. A joint arrived. He sucked, passed. His mood shifted. He felt love. And hate.

He had decided: Parsons was a shit. He had the face, legs, arms and guts of a shit. When they did LSD, Parsons knocked over a beggar and left him lying in the street. Muir picked him up and gave him five rand.

Muir took another biscuit. Smoked another joint.

Top to bottom, Parsons was a drug-dealing shit. The shit arrived on the same ship. Where was he? There, talking to a young woman in hippie clothes. Muir wanted to warn her, say, don't talk to him, he's dangerous, I have been travelling with him for weeks and I know him. When he leaves our flat, guess what,

I can still smell the shit. And another, something else, can't pick it, something from my memory, a smell from the farm shed, where we kept all the poisons.

Parsons had money. No idea where it came from. Yes he did, drug dealing. Trapped with him but didn't have to be. Could be free, away from this place, all Muir had to do was make a call home. No, couldn't, would never call when desperate. The shame of it.

Voices rose in mad rushes inside his head.

Let me set you free, said one.

Who the fuck are you? said another.

Who the fuck are these people?

You're in fucking Africa, where are the black faces?

You left home for this shit? Fuck you.

Muir looked for Parsons and the hippie woman. Gone. Tin arrived. Another biscuit. Drifted, floated, felt sick. Unhappy stomach. Water. Only water. Nothing but water. He knew water. Something about water. The way it fell over the body. Caressed. Cleaned. Soothed the skin.

Someone was talking.

Jack, you okay?

He liked Etienne. A big, brutal, hairy, kind face. Big hands too. Knees, shoulders, feet, all big.

Jack!

You are Afrikaner? Jack asked.

Yes.

Can't believe it.

Why not?

You are not like the others.

What others?

All the other Afrikaners I have met.

The great tragedy of this country, Jack, is that it is based on the myth that something as superficial as skin colour can determine a person's intelligence, their capabilities, their ability

20

to complete a task and to function in a civilised society. Do not fall into the trap of lumping us all together, whatever our skin, our origin, our religion, our language.

Muir had to run then. Something stirring. Ran, vomited, the back arched, the guts screamed, emptied, forehead damp, face dripped sweat. Arched. Vomited. Arched. Vomited.

Then, peace. Muir basked in the aftermath of the violent, cleansing chuck.

Before Muir left Johannesburg, a Zulu man gave him a lift and then invited him to visit his house and family in Soweto. Muir took up the invitation because he liked the man and he had never spoken to a white person who had visited the sprawling suburb. It was always spoken of in a hushed tone, a no-go area for white people. Muir was determined to stamp his foot on the jackboot of apartheid.

Cothoza found him waiting on the pavement outside his apartment. Muir climbed in the front seat where they clasped hands gently. No violent shaking. On the outskirts of Soweto, Cothoza stopped and rigged up a box for Muir to lie under, because Muir had no pass, no right, to enter such a place. Then Cothoza put the box over him and various items on top – cartons of groceries, clothes.

Once on their way, Muir noticed the sounds and smells changing – the sounds mixed, muddled and confusing, and the smell an overpowering, nauseating stench. Pushing their way through the cacophony, voices, hundreds of them, yelling, arguing, mingling with the barks and squeals of dogs and sometimes engine noises, as though people were fixing cars, trucks. Banging, crashing, things being driven into things. Things falling over.

The car slowed, then stopped. Cothoza opened the door and Muir slipped out from under the box. They walked calmly but quickly to his house. Up and down the dirt road, Muir saw a mad throng, a tide of humanity crushed and crushing, in and out, weaving, dodging. Rubbish, animals, balls, vehicles, gangs. He wasn't always sure.

We must move quickly, said Cothoza, there are spies everywhere.

Muir could sense the spies and wondered if he had made a mistake in accepting the invitation, that the spies already knew his name, that he was an associate of drug dealers.

Cothoza's wife, Amhale, met them inside and took Muir's hand in welcome. Her hand was firm and her skin, not rough, but not soft. Muir could see a handsome, strong woman looking right back at him. Their children were polite, tall, muscly and good-looking. The house small, four rooms only, spotless, and Cothoza took him out the back to show him the extension he had built out of corrugated iron – an extra bedroom for the two older boys. Alongside the extension was a garden with vegetables and flowers. And a tree.

Inside the house Amhale had laid out a meal on the table and as he ate, Muir imagined he was in a Genoralup farmhouse, one a long way out of town where the farmers struggled against the odds to make a living but when visitors arrived their table showed the best they had. He ate everything on his plate, even the meat.

On our way out, said Muir, I want to sit in the front.

Please, Jack, said Cothoza, it's too dangerous.

Cothoza, you wanted me to see how your people lived here in Soweto. How can I if I'm hiding under a box?

After they had said goodbye to his family and were facing the car Cothoza said: Okay, Jack, let's see what happens.

He drove through the stench of Soweto, the dust, tin shacks, piles of rubbish. He could feel the nauseating odour penetrating his clothes, the pores of his skin; he noticed his fingers scratching at his arms and then he saw what it was – raw sewerage oozing into the streets, into houses, into nostrils, into guts, heads, a person's sense of self. Endless lines of busted cars and makeshift electricity cabling and shit – all encompassing, all embracing shit. Soweto hid nothing.

Makeshift. Everything. Easy to move on, demolish, destroy, obliterate. Some houses were slabs of cardboard nailed or tied onto lengths of sapling. On one ramshackle tin house someone had written in big letters: BE A VISITOR, NOT A SPY.

As they approached the police station, Cothoza stopped and insisted Muir got back down behind the seat.

Cape Town 1

The young Muir spent a lot of time on the road in South Africa. He would almost settle in a place, then something would go wrong, and he'd run. He was good at running, and hitching. He hitched back and forth between South Africa's three major cities – Johannesburg, Cape Town and Durban – smoking large quantities of Durban Poison in Durban and Johannesburg, and dropping LSD in Johannesburg. Most people who dropped LSD in the 1970s did so in a forest, or a hippie commune, maybe a city full of revolutionary young people – Sydney, San Francisco, New York, Paris. Not Muir, his tab fell down his throat in one of the nastiest cities on the planet.

On his way to Cape Town he accepted a lift out of the Karoo desert with two men in an ancient and battered truck. They were not white men, or black men, somewhere in between, and clearly not happy with their social standing.

It was a shambolic, dishevelled truck that chugged and choked and drove past Muir and stopped one hundred yards down the road. A face appeared from the passenger side and called out to him in Afrikaans. The door opened and Muir ran, eager to leave the desert. He threw his pack in the cabin and climbed up behind it. Inside were two unpleasant-looking brown faces, but he needed a lift, after two nights sleeping out in the cold, under threat from stalking baboons and his throat dry from an impending cold.

Dankie, he said.

Three miles down the highway, the truck stopped. The men ordered him out, took down his backpack from the cabin and emptied it on the side of the road. They took his remaining orange, frisked him roughly, found his wallet, took the twenty rand, went through all his belongings, all he owned, dismantled his life and left it on the ground, laughing, as though it was a meaningless and sad life and not worth their while. They opened everything, except the pouch he wore under his t-shirt, shirt and arm, close to his skin, the one that contained his passport and traveller's cheques.

One of them rushed Muir and slammed his fist into his stomach. He bent towards the dirt, dropped to his knees, thankful for the sit-ups he had been forced to do in school. The man kicked him in the ribs and he fell all the way. As he lay waiting, the man came again with one more kick, in the thigh. Muir could sense he was not done, so when the man came again Muir jumped to his feet and dodged the punch. This surprised the man and he wasn't sure what to do next. The driver got up and walked away, motioning to his companion to follow.

As they climbed into the cabin, Muir picked up all his possessions one by one, checked for breakages, stuffed them in the pack, tied on his coat and sleeping bag and stood, staring at the truck. It didn't move and he was sure he would be safe enough, that they had had enough fun at his expense, that if they had intended killing him, he would be dead. No sign of any traffic, from either direction. He climbed up, sat, and turned to look at the men as the one beside him raised a hand and slapped his cheek. Muir smiled, said *dankie*.

When the truck stopped in the next town, Muir climbed down, took his pack, looked at the men in the cabin, offered one more *dankie*, closed the cabin door carefully and watched as they drove away.

The next lift, four brothers collected him outside of the city, offered him biltong, which he refused, then cheese, which he ate, gave him beer, marijuana and then added to his bruised and battered body by rolling their Ford Fairlane off a major highway, over an embankment and into a tree.

Are you all right? said Tommy, the oldest brother and the driver who had given up his wheel to his younger sibling, who did not have a driver's licence.

I am so sorry, brother, he said, I thought he could drive. Now we must run in case the police come and arrest us all for being coloured. But you will be okay.

Tommy, look at my blood, said Muir. And yours. We are the same colour when we bleed.

How do you know?

Look at your hand, you too are cut.

Tommy looked, laughed, and took Muir in his arms.

You are my brother, brother, he yelled.

Etienne was right, thought Muir, don't judge by the superficial. Two lifts, two sets of so-called coloured people – one set brutal and criminal, the other kind, welcoming and generous.

In Cape Town, he searched for the ship he knew would not be there, stayed in a boarding house until his room was raided, or robbed, then hitchhiked back to Johannesburg to find the apartment he had shared with Parsons in Hillbrow locked, boarded and a crime scene. He fled, of course, back to Cape Town, where he decided he wasn't a vegan, just a vegetarian, and where he found a new boarding house and the courage to change the course of history.

Cape Town 2

What is not widely known, is that this younger Muir, small in stature, wiry and from a south-western Australian village, single-handedly embarrassed the police state of South Africa. His actions may well have been instrumental in its final collapse.

When Muir got off the *Fairstar* in Durban, he was not ready for the sights, sounds, smells, the way people looked at each other, didn't look at each other, segregated themselves from each other.

Five days into his stay, somewhere close to midnight, from the fourth-storey apartment he shared with Parsons and the spoilt lazy hippies, Muir had heard screams, growling dogs and commands yelled in Afrikaans. He ran to the window that opened onto the street below and watched as two Alsatians mauled a man to death while two huge white policemen yelled at him to stop crying, to admit the error of his colour, or to hand over the five rand he stole from the pavement.

When Muir cried out, What the fuck are you doing? his hippie flatmate assured him they were within their rights because the black man was out and about after curfew.

Curfew? asked Muir.

Yes, said the hippie, they must be out of the city by ten.

There were other incidents along the way from Durban to Johannesburg, Johannesburg to Cape Town, and Cape Town all the way back to Durban and Johannesburg, and all of them caused Muir to think the apartheid system was a monstrous and evil imposition and he was determined to destroy it.

The Cape Town General Post Office on Adderley Street was an impressive building, full of colonial power and glory. People rushed in and out as though there was nothing to gawk at. But Muir gawked at the grandeur, the opulence, the wealth, the oppression. Then he made his way inside, clutching the parcels from the wholesale bookseller where he worked. The mother of a young woman he met offered him a coloured man's job while the coloured man was on holiday. Muir gladly accepted, along with the coloured man's rate of pay. The important result of the arrangement was that Muir worked; the money was irrelevant. He needed money, of course, but work in South Africa had been hard to come by because Muir did not have a trade. Most people who disembarked in Durban had trades and were quickly employed. Many of them seemed to fit easily into the South African way, the white way. Muir had lived in Papua New Guinea and was used to mixing, but in South Africa, Muir discovered that separation was not a simple matter of black from white. In the Afrikaner community, there were those descended from Dutch migrants – lower class – and those from French – upper class. There were other white groups too: English, German, Portuguese. There was also a Jewish community, mostly from Lithuania, and several of the younger Jews had lived and worked on kibbutzim, farms run on socialist ideals, in Israel. Jack listened to all their stories.

It was very complicated, but once inside the post office, Muir was aiming for simplicity – he had parcels, the parcels had to be posted.

There were many queues, some pure white, others almost black and others, shades of white, brown and black. Muir chose a queue laden with parcels. It seemed the most practical, given he carried parcels he could vouch for, since he had prepared them himself. This caused much consternation among the postal workers, they yelled at him, waving their arms. Muir smiled and returned their waves. In his queue, men laughed and pointed and jabbered.

An official-looking man appeared from behind the counter and approached.

Excuse me, sir, he said, but you are in the wrong queue.

No, said Muir.

But this is the non-white queue.

This is the parcel queue and as you can see I am carrying parcels, so this is the right queue.

The man was dumbfounded.

Ja, ja, of course, but even so, you can post parcels from the whites-only line.

I recognise no colour, said Muir, only shapes. These items I carry are shaped like parcels and this is the queue for items of that shape.

Muir stood his ground. It was a great day, the day a man stood up against apartheid and the bureaucratic machinery of the state. People of all shades shook his hand. The post office buzzed, and as he moved up the line he imagined a story being told for generations to come, the story of the white man in the non-white parcel queue, the white man who broke the back of apartheid. And as he moved up the line, he could see a great future in the new world of peace, love, kindness and equality, and he became a legend and those who were there that day told their children, who told their grandchildren, and when the system collapsed, the new city fathers and mothers, made up of all races, creeds and body types, decided that it all began back on that day a strange, long-haired, pink-coloured, white boy made a stand in the Cape Town General Post Office, and they arranged for his statue to be erected on the pavement at the front of the building, but because there was no record of him, no photograph and they had no idea where he came from or what he looked like, they erected a likeness gleaned from the memories of those who were there – a tall, handsome, blond man with straight, wide shoulders, who looked surprisingly like Clint Eastwood.

Camps Bay

He met Shoshanna, a Jewish Buddhist socialist, outside his Camps Bay room, in Cape Town, as she walked away from the laundry along the veranda. They locked eyes in the hippie way, nodded, and then he was in her Vanguard van as she drove along the coast to Llandudno Beach where she parked and lit a joint. They smoked and she told him about her *zayde*, grandfather, and how he escaped from the pogroms that followed the assassination of Alexander II of Russia in 1881.

Zayde was a Litvak, she said. About forty thousand of them came from Lithuania to South Africa before World War I. Most of them on assisted passages run by the Castle Line from London. He was a tailor and my father is a tailor and no doubt my young brother will be a tailor and the business will go on forever.

You think so?

Nothing lasts forever. They would have thought they would be Lithuanian forever and here we are in Cape Town.

They never wanted to go to Israel, or America?

America, yes, but not Israel. It was nothing then. Now they all want to go, to visit, but not live. They don't believe it will last as a nation. Some of them don't believe it should have become a nation.

She looked at her watch.

I have to go, to visit my parents.

She drove back to Camps Bay and as Muir left the Vanguard she said: Wait a minute, take this book.

Siddhartha? What's it mean?

Read it.

In his room he opened the book and didn't put it down until the last page. Three days later Shoshanna picked him up and took him to a vegetarian restaurant full of people who looked at them and nodded, and Muir thought he belonged to a worldwide movement of like minds. That night she took him to a play written by a man called Pieter-Dirk Uys.

This is a new world, thought Muir, a long way from Genoralup and Perth.

It didn't last long.

When he came home from an afternoon on the beach at Camps Bay, he found his room in a mess. Items thrown in one corner as though whoever searched it thought: I'll throw all his shit over there so he'll know I've seen it. It was no brief look over his belongings, it featured heavy and angry hands. The intrusion unsettled Muir. Why? He was not dealing, not causing trouble, although mixing with the wrong people on the wrong side of apartheid and the drug laws. How did they know he was there? Who knew? Parsons knew.

It's not our Jack, his mother would say. It's the company he keeps.

After the raid, he walked into the city, hard, fast and aimless. He had no idea how he got there, in the flea market. He stared hard at all the European men. Was it one of them? Is that one following me? Then he saw her among the leather bags. She was Indian, beautiful and reminded him of the sister of Suresh, the sister he longed for but never met. She saw him looking.

That bag there, he said. Can I buy it?

Would you like to hold it? she asked in a voice that suggested heavenly connections.

I would like, he thought, to hold you, to embrace you, put my lips on yours and suck in your life force and beauty because I have never seen such beauty, not in eyes, nose, cheeks, neck or even arms.

Are you all right? she asked in a voice that suggested concern, and it confused him, and he could feel the blood in his face forcing him to drop his eyes, turn away from her and rummage in the bags on the other end of the stall. They were not in the same class as the bag she held, but he was not yet ready for her.

Are you from Australia? she asked.

How can you tell?

Your accent.

My name is Jack and I am from a small town in the deep south-west where the trees grow tall and the men are shy.

She laughed and held up the bag.

My name is Lakshmi and I am not so sure about the men being shy. I have not yet met a shy Australian.

Did one ask you to join him for a coffee yet?

Many, but this is South Africa and such meetings are not allowed, by law.

Damn the law.

Don't be so brave. There are ears everywhere.

He took the bag from her hands, carefully, making sure he touched her fingers. He felt her soft skin and a deep part of him stirred, rose up inside him. He smiled at her, nodded, put his bag on the counter, bent over it as though having trouble finding his wallet, closer towards her, not too close, but enough to smell her, know her scent, hold it. The deep stirring moved again and he knew it was time to leave.

Lakshmi, he said, I have just read a book called *Siddhartha* and in it is a woman called Kamla.

She put her hand on his and said: Kamla is another name for Lakshmi, a consort of Vishnu, the God of Perfection.

He could feel the tear ducts open in his eyes. He thought he loved her, was sure he could. Young Jack seemed incapable of meeting beautiful women who smiled, perhaps offered a kind word, a brief touch of finger to hand, without the dream of a perfect love flooding all other thoughts and, occasionally, restricting his respiratory processes.

He turned quickly to hide again and to replenish his lungs but was unable to resist one last look.

I will not forget you, Lakshmi, he said.

Of course you will, she replied. But, just in case, always sleep with your windows open, as we Hindus do, so the real Lakshmi can come in.

And that is why both young Jack and old Jack, even in the noisiest of cities, have never slept with a window closed.

The day before he left, Shoshanna drove him up Signal Hill overlooking the city. They sat on a bench and smoked a pipe packed with *dagga*.

Is it possible, he asked, to be Jewish and Buddhist?

Shoshanna had a big laugh and she used it to draw the laughter from him.

I am a Jew, but I don't go to synagogue, she said. I'm not Judaist. Most of the first Christians were Jews. Why not? And you, what are you?

I don't know. I was beginning to think I might find out in Cape Town. It's not like the other cities I've lived in. I feel different here.

Someone is after you, Jack. Who knows why? They don't need a reason to raid your room. Maybe they saw you with me, because I am on their files with all the usual Jewish left-wing suspects. What a joke. That bastard, Prime Minister Vorster, was a Nazi in the Second World War and Jan Smuts threw him in prison for two years. He hated Jews and wanted us all dead, now he's sucking up to the Israelis because they have weapons.

What should I do?

Leave. Go to Israel, join a kibbutz. No-one will find you there. On my kibbutz, all kinds of people were hiding, from ex-wives, husbands, police, the CIA.

Come with me.

What, as your lover? We haven't even kissed.

My sister. That's how I think of you. From that first day we met, you have taught me things I never knew, never even contemplated.

The sun was forming a red ball and readying itself to slip away into the Atlantic Ocean. There was just enough light for Muir to turn and look at Shoshanna. She had strong features, sharp eyes, long curly hair rushed down her cheeks to fall on her shoulders and her solid arms. He had never seen her legs, as they were always hidden under long dresses that ebbed and flowed as she moved. In another place, another time, he would have imagined, maybe attempted, a sexual encounter, but here it had never crossed his mind. She was the older, wiser sister he never had.

Garden Route

Muir packed his pack again and found the road out of Cape Town. It was not a long wait before Jacob arrived, a Jewish man recently returned from Israel and on an unnamed errand for his father. Jacob was small, wiry, with crazy eyes and quick hands that darted around the dashboard and all over the steering wheel.

Where are you going when you leave South Africa? he asked.

Maybe Israel, said Muir.

What are you? *Meshugge*?

What?

Crazy man. You have to be. I have just come home after three months on a kibbutz and those Israeli bastards made me work my guts out and paid me peanuts. I mean it, peanuts. At the end of every week you go to the kibbutz shop and get a packet of cigarettes and a bag of peanuts.

Jacob lifted his hands off everything and rocked his head until the car swerved and Muir grabbed the wheel.

Jacky, said Jacob, you must ready yourself already. The Jews in Israel are not like the Jews from other places. Do you know any Jews?

I went to school with Jews.

Must have been a very expensive private school.

It was.

And did the Jews participate?

In everything except chapel and divinity.

And you liked them?

I did.

Was there any anti-Semitism in that school?

There must have been but I never saw it or heard it. I think the Greeks took more flak than the Jews. Being a Jew was no big deal.

No big deal to be a Jew? What kind of Jews were they? There is no bigger deal than being a Jew. Unless, of course, you are Zulu, or Basotho, or Afrikaner, or English, or Australian, or German, no, that's embarrassing to be German.

Jacob, you should have been a comedian.

You think comedy needs another Jew? You take the Jews from English and American comedy and what have you got? A couple of blacks, some half-blacks and one Catholic. Did you have any Aboriginals at that school?

One that we knew of.

That you knew of?

There was one kid there who was Aboriginal and maybe there were others but they didn't say.

Didn't say? What kind of a country is that? You have to say if you are Aboriginal? Do you have to say if you are Greek?

Yeah, because you could be Italian, or Yugoslav, maybe even Lebanese.

No, no, no, you people have it all wrong. Next you'll be telling me you only knew the Jews were Jews because they said they were Jews.

Of course.

You mean, you don't have race police coming to your house and taking hair samples and telling you who you are or what they want you to be?

No.

Jacob slammed the brake pedal. Muir managed to manoeuvre the car to the side of the road. Jacob held his head in his hands.

You people! he screamed. What a country!

Jacob reached across Muir, took a piece of paper from his glovebox and wrote down an address.

When you get to Tel Aviv, go to this office, he said. These people will assign you a kibbutz. And here, my full name, Jacob Rubenstein and my kibbutz, Mitzpeh Dovrat, and my kibbutz father, Zvi Silverman. This will show them that you are not coming without knowledge, or without connections. Connections are important in Israel.

In Johannesburg, Muir visited the central branch of Barclays Bank only to find his money had not arrived. His father had promised to send the proceeds of the sale of a block of land Muir had owned, land he had bought thinking he would build a house, settle down, find a wife and make a family. It was all that was left of his capitalist past, his connection to the profit motive. And he needed the money. Without it he was stuck in a place with secret forces hounding him. He called his father from a post office pay phone.

Dad, it's Jack, he yelled. I need the money.

Sorry, son, said his father. The sale was postponed because the bloody buyer didn't get his loan through in time. Settlement will be in three weeks now. We'll wire the money as soon as we get it. Hang on, your mother wants a word.

Jack pressed the handpiece hard on the side of his head. He waited for his mother's voice, thought he was ready, that he would remain calm, wanted to say that he loved her.

Mum.

He could hear sobbing.

Jack.

He could hear his own sobbing now.

He managed to say, Love.

Yes?

You.

Then silence. Then his father.

Bit much for her, Jack. Might be best if you write.

Rhodesia 1973

1

Short of money and running out of places to hide, Muir decided to hitchhike to the newly named Republic of Rhodesia. His second lift out of Johannesburg warned him not to continue. The man, a large, hairy Afrikaner farmer driving a Toyota Land Cruiser with a fridge tied on the back, said a war had begun over the Limpopo River, the natural border between the two countries.

The *kaffirs* are killing farmers, he said, and that Prime Minister Smith better get a move on and crush the terrorists. And you, my friend, are telling me that you sleep on the side of the road?

Yes.

And you are tramping to Rhodesia because you want to see Victoria Falls?

Yes.

If you get killed, don't say I didn't warn you. *Ach* man, you Aussies are crazy and it's for sure without you the English would never win all those wars.

Muir slept on the side of the road that night. It was an uneasy sleep and he kept the hunting knife he bought in Cape Town in his preferred, left hand.

At the border, the guards hassled Muir and Kevin, the New Zealander who had picked him up in South Africa. The guards made a fuss about terrorists and how it was not safe, but Kevin told them they were Anzacs and knew how to look after themselves.

His next lift was with a man whose neighbour had been murdered the week before.

Terrorists, the man said. Animals. *Munts*.

What's a *munt*?

Down there, where you've come from, they call them *kaffirs*. Up here we call them *munts*. Well, not all of them, many of them are good chaps, but these communist terrorists, they are the scum of the earth. What do they want? This is a beautiful country and if they would let us get on with it, we could make it great. They murdered my neighbour and his entire family. Hacked them to death with machetes. What did Tony ever do to them? I'll tell you what he did, he made a productive farm and grew vegetables and mealies and created work for twenty people.

Muir did not need to hold his tongue, it had nothing to say.

An agricultural scientist stopped and drove him into Fort Victoria and told him about the ancient city of Great Zimbabwe. From Fort Victoria, Muir found the road out and walked. There were few cars and none stopped. Muir thought it was because of the heat, that the last thing drivers wanted was another sweating, stinking human in their car. He had always enjoyed a good sweat and stopped to feel it run off his head, down the neck and form small pools in his family mark – the dip between the breasts, the concave chest. At the sign to Great Zimbabwe, he turned as a tourist bus pulled up beside him. The driver offered him a lift. He climbed on board.

At Great Zimbabwe he walked the long narrow alley between the mortar-less stone walls and stone buildings that featured stones chosen for their size and shape to fit with exactitude. It was not a city built by dumb savages, thought Muir, but a civilised people with intelligent design and building capabilities. He guessed that Great Zimbabwe did not exist in isolation from other civilisations, and probably traded with cities in nearby regions. In some places the builders had used huge boulders as extensions, additions and central sections of a structure. It was a wonder that after all the wars and battles fought in that part of Africa – tribe against tribe, kingdom against kingdom, nation against nation – there was any sign left of human habitation. He knew nothing and there were no signs, or guides, to tell visitors what they didn't know. When did the city state flourish? Who lived here? How many died here? Who ruled? He ran his hands along the neat piles of dark grey rocks slotted with precision that had stood longer than him and the other three tourists who had passed him with a nod.

Back on the road, with his index finger out, a Volkswagen Beetle swerved into the side of the road and reversed at speed.

A black face appeared from the passenger's side: Good afternoon, my good man.

Three young men in a Volkswagen. A man got out of the passenger side and let Muir onto the back seat. They told him they were on a break from the University of Rhodesia, Salisbury, a campus open to students of all races. Their English was impeccable.

That place you visited, said Reggie, it was built by our people, the Shona. There was once a great civilisation here, right in the middle of this heat and dust and where the white man claimed there was nothing but warring, mad naked savages yelling, screaming and thrusting *assegais*. Then that man Rhodes and his gang turned up with gunpowder, good manners and bibles, creating vast farms and huge holes while digging up precious minerals to feed European greed. But the Europeans won't have it. They say it could not have been built by our people, but only by a more sophisticated civilisation, like one from Europe, or Arabia. This is another attempt to remind us that we are inferior. And soon everything up here will be like down south. Ian Smith and his government are changing laws and bringing in an apartheid system.

Arthur, the driver, swung his head around and yelled: They are all bastards!

Reggie and the other man, Tom, yelled together: Arthur, keep your eyes on the road!

Reggie turned and looked behind: Arthur, I think that car wants to pass.

Does he? said Arthur. He will not get past me. I will never let them pass, the white bastards.

Arthur manoeuvred his car from the legal left to the illegal right side of the road as the vehicle attempted to pass. Reggie implored Arthur to allow it through, but to no avail. Arthur was full of alcohol, anger and hate.

This will end badly, said Reggie. We can't stop him drinking, but we should not have let him drive.

The three white faces in the car behind were not happy. The driver waved a hand. Arthur waved a dismissal over his head. No-one was ready for the next move. The car pulled out quickly, ran into the rough on the right-hand side of the road and the passenger held up a badge.

It is the police, yelled Reggie. Arthur, you idiot. Stop the car.

As Arthur pulled into the side of the road, the police jammed their car in front, three doors opened and two plain-clothes and one uniform rushed out – two men, one woman. The men dragged Arthur from his seat, threw him against the Volkswagen and worked him over. The policewoman ordered Reggie from the front passenger seat into the back with Muir and Tom. As soon as the men had Arthur in the unmarked police car, the policewoman took the Volkswagen wheel and followed. It was a silent drive to the Fort Victoria Police Station.

The inside looked like a police station – a long counter with uniformed men behind it, sitting at desks with typewriters, others standing around, staring at the newcomers. Muir and his two new friends were told to sit on the bench along the wall facing the counter. The policewoman lifted the trap at one end, walked behind the counter and into an office.

When she emerged, Muir asked: Where is Arthur?

They will have gone around the rear of the building, she said. That's where they take all those in custody. You can leave now. This is no concern of yours.

What will happen to him?

She is right, said Tom. I am sorry but Arthur has brought it on himself. He was drunk and became aggressive. If he had let them pass, none of this would have happened.

I don't want to go.

Maybe not, the policewoman said, but you must. You have nothing to do with this, or these people. They picked you up from the side of the road. You do not belong here. Go.

She took his arm and moved towards the front door. Muir resisted, with no plan, no idea, no sense. One of the policemen returned.

Look, he said, you can go now or you can stay and we will take your passport, run a check on you, hold you in a cell overnight, maybe longer and then send you back where you came from.

Tom and Reggie stood and put out their hands.

There is nothing we can do, said Tom, and even less you can do. It was a pleasure meeting you and spending this short time with you.

The policeman followed Muir out, walked him down the steps to the last, then turned and walked back.

There was a noise, a yell, a scream. Muir walked past the station building and looked through the trees. Behind the building there was a large wire cage, at least twenty feet high, as though built to house wedge-tailed eagles. He walked towards the fence and, inside the cage, saw Arthur on the ground. Around his neck was a strap, or belt, and holding the other end was a huge black policeman. Beside him the other white policeman from the car, holding a truncheon. The strap was tight around Arthur's neck. Veins were filling with blood. It looked like they were strangling him. The black policeman leant back and moved forward, quickly, with violent intent and struck Arthur across the back with a small whip. The white man followed with a crack across his thigh.

Muir shrieked: What are you? What kind of place is this?

A policeman appeared at the front door of the station: Leave, he yelled. Your last chance.

Muir walked away, as though on a mission. He put his hand on his knife, poised, ready to attack, to save a life, start a revolution, he didn't know, and he had no idea where to start, what to do, how to go about it. He felt sick, in his stomach, head, heart, soul. He understood all the sick bits but not the stomach – he had hardly eaten more than a handful of nuts a day since leaving Johannesburg.

Jesus, where are you when injustice reigns? Muir could hear his voice. And again – they were killing a man back there, why? Because he was a drunk driver?

Something moved. Deep. Rising. He stopped, let go his knife, leant over a fence, looked down on a neat and well-kept household garden. Up it came, the nuts and dried fruit, along with thoughts, desires, dreams. He stared at the tiny pile beside a bed of roses.

His last lift out of the Mafungabusi Forest and into Bulawayo was with a widower and her two children. They had not gone far when they were obstructed by a bull elephant. They sat in silence in the tiny Volkswagen while the elephant prepared to discharge his entire waste in the middle of the road.

And then the woman opened up, slowly at first, then in a rush, as though Muir was the first person she had spoken to in a long time.

I lost my husband, she said, eighteen months ago in one of the earliest terrorist attacks. The police referred to it as a murder-robbery. It wasn't. They were filthy communist terrorists.

She had been in the capital city of Rhodesia, Salisbury, when they attacked her husband on the farm out of Bulawayo. They hacked him to death with machetes, along with all the farm workers there on the day, five of them.

The killers were Shona, she said. Our workers were Ndebele. They want us out of this country, our country, all of us, even the Ndebele. I have kept the farm running with a manager and only visit from our house in Salisbury. I have to leave, for the children's sake. Maybe try and get to Perth. This war will end badly, for all of us, whatever group we belong to.

They all jumped as the elephant raised its huge head and trumpeted. Another jump as the bull elephant roared again, made a sudden forward movement, lifted a huge foot, stamped it, turned and walked into the jungle.

Back home, thought Muir, people died in hospitals, bedrooms, or car accidents, but in Africa they died in front of you, in the jaws of dogs, trampled by elephants, hacked to death by terrorists, or beaten and hung by angry cops.

Three lifts later, Jack remembered Rudyard Kipling – at last he came to the banks of the great grey-green, greasy Limpopo River. Over the river and the border into South Africa.

A car stopped in front of him. Muir got in. The driver was a young minister from the New Protestant Church and he told Muir he was the first NPC appointment in Rhodesia. He was a handsome yet shambolic man with unkempt hair, deep blue eyes, a heavy scar on the top of one ear and hands that belonged to a farmer.

The NPC is a breakaway from the Dutch Reformed Church, he told Muir. The DRC rejected soldiers who fought in the Second World War for the Allies, because many DRC members supported the Nazis. They also believe only certain people will be allowed into heaven.

It was as though the minister had just come out of a vow of silence and now he had started talking, he was unable to stop.

Prime Minister John Vorster was jailed for his activities in support of Nazi Germany during the war, the minister said. I have also heard rumours his government is doing business with Israel.

I'm going there.

Israel?

In a couple of days.

Are you Jewish?

No.

Christian?

I don't know anymore. I think I'm a socialist. I'll probably live on a kibbutz.

You can be a Jew, or a Christian, *and* a socialist.

And a Buddhist.

We are all children of Abraham.

What does that mean?

Metaphorically it means we all came to our God through Abraham, that's Jews, Christians and Muslims, and given that there is only one God, it should not matter what we call him – Yahweh, Allah, or God. You are going to the hotbed for all three religions, and over the centuries each one has tried to make it his and his alone. We are now in a period of Jewish domination. I have never been there and I'm not sure I ever will, even if it has such significance for Christianity.

As the young minister spoke, Muir gazed out the window at the changing landscape, shifting from subtropical bushland to open farmland. There were more people in the south and more villages and towns to house them. As they passed through one settlement after another, all seemed peaceful and quiet but he was sure he could still smell the hatred.

My Christianity is a personal journey, said the minister, and does not require me to live in any particular country, just that I live by my codes and values.

When he stopped the car and Muir got out, they looked into each other's eyes and held hands for what seemed like minutes, then the young minister put both his hands together and bowed slightly. Muir did the same, believing it to be a kind of blessing and deciding that he liked it.

Muir's last lift was with a fat, drunk, black man who laughed at nothing and everything. Unlike Arthur in Rhodesia, he drove slowly, letting every car that came up behind him pass, with a polite wave. After stopping for a piss at the side of the road, his car refused to start.

You get back behind the wheel, said Muir. I'll push. Once we get over that rise, it'll be easy to kickstart.

The man laughed so hard he had to pull at his trousers for fear they would fall. But he got in and Muir pushed. Over the rise the car kicked, jerked and roared. Muir ran after it and climbed in.

Lucky no Afrikaner drove past, said Muir, or he would have shot both of us.

Johannesburg 1973

Muir's first task when he returned to Johannesburg was to make sure he had money. The transfer had come through and the teller at Barclays arranged it all in traveller's cheques and then handed him a note from a young family friend from Genoralup. Muir's father, Andrew, had told her to leave a note at the bank as the younger Muir would be calling in to pick up his money. Last time Jack saw Evie, she was still in high school and he was eager to see how she had grown. On leaving the bank he went straight to her address in Hillbrow.

An attractive young woman opened the door to him.

Evie, he said. I wouldn't have recognised you.

Me too, she replied. Look at you with the hippie hair and beard.

There was an awkward moment when they were not sure what to do or say next. Evie made a move, opening her arms wide to hug him.

Let me take you to lunch, he said. My money arrived from the old man.

Hang on, she said, first put down your backpack. When are you flying out?

Day after tomorrow.

You got somewhere to stay?

Not yet.

All right, why not here?

They went to his favourite little café, Cabbages and Kings. He ordered fish, deciding he would be a fish and egg eating vegetarian. She told him all about her life since he had seen her last, how she had finished high school with average marks, gone to secretarial college, dropped out, worked in a restaurant, then a spinster auntie had died leaving her and her sister enough money for a deposit on a house or to travel the world. Her sister chose the house and Evie chose travel. While she talked and laughed, Muir found himself nostalgic for his old life, full of secretaries, aunties, mortgages and a simple life without drug dealers and complex social systems.

Evie had grown into a mature young woman with cheeky eyes, full lips and a compact body. Muir tried hard not to look anywhere but her eyes and he was sure she noticed. He also had to concentrate on the conversation because her voice was deep, resonant and seductive. They followed lunch with a visit to a bar for a few beers, stumbling out after dark to find their way back to Evie's small apartment. All the way Muir made sure he was alongside her so as not to drop behind and fall prey to inappropriate thoughts.

It all changed after they arrived, entered, removed their coats, and stood staring at each other. Before he could remind himself that Evie's mother was his mother's best friend, Evie's lips were on his and his hands were in places he had tried not to imagine, their breasts were bare and hard against each other. Hers were upright, firm, glorious and reminded him she was recently a girl and he pushed her back and said: Evie, I'm sorry, our mothers are best friends.

They both laughed, covered their bodies, made coffee and watched television. Later, they kissed quickly before she went to her room and he laid out his sleeping bag on the living room floor. Before he lay down, he checked the room's only window and opened it wide to let in the late-night sounds of inner-city Johannesburg.

On his last day, Muir thought it best to keep his distance from Evie's house and went for a long hitchhike out of town. One of his lifts was a young Indian man who took him to his house in Fordsburg.

Raj lit a joint and asked if Muir had met the world's greatest cricketer, Sir Donald Bradman, and was it true that the new prime minister had ended the White Australia Policy and if so would he be able to migrate to Australia and start up a new business selling clothing made in India with the finest cotton?

Probably, Muir said, but he wasn't sure because his family had a rule never to discuss politics, sex or religion and so there was no news from home about what was going on in Canberra, who was having an affair, or what the Pope said last week.

They smoked until Raj fell asleep and Muir stood and walked softly to the kitchen and fronted the sink. It sat embedded in a short bench cluttered with every type of bowl imaginable and unimaginable. One tap. No hot water. But a saucepan. He filled it, boiled it, poured it, got to work.

He would leave the next day and he felt no disappointment. He hadn't thought of it before, but as he washed in the sink and rinsed in the saucepan, while remembering his encounters as a hitchhiker on the road and his meetings with Shoshanna, Lakshmi and Evie, it came to him that he had left Genoralup looking and longing for love. He had, of course, known the love of a mother, a father, three grandparents and a small collection of aunties and uncles, although none of them had ever said the words I love you. But he had never known the love of a stranger to the family, someone who looked at him with eyes so deep he wanted to dive in, knowing he could not reach bottom, someone who held and hugged with a passion, maybe need even, and when he lay naked beside her he would cry. He wanted that kind of love.

The dishes done, he stood back and admired the way he had carefully placed the bowls first, allowing him to rest the plates up against them, for more efficient draining of excess water. I have never met anyone who enjoys washing dishes as much as me, he thought. One day it might help me find someone to live with.

The Jan Smuts International Airport central hall was full of people all colours and shapes. Except, of course, the departure queues – there were no black skins there. All the non-white skins were standing around with brooms and buckets and cleaning, or readying themselves to clean up after the white skins, who made a mess in toilets, dropped lolly wrappers, newspapers, sodden handkerchiefs and even, Muir noticed in one corner, a smelly bundle that looked like a nappy. The whites were flying out and flying in, but the others were staying put, there to tidy up and even if they had wanted to fly, there were no queues for them. And air travel was for the wealthy.

Then he remembered he wasn't. Or hadn't been. The difference between him and the handsome young man standing outside the male toilets with a mop, was that all Jack Muir had to do when he ran out of money was to call his father and ask him to send more.

He entered the toilets with a nod to the handsome young Zulu. He was sure the man was Zulu, because he stood with a proud, strong body and looked Muir in the eye as if to say: You might be white, but you ain't no Zulu.

As he left, he turned to the man and handed him five rand. The Zulu took it, nodded, put it in his pocket, all without a *dankie, baas*. Muir was not offended, but pleased the man had confirmed his Zulu heritage.

He made his way to the café, bought a coffee and sat at a table. South Africa, he thought, was a country based on the violent separation of people according to skin colours. What could be more superficial than a skin colour? What kind of human could design, then manage and implement the laws of apartheid? Although Muir had met people like Etienne who were not perpetrators and upholders of the brutal system, all players – the oppressors, the oppressed, bystanders, visitors – became victims

I am not a victim, thought Muir, I have passed through this pit of hatred and received an occasional buffeting by those unable to restrain their anger and bitterness.

He looked around the airport waiting lounge, becoming aware of an increasing distance from events before him and his disconnection from them. It was as though he had entered a dream with accompanying sounds and physical sensations, and when his flight was called he broke from the dream, stood and re-entered the real world.

Kincannup 2018

I took a job at a local café. I didn't mean to, but early one morning, right after a swim in the Southern Ocean off Binalup, the place where the sun comes up, the owner, a friend of mine, stormed out of the kitchen complaining about his casual kitchen hand, a backpacker from London.

Show me the sink, I said.

What?

Come on, Tony, you've got a full house, the cups and plates are piling up, so I'm stepping up.

Sorry, Jack, you're not covered.

I'll wear an apron.

Insurance.

I grabbed a napkin, took a pen, and wrote: I, Jack Muir, of sound mind and body, hereby waive all workers compensation claims due to injuries incurred while washing dishes for Anthony Roberts at Whalers Retreat Café and Restaurant.

I signed it, asked one of the other swimmers to witness, and Tony showed me the sink. It was a double, with long benches on either side.

This little thing here, said Tony, is a dishwasher. You can shove as much as you can in there, but, because of the back-up, and because we can't afford a massive industrial dishwashing complex, you'll have to dirty your hands.

He did not know how much I would enjoy myself, but he soon saw.

I've seen many a domestic and commercial dishwasher attack a sink as though it was the enemy. Not me. With apron on I stood and looked at the scene – full bench alongside the stacked sink. Only one way to approach – rearrange everything into like stacks. Clear the washing tub, wipe it over, make it shine, listen to it sing. Turn on the tap, make sure the water is hot and soapy.

Let the music start.

Dump in the cutlery, let it soak. While the water is untainted with liquids and solids, wash the glasses and rinse them in the clean, clear rinse. Pile in the saucers, the side plates, follow up with the larger, finally, the cups.

At two o'clock in the afternoon, over a late lunch and coffee, Tony asked: Where the hell did that come from, Jack? You and the dishes?

Started in Genoralup, I said. Then I just kept washing wherever I went. Had most fun on a kibbutz in Israel. Washed one night for over six hundred people.

Some sort of communal farm, was it? Or a hippie commune?

The volunteer community was hippie-like, but the others, the kibbutzniks, were hardcore socialists. It's where I met my wife.

Israel 1973

Gavrot 1

She was in the peaches. Then the apricots. Then she stood in front of me and asked if I was the Australian the others had been talking about. Her long brown hair was tied in a bun at the back of her head and her skin was brown, smooth and shiny. Her arms showed signs of muscle and although I couldn't see her legs I knew they were hard and strong. She didn't look like any Jew I had ever seen. Nothing like the girls who went to the private schools in Perth, or Shoshanna, the dope-smoking, Jewish Buddhist I hung out with in Cape Town. She looked like a Pacific Island princess. The thought surprised me, because I had believed I never dwelt on stereotypes and the only way I had ever known a person's ethnicity was when they had said what it was.

What are they saying about the Australian? I asked.

They say he is like all Australians, she said, thin and strong and can do anything with an axe, or those things they use under the apple trees to dig the weeds. They think he would look right on a horse, a tractor and with a gun.

I think they are talking about another man.

But there is only one Australian on the kibbutz. It must be you.

Maybe it is me and I can do some of those things but not all.

Her eyes never left mine and mine never left hers.

All that took place after five weeks on the kibbutz. I had not seen her before because she was in the army, stationed much further south and now home was a place she visited. Neeva saved my kibbutz life because my first weeks were boring, irritating and I found myself planning an early departure. The volunteer community, those from London, New York, Paris and Buenos Aires, were lazy, selfish and refused to wash dishes or clean the community toilet and shower block. As soon as I heard about the dishes I went to Zvi, the man responsible for the volunteers. Zvi was a short ugly man with a bent back and hair that looked like a bomb had gone off inside his head and blown everything out. His office was a room barely big enough to house a cistern and toilet bowl, yet he seemed comfortable and he occupied it as though it were a tiny kingdom.

Shalom, Jack, he said. *Ma kara*? This means, what has happened?

You have a problem with the dishes?

Me? No. But the volunteers, yes. They don't want to work in the kitchen. They think it dirty work. Not for them. What, they think this is a holiday camp? We cannot force them but if it continues, we will make a decision. Here in the kibbutz, we respect people who work. Work is the heart of kibbutz life. It is why we Jews came home so we could have land to work, to grow food, to become whole, become human, men and women. Work, what we call *avoda*. We will not shoot them, of course, we are not Nazis, but we will do something. Why do you ask?

I will do the dishes.

You?

I just said.

You can start tonight.

One more thing. I need cleaning equipment for the toilets. The volunteer toilets are disgusting.

You are a crazy man, Jack Muir, but I like you.

There were twelve volunteers living on Gavrot and not one of them had cleaned a toilet. They came from homes where toilets were cleaned for them and if ever they needed a toilet outside of their home, that was also cleaned for them. In some houses the cleaning would have been done by a mother, or perhaps a father, maybe servants, and the toilets outside their homes, well, what did they care. Each day they went to the volunteer ablution block, sat on a toilet, stood above it, shat, pissed, wiped no spillage and added to the stench and degradation. Inevitably, the bowls blocked up, overflowed, and sent filthy water full of shit, paper and unrecognisable items back, over the rim, on the floor and, occasionally, out the door onto the path. With a blocked bowl, the arrogant brats made no attempt to clean the mess, but simply wiped their arses and dumped paper on the floor. Then left, oblivious. Not quite, because they did complain about the filthy toilets. When told the cleanliness was their responsibility, they rejected it. Such was the state of the volunteer community, full of spoilt, self-indulgent, pretend hippies.

The setting was perfect. I had arrived after nearly nine months living a self-indulgent and degraded life in a police state. In Durban I lived in an apartment near the beach where we smoked dope, ate yoghurt and ice-cream and I cleaned the toilet once. In my house in Genoralup, I cleaned the toilet. No-one else cleaned my toilet. I decided if I ever had a child, that child would be taught, from an early age, to clean a toilet.

For two weeks I went to the orchards at six o'clock in the morning, slogged for seven hours, and at five o'clock in the afternoon went to the kitchen to wash dishes for the masses. My workmate was often Avi, a fat and greedy man. When filthy plates came over the counter, I could see the light in his eyes when he spotted favoured tasty morsels and it never ceased to astound me that he resisted the temptation. Before he could touch a scrap, I snatched plates and pulled them into the huge tubs on wheels.

Relax, my friend, he said on day three. There is not so much hurry. The dishes will not disappear.

What is it with you? he said on day five. I never met anyone who can wash dishes like you. No-one wants this work, but you love this work. Or hate it. I am not so sure which. You are one crazy Australian man.

Kibbutz Gavrot did not live up to my socialist dream: from each according to his ability, to each according to his need. Each volunteer had the ability to wash dishes and clean toilets, but they did neither. Each volunteer had a need for a clean plate and a clean shit bowl, but they believed their need should be catered for by others. This was a classic response of the spoilt children of capital accumulators: from each according to my need and want, to each according to a tenant of economic rationalism that requires I build profit margins and amass vast sums of money.

The response to the lazy volunteers was classic kibbutz: Zvi called a meeting. Those in attendance were Zvi, me, Israeli Chava, who once managed the volunteer community, English Jim and American Dave. We talked for hours, each one of us had our say, then, when each one had their say, the rest of us had to have another say and so on, and on. English Jim was a philosophy major in a northern university I forgot the name of as soon as he mentioned it. Every Sunday evening we met in the dining room before the evening meal, our voices not cushioned by other bodies, voices, plates, bowls and utensils, and as our voices rose they bounced off walls and the ceiling. No-one from the kitchen came to watch, to check, to listen.

We have to remember, said Jim, that the kibbutz is a socialist experiment and that experiment is continuing. This kibbutz itself is not yet twenty-five years old. Those, like Zvi, one of the founders, will be passionate about the original ideals. Those, like Chava, who came later, will have brought another experience to the debate. But both of them will be well versed in the collective spirit, whereas those of us who hail from the western capitalist, individualist experience are essentially, by definition, self-centred, and that makes thinking for the collective hard work.

You can speak for me? said Chava. You know nothing of me.

Jim, I said, the dishes need to be washed and the shit from the toilets needs to be cleaned. How fucking hard is that to grasp?

Jack is right, said American Dave, but maybe if we offered them an incentive?

An incentive? You must be joking, Dave. Incentives are not a part of socialism. You do what you have to do because it has to be done. What's more, how do you think your ancestors arrived in the United States? Or mine in Australia? You think they looked around for people to do things for them? No, they got on. Unless they were aristocratic shits who arrived with slaves or servants. There were others, of course, from both countries, who enslaved locals.

If they don't begin to do dishes, said Zvi, we must ask them to leave.

That's an overreaction, Zvi, said Jim. And seems to suggest some intolerance, which is not what the kibbutz is about.

What do you know? said Chava. You have lived here one minute of your life.

Chava did not like Jim. Jim was English, symbolic of colonialism, the British Mandate to rule Palestine, which it did, from 1923 to 1948 and, as Eliezer, my co-worker in the orchards, had said: When we fought for Israel's independence, we had to fight both the British and the Arabs.

On and on went the discussions. And when we were done, we all went back to our rooms. And the next day my head was in a dunny and my hands in a sink. I grew to despise that group of volunteers and my loathing forced me to crave relationships with kibbutzniks, the people who founded the community, made it, were born in it, and lived it as a dream come true.

Gavrot 2

Kibbutz life in the volunteer community seemed like it would be the same forever – you worked, you ate, you slept, you worked, you ate, you slept. Then everything would change, suddenly, no warning, and you'd be stuffing chickens into a small crate for the city market. Or sweeping the bottom of an empty, recently repaired swimming pool. Or ironing shirts in the laundry at 5 am, but only if you were a woman. And that was something I noticed – the men mainly worked the fields, the productive units, and the women mainly worked the kitchen, laundry and the children's houses. Unless you were a volunteer and then you went where you were told. It was different for me, because I volunteered for the dishes, and on my first day in the apple orchard I showed my ability with hoe, spade and scythe.

Yigal, the warrior orchardist, handed the eight volunteers a hoe each. Most of them looked at it, puzzled, but I took it, weighed it and used it as though it was an extension of my arms.

You know this? said Yigal.

Of course, I said. I grew up on thirty acres of Granny Smith apples and we used this to dig weeds and bushes from around the trees.

The others watched me and tried hard, but I was the only one who lasted and the only one to be called for, day after day. The others moved from one odd job to the next, depending on demand, never skill. Most of them failed to stay their full three months, leaving after one, or two, and then our little community would be all abuzz as a new lot arrived, sometimes in groups, often alone. Mostly they were like the lot that recently departed, but not Arieh the Iranian.

What's that? I asked him.

Arieh had a long, thick scar running down his left cheek, from just under the eye, almost to the jawbone.

A friend cut me, said Arieh.

Friend?

I grew up in a slum.

I don't believe you.

What, all Jews live in big houses surrounded by other rich Jews? Not us, *chaver*, my friend, we lived in the middle of the shittiest hole in Tehran. When you meet my mother, you will meet a Jew from the ghetto.

We were as high up two trees as we could climb, side by side, yelling through the branches at each other. They were Australian eucalypts, planted right outside our huts. Arieh lived in a hut with a Frenchman and a Colombian. I lived in the hut next door with an American and a Frenchman. None of them liked each other and they looked at Arieh and me with concern. We climbed those two trees every day after work, Arieh climbing the taller of the two because it was an easier climb. I climbed the other because I had climbed trees all my life. My tree required a climber to jump, grab the lowest branch and pull himself up, like a monkey. It was how Arieh wanted to climb but his arms wouldn't do it.

That's what comes from being a city Jew, he said. We know all about money and nothing about trees.

You said you were poor.

We were, but we still knew money before trees.

Tell me about your scar.

He didn't tell me up the tree, he waited until after dinner when we drank Turkish coffee in the kibbutz coffee house, the *moadon*. I liked Arieh, his talk, his walk, his smell. He had a swagger, a confidence, and his talk was accompanied by a gentle head movement, not quite the Indian roll but more of a tiny Middle Eastern dance. His smell was earthy, as though he slept every night in the field nestled among fruit trees and long grass and not in a bed with sheets and blankets.

He sat outside on the low wall that divided the coffee house from the kibbutz gardens and invited me to sit next to him. His Hebrew was serviceable and his English wasn't much better, but we got by because he used both, and his face and hands filled in the rest of the story.

In Iran, there are maybe one hundred and fifty thousand Jews, he said, and maybe a few hundred of them are rich, really rich. The rest of us are between rich and poor. We were just above the poorest and we lived among them. If you want to survive in a ghetto, you have to have protection. This means to join a gang. If you join a gang, you don't have to think who your enemies are. Are they Kurds, Arabs, Azeris, Persians? You don't have to think, because you take the enemies of the gang. My gang wanted to protect its territory and they sent me to scare a member of the next gang, in the next suburb. I told him to be careful because we were the first gang in the area and he should keep out. He takes a knife. My knife is quicker. I stab him. He stabs me. I stab him more than he stabs me and when I leave, he is lying in blood. Maybe he died. I don't know. Some days after, I hear the police want me, his gang wants me, everybody wants me. Except my mother. Okay, also my mother, but she wants me to leave. She was talking for a long time about coming to Israel. This was the time, she said. You go, we will follow.

You said he was your friend?

That was my joke.

When Arieh told a story, I watched, mesmerised by his tonal rhythms, the play of the tale in his hands, his head dancing, and there was something else, a kind of joy, which I thought might be Persian. He, like most others on the kibbutz, did not fit a Jewish stereotype. His hair was thick and curly, his eyes intense, dark and under heavy black eyebrows. His nose flat and wide, above a strong and full mouth. His face marked with deep lines and his body stocky, solid, muscular. We often ran to the swimming pool late in the day, after dark, and wrestled, sometimes naked, like two Greek warriors. No-one won. We were equal. He had wrestled as a sport in school and I had wrestled in boarding school to defeat stronger, bigger boys.

You think the police and the other gang were working together? I asked.

Who knows. It was Iran. The West sings sweet songs to the Shah but he is a corrupt *ben zona*, a son of a bitch, and if the man at the top is corrupt, then the corruption goes all the way underneath. Many Jews like him because he made life easier for them, but we were not Jews that the Shah helped. There is one question I always ask – Were the police after me because the other gang was paying them, or because the man I stabbed was dead? I never knew. I can never know, never go back. Here I am, in the land of my forefathers, Israel, the homeland of every Jew, even if he stabbed or got stabbed, rich or poor, ugly or as good-looking as me. My luck is that the man I stabbed was not a Jew and so I won't run into him here. If he lives. Or his family, if he doesn't.

As far as Arieh knew, his own family had been in Persia since Cyrus the Great, creator and king of the first Persian empire, the man who released Jews from Babylonian captivity and who decreed that the Second Temple be built in Jerusalem.

Most Jews went back to Judea, he said, to rebuild Jerusalem. My family stayed and went nowhere. The history tells us that the Babylonian king Nebuchadnezzar II took nobles as hostages and maybe he took my people too and they never made it back to nobility. My grandfather worked in a furniture store fixing broken chairs. And me, I learnt to wrestle, run, street fight and fix motorbikes.

When I told Arieh about Neeva, he said: She's a *sabra*, Israeli-born? You are a brave man, my friend.

Yizrael Valley

Her work sometimes took her away from Gavrot for up to three weeks, but, more usually, one or two. She said she could not say exactly what she did in the army.

I work in administration, she said. With a general. He has important work and when he travels, I must go with him.

Like a secretary?

Maybe.

When she returned to the kibbutz, we fell into each other's arms and when we had free time we hiked on trips with the orchardist, Yigal. He took us up high towards Mount Hermon in the tight corner where Syria, Lebanon and Israel converge. We swam in a cool pool and walked up the mountain again to watch vultures.

This is a war zone, said Yigal. They patrol the sky, endlessly, knowing something will die, if not now, then soon, and be ripe for feasting.

We walked through filthy mountain streams and stagnant ponds, and touched rocks that had been touched by Jesus, or his disciples, or Saul, David, Goliath, any number of ancients who had inhabited Judea, Israel, Canaan, all the lands of the Bible. I dreamt of them as we wandered and we slept.

On another trip, just the two of us, we went to the Kinneret, the Sea of Galilee, and walked through a beautiful valley with lustrous vegetation, clear waterfalls and large pools. We swam and jumped and lay in the cool and slept a little. We did not want to leave. We forgot to eat. Outside of the valley all was dry and barren, harsh and hot, but we had to move on and so left the fresh air for the harsh heat and found little solace in the warm waters of the Kinneret. We swam until exhausted and slept on the beach that night and the next day hitched a ride to Nazareth with an Arab man who offered me money for Neeva. I put my hand on the South African hunting knife I wore by my side and told him I was from Australia and we didn't do that there. He laughed. I told him to put us down beside the road as I slowly pulled the knife until it was sitting snug in my fist. He saw the movement and the look in my eyes and stopped the van.

As we climbed a hill to a forest named after Churchill, Neeva asked: Would you have used that knife?

It was enough to pull it, I said. He was not a warrior, more a sexually frustrated small businessman.

We sat and looked out across the Yizrael Valley and when night closed in, we opened our sleeping bags off a road in a small clearing among shrubs, snuggled up close and gazed at the universe above. We talked of love and dreams and our endless future together. Eventually we slept, tangled in each other, fully clothed and wrapped in our bags.

A long time before light, we woke to the sounds of angry voices. My left hand searched for my knife. The voices belonged to faces above hands holding double-barrelled shotguns, and if the fingers on the triggers had pulled, both our heads would have disappeared into the universe we had fallen asleep admiring. Neeva responded quickly and I heard the words *Kibbutz Gavrot* and *Australian*. Both words calmed the men and one of them said something about Australians and laughed.

When the men had gone, Neeva said they thought we were Arab infiltrators hiding out, maybe planning a sabotage operation.

He said we could sleep, but to take care next time, she said. He said he liked Australians and asked if we needed water.

I found my long knife and laid it beside me, knowing it

would have been useful against the Arab man who wanted to buy Neeva and pointless against the shotguns. We snuggled up again in our love, clothes and sleeping bags, and slept as though the world was a better place because of it.

Gavrot 3

Neeva's mother had a pale blue tattoo on her arm. Everyone knew what that meant – she had survived Auschwitz, the mother of all camps, where over one million Jews had been killed, murdered, exterminated. Forever a symbol of humanity's ability to produce, from sick and deranged minds, a monstrous evil. The number on her arm was clear to all who saw it, as Auschwitz was the only concentration camp that tattooed. There was no need for the question, which camp were you in? And if the question was necessary, surely only another survivor, one who had known such horrors, could ask it. They had been, in the words of a French poet, Louis Aragon, *Branded like livestock, and like livestock to be butchered*. I found these words written on the wall of an abandoned building in Haifa.

As if that wasn't enough suffering in one family, Neeva's father was a sole survivor of a Polish family that had hidden under floors, in attics, and, finally, in holes they dug in a forest. One day he went out to forage for food and when he came back to his hole, there was no hole. Someone, or some monster, had filled in all the holes. His family were nearby, in a neat line, one had fallen one way, another had fallen the opposite, as they were cut to pieces by Nazi machine-gun fire. How could I face these people and ask them to trust me, a gentile, a non-Jew, a symbol of the evil they had survived? How could you ask them to share their daughter, their kibbutz, their country, with anyone other than their own? I asked anyway. Because I was in love.

I saw Neeva's father Haim walking towards the dining hall.

I had been waiting for him, knowing he would approach from that direction, from the chicken house where he worked. He didn't see me until I was next to him.

Haim, can I talk to you? I said, putting my hand out, in a gesture of reconciliation.

He struck out, hitting my hand away, increased his pace and said something to the man with him. I couldn't hear but I guessed he might have said: Fucking *goyim*, what the hell are we doing allowing them on our kibbutz? We don't need them. We can't trust them. We can do without them. And now they want our daughters.

Their feet seemed to land heavy on the ground. I couldn't hear them speak but I could hear their feet strike the earth. They did not look back. It was the first time I had looked him in the face. He was a handsome man with sad eyes. Not much shorter than me, he carried himself as though the ground was a danger to his feet. Almost as soon as they struck the earth they seemed to jump back, like naked soles on hot sand.

I did not eat that lunchtime, thinking to spare him my face in the dining hall.

At three o'clock the next morning, he broke Neeva's door down and charged in, screaming: Where is he? I will kill him.

All he found was his daughter sitting upright in bed. He cried and held her and pleaded with her. She told him he didn't understand, that I was a good man, that I was in Israel because I believed in its right to exist.

Neeva's mother called a family gathering and said: We know this world is not the world we grew in and so you have to make your own choices, to be with this man, or not, but know this, if you choose to be with him, then you are no longer our daughter.

I had left the theatre of South Africa, ruled by leftover Nazis, only to find myself in another theatre, one dominated by victims of the Nazi war machine, rendered incapable of recognising their daughter's lover as a man of good intentions, sound morals and a belief in their way of life and their right to it.

Two days after the family meeting, I found the note on my bed: *Jack, do not try to meet me, and if you will see me in the kibbutz, think that you do not know me. I will come to you in the night. Sad. Neeva.*

Leaving was the only way out.

Gavrot 4

I had three responses when threatened, or under pressure – hide, run, or work harder. In that last week on the kibbutz, I stayed in the orchards long after it was necessary and volunteered to wash dishes every night in the dining room where four hundred and fifty people threw plates at me, relentlessly, vigorously, and I encouraged them.

Come on, I yelled, is that all you can eat? Go back. Eat more. Give me your filth, your unwashed, your debris, I will wash everything and anything.

When I told Arieh to join me up a tree, the same tree, so I didn't have to yell, he knew it was serious.

I'm leaving, I said.

It's her parents, right? he asked. So many of these Israelis came from Europe and, even if they don't have a number on their arm, they wear a deep scar. This makes them full of hate for anyone not a Jew. For me, I think a Jew can live anywhere, and maybe it's best to keep quiet about being a Jew. Why am I a Jew? Because of my mother. What about my father? Was he a Jew? I don't know. He left early and she won't talk about him. I will not be marrying a Jew, no, I think I will marry someone from Norway.

Why Norway?

It's a just a place that came to me. No reason. Maybe because I never met a Jew from Norway and maybe they never heard of a Jew in Norway, or they don't care about Jew or not Jew.

I will miss you, Arieh, and this tree.

I hear Norway's trees are very tall and good to climb.

No tree will be the same again if you are not in it, Arieh.

And you, Jack, where will you go?

I will use my onward ticket to London and from there I will fly home to Australia.

When I came down from the tree and entered the dining room, the volunteer coordinator handed me a letter from Shoshanna in Cape Town. Inside was a newspaper clipping. The news was not good. Parsons had been arrested with one and a half tonnes of marijuana in the back of a truck, taken before a South African court and sentenced to ten years hard labour. Shoshanna offered no news of herself. If I had stayed, Parsons might have sucked me into the maelstrom.

I ran from South Africa just in time, only to run from Israel. I ran from South Africa because of hate and I was running from Israel because of love. There was no way I could see, or the one I loved could see, that our love could work, could fulfil its dream, not there, not then.

We left the kibbutz for a week on the coast together, to confirm our love, well away from her parents and other disapproving faces. Neeva and I were in the right place to distract ourselves from our pain, a place of misery, slavery and brutality, an ancient Roman fort.

We were employed by a hippie, Eli Avivi, on a site that had been an Arab village, a Canaanite city, a Phoenician town, overrun by Greeks, Romans, Persians, Crusaders, Ottomans and British. I imagined it a place Titus and Vespasian might have unloaded timber from Macedonia, timber required to build the war machines they used to pummel Jerusalem in 66 AD.

Avivi was a Persian Jew and was on his second build, the first construction having been demolished by Israeli government forces a little more than twenty years after they had demolished the Arab village, claiming his buildings were illegal. After the demolition, Eli moved back and declared his independence from the state by creating a tiny nation called Akhzivland.

My job was to lug heavy stone blocks up the steep bank from the Mediterranean foreshore to the construction site. I imagined Roman slaves crafting the limestone blocks two thousand years before, under the supervision of stone masons and soldiers with whips. The slaves might have been Jews, Greeks, Gauls, Assyrians, or men from any number of countries conquered by Rome. It was clear the stones were well used and that every occupier since had taken advantage and used them to build in their own image.

I used the imagined misery of others to force myself to work harder, to make sure I spilt more blood one day than I had the day before.

Avivi, a blunt man, offered accommodation even blunter. The toilet was a hole in the ground inside a stone building. This did not bother me, as I was well accustomed to squatting in an orchard, or behind a bush, in the land of my birth when a long walk to a toilet was too long to wait. The shower was outside in the open and the bed was a raised stone slab. Each night Neeva and I lay down exhausted, but sleeping was not easy. It was hot, nasty weather and the casual dips in the Mediterranean provided only short-term relief, but allowed us to wash the blood from our shoulders. I embraced it, needed the brutality of it, the chance it gave me to remember Rome, that ugliest of empires that once molested Palestine and all that surrounded it. And to forget the hate of Neeva's parents.

One night, as we lay beside each other on the slab, Neeva told me about Avram.

He was my boyfriend, she said. From the kibbutz next door and we have been together since high school.

Does he know about me?

Yes.

What does he say?

He says he will wait for me.

That makes two who will wait for you.

When the weather turned, the Mediterranean pummelled the shore and work was called off. Neeva and I went for a trip to the south. We made for what she said was a popular beach. There were people there, but none in the water, even though the strong wind was delivering good-sized waves. I stripped off, dived in and took every raging whitecap I could, waiting until the last second, catching the lip and allowing the force in the wave to dash me towards the sandy floor. Something mad rose in me. For the first time in my life I had experienced true love, and the forces opposing it were mounting – the parents, the ex-boyfriend, and the State of Israel.

You might love her, Avivi had said, but you will never marry her, not in Israel. It only allows marriages between Jews. But here, in Akhzivland, anyone can marry.

From the water, I heard screaming but ignored it. It got closer. I looked up and saw a man running at me, waving frantically, babbling in Hebrew.

Lo Ivrit, I yelled back. English.

You cannot swim here. It is dangerous. There are rips.

Chaver, I'm Australian. This is good for me.

He turned laughing and ran back to shore.

When I came out, dripping and happy, Neeva said the man had told her: Your friend is crazy, but I have seen these Australians before in the surf. He will live.

Genoralup 1973

1

There was a war raging in Israel and Jack Muir was living with his parents in Genoralup, a small town in the south-west of Western Australia best known for its gentle hills, lush forests, music festivals and lingering deposits of DDT.

The war raged and Muir raged, against himself, his parents. He hated everybody he met, in the bakery, in the front bar of the Freemasons Hotel and at the Kookaburra Café. He particularly hated the owners of the Kookaburra Café. Who would name a café after an intruder, a bird his grandfather said was introduced by Premier John Forrest who was afraid of snakes and because he had once seen one eat a snake in Melbourne, he ordered a family of the predators be brought back west?

IT's A BAD WAR THIS TIME.

That was the headline screaming from a newsstand when he arrived in Perth. Jack Muir bought a paper, wept, walked into a travel agent on St Georges Terrace and asked to be booked on flights back to Tel Aviv.

I can get you to London, said the agent, but you won't get into Israel. Tel Aviv airport is closed. There are no planes in or out.

Muir had caught the Australind passenger train to Bunbury and hitchhiked to Genoralup. His progress was constant and safe. There was no attempt by angry men to rob him, beat him, or by wild animals to trample him to death. The conversations were monosyllabic, boring and lacking in curiosity, from either party. He told no-one he was coming home. His final lift dropped him at the family farm and he walked through the orchard, across an open paddock, along the dam wall, up to the house and in the back door. Although his mother was in the kitchen, three rooms and a hallway away, she screamed at the sound of him, ran and flung herself at her son. They wept, fell to the floor, and wept some more.

What an idiot, Muir said, whenever he walked past the café and looked in to see it full of other idiots who had no idea what was going on in the world, the wars, assassinations, mass murders, invasions, suppression of freedom. The café ran long and narrow, with a service counter down one side, behind which stood the owner, Constantine Paradopoulus, a man who once played football for the local Australian Rules football team with a grace and poise never to be found behind his counter or in his milkshakes, coffees or toasted ham sandwiches. Muir didn't need to buy any of it to know it would be shit, but he went inside once to follow the sultry Sally Thompson, who he thought liked him, and maybe she did but when she turned in response to his hello he realised she was another idiot.

Where have you been, Jack? she asked.

Israel, he said.

Thank goodness you're out of there. I'll bet your parents are pleased.

He wanted a coffee but he had no patience for empty conversation with people who thought a kookaburra was a bird native to the west. When Muir wanted a coffee he made it himself, at home, strong, black, in a saucepan, with Turkish coffee out of a packet he bought in one of those city shops that specialised in products from Italy, Greece and the Middle East. It wasn't the same as the mix he drank in Israel, *botz*, they called it, or mud. That mix included powdered cardamom and when it was his turn to make a pot he stood close, with his nose in the steam, sniffing, holding the memory. He rarely made a pot in Genoralup, there was no cardamom in the mix, but his nose made sure the memories came with the steam. There was another ingredient that went with coffee – conversation. On the kibbutz they made *botz* in the old tin shed out in the fields on top of the valley that ran all the way down to the Jordan River and they told stories that may have been true, or may not, it didn't matter, and sometimes they argued, often about America and its power and evil and support of Israel.

If America did not support Israel, said Chuck McKinlay, it would not survive.

Slicha, excuse me, said Elan the kibbutznik, you know how much help America was during the Second World War, when Hitler killed six million Jews? It is nice that America helps, but, don't worry, my friend, we could do it all without America.

What about all the money from American Jews?

Nu, so?

That's not American help?

Those Jews, if they did not live in America, they would live somewhere else, Argentina, Australia maybe, and they would still contribute.

Muir missed intense conversation, peppered with universal issues of war, revolution, and global alignments. There were no conversations in Genoralup, only people making statements at each other. Or arguments between people who agreed with each other but couldn't see it, or people who didn't agree and could see it. None of them understood. They knew nothing. They talked about the weather, the stock market, the Potato Marketing Board, religion, where to buy the best cheesecake, or sport. He didn't bother going into the Freemasons Hotel front bar where only men stood, leant against the solid jarrah counter with one leg up on the spit trough below, and indulged in the same chatter as yesterday, the day before, always the same, ever since there was a bar and men in it – sport or sex. Sex talk was gossip about who was up who, jokes, or complaints about wives, partners or girlfriends. If Jack met any of them in the street they might mention the war to ask if it was still on, or if he knew anyone dead, or to make a statement: They're all bloody mad over there, aren't they, Jacky boy?

There was no-one in the Kookaburra Café, or a front bar in any of the town's three hotels, who could talk about important political figures – Yasser Arafat, Moshe Dayan, Golda Meir, Richard Nixon, Leonid Brezhnev, Che Guevara. Or the writers and thinkers he had discovered – Carl Jung, Hermann Hesse, Jean-Paul Sartre, Albert Camus. Muir was stuck in a cultural vacuum while the people he thought of as his people were in a battle for their lives only a few kilometres from the Syrian and Jordanian borders. He saw now it had been a cowardly dash from a country about to be invaded. He should have stayed and suffered and fought and proven his love for Neeva, his commitment to the continued existence of the State of Israel and his determination to fight for the kibbutz – the reality, the ideal. Love caused him to run, and love was burning holes in his soul.

Sally Thompson bought a Coca-Cola and Muir left the café in disgust. As he walked up the main street, he tried to figure out if he was more disgusted with Thompson – the shallow, yet fashionable local – or himself, for following her inside the café. He decided he was most deserving. He had no real interest in Thompson but he missed the company of women, their smell, their softness. And he missed Neeva, his girlfriend, who lay awake at night while men killed other men who were trying to kill them. What kind of a man left the love of his life behind in a war zone? He wrote every day. She wrote every week. Letters rushed back and forth. It wasn't enough to ease the guilt he felt for leaving her but it paled compared to the guilt he felt for attempting to steal the daughter of Holocaust-surviving parents.

Muir's own parents were at first pleased he was home and out of danger and then that pleasure morphed into concern that revealed itself in their words and faces. Muir could see the disappointment again in his father's face, the father who never thought he would amount to much, until he arrived home from Papua New Guinea drunk and broken and then he was sure he wouldn't. After Jack took control of the family business and turned a fading supermarket into a raging success, Andrew Muir changed his mind. In Andrew's face, Muir could see that mind changing again as he looked on the long-haired, bearded, miserable man before him.

What do you want to do, Jack? he asked.

The good man Muir looked at his son and wished he could help, wanted to, did not know how. His other sons were easier, their demands simple and usually involved money, or practical assistance with a purchase, or help fixing a piece of machinery. Andrew Muir knew when Jack put his mind to a task, he was determined and relentless. The household dishes were already shining from his attention.

Muir dug deep and found the answer his father would appreciate.

Work, Dad, I have to work.

2

Muir did not own a camera because it was a material object, a symbol of the capitalist plot to keep people complacent, satisfied, and stupid. Shower them with material objects – entertainment, chocolate and lollies – that way they will not protest, or revolt against the ruling elite.

There was a man in Genoralup Muir would have shown photographs to, but all he could do was explain what he had seen, what he knew, and what he could remember. Tom was a hippie. He had moved into Genoralup after Muir had left. He was one of an influx of young city people seeking alternative ways of living. They were part of the movement Muir had thought he was part of when he left. He was beginning to think there was no real movement, just a gaggle of young people wanting to get as far from their parents as they could and that meant buying or renting small blocks in small towns where they ate a lot of homegrown lettuce, washed once a week and ignored personal grooming. Like him they were not part of any organised movement, not like the great student uprisings in Germany, France or England, maybe Sydney, but more a mishmash of individuals wearing mainly cheesecloth and sandals they made themselves. They had no concept of socialism, of collectivism, because none of them had lived on a kibbutz. Only Jack Muir knew. He had lived the dream, worked the fields, lived like a pauper, argued with great vigour about existentialism, the destruction of the Second Temple by the Romans, and the poisonous junk marketed as food that came out of the United States, all designed to create a world dependent on its muck and to make outrageous profits for its capitalist monsters.

Say that again, said Tom.

The entire community meet once a week, said Muir. In the communal dining room, where they argue like hell and then vote. There could not be a purer form of democracy. Here in Australia we only get to vote every three years and our choice is limited to who the major political parties thrust in our faces.

And who is in charge?

They all are.

But they must have a president or chairman, or a group of leaders.

The two most important people are the social secretary and the financial secretary.

And these blokes, when they get the power, they never give it up, right, and stay there as long as Bob Menzies?

They have set two-year terms and they can only do two terms before they have to stand down, making way for the next two secretaries.

Tom was having difficulty absorbing the kibbutz infra-structure, so they smoked a joint.

Muir was still an immature smoker. He had started with joints on the ship over to South Africa and there he graduated to bongs and packed bottlenecks the locals made by soaking string in kerosene, wrapping it around a bottleneck, lighting it, and when the flame had died, cracking glass from glass. The result was always a clean break and, with some filing, no sharp edges.

Tom packed the joint with marijuana and tobacco. Muir watched, admiring Tom's dexterity, and guessed his friend would probably prefer the South African experience, where tobacco was never used to dilute the dope of all dopes – Durban Poison.

You know what, Jack? said Tom. Your father is the only businessman in town who stops to talk to me in the street, ask me how I am and if I need anything. Some fuckers yell at me to get back in the hole I climbed out of and one bloke last week yelled: You fucking poofta! Why don't you fuck off and fuck yourself?

It wasn't a Muir was it? Because they're all my cousins. Or uncles. Or brothers.

Looked more like one of those Robinsons.

They often met up in Tom's shed on the outskirts of town. The first time Muir walked all the way out, he started from his father's business. His mother had given him a lift into town and on the way she let loose her fears.

Your future was assured here, Jack, she said. Everyone said you did well in the business and on the farm. You had everything you could ever want and I know a lot of the young girls were keen on you. We understand you need to find yourself but how long will that go on? At least you're not taking drugs. That would be our biggest fear.

As she spoke, he leant down and adjusted the lump of hash tucked into the top of his above-ankle boots laced tight and every day reminding him of South Africa. He had bought them in Cape Town, along with the hunting knife he bought to protect himself from inner-city beggars and outer-city baboons.

Believe me, there are other fears, she said, that you have a child out of wedlock, or even worse, an abortion, are arrested for a serious crime, spend time in jail or, heaven forbid, get killed on one of your adventures overseas. As if it wasn't enough that you were arrested for being drunk and dangerous when you came home from Papua New Guinea.

She stopped then. She always stopped then, it was a period of great shame for the family, the Muir name splashed all over the front page of the *Sunday Times*, alongside a photograph of his father's Holden Premier sedan, crushed, smashed, an insurance write-off. The car was pictured beside the snapped power pole with the news that his destructive escapade had denied electricity to Claremont, Cottesloe and Peppermint

Grove, three of Perth's most prestigious suburbs.

I should be back in Israel with Neeva, he told her, helping defend the kibbutz.

Are you depressed?

Probably, but I won't let it get me down.

She almost laughed through the tears. He knew that she knew about depression. It was an unspoken, shared burden, and perhaps what caused their emotional outbursts, especially if Muir failed to keep a commitment.

Bugger you, Jack, she would yell. I said we needed the car at nine thirty. It's now ten thirty. When will you learn not to be so selfish?

Shit, he'd reply. You're only visiting friends. What does it matter?

Shit to you, Jack.

He had never heard her say shit. He was shocked, pleased and worried. He wanted her to admit her depression, but she wouldn't.

Have you ever been depressed, Mum?

Don't be silly, dear. I haven't got time for that sort of thing and your father would not allow it.

She dropped him off outside the family business, right in the middle of the main street, an easy but long walk out of town to Tom's shed. He didn't have to look back to know his mother would park her car and stroll from one end of the main street to the other, buying at least one item in every shop. The town was blessed with two bakers and two butchers. She would buy chops in one, steak in the other, then a loaf of bread in one bakery and buns in the other.

We have a duty, she would say, to spend money in all the shops, to help keep the town afloat.

That sounds like socialism, Jack said.

Don't be silly. Now off you go and visit that odd friend of yours. Although I wish you would spend more time with your old school friends.

Most of Muir's old grammar school friends were in real estate and property development and the thought of spending time with them repulsed him, as there was no more obvious example of capitalism at work and no greater enemy of the committed socialist.

3

Tom was a small, wiry man with long hair and beard. His lips were thin and tight and his eyes piercing. His hands were in keeping with the rest of him, small, but strong, and Muir knew why as soon as he entered the shed for the first time.

Jesus, Tom, he said, where did you get that?

There was a piano up against the back wall, the one that faced the jarrahs that grew all the way down to the riverbank. Before he answered, Tom sat on the chair, lifted the lid and played. He could play. Muir didn't know what he was playing but it was a classic and then Tom played a jazz piece, and next sang 'The Long and Winding Road' and Muir remembered the guitar he bought before he left home, the lessons he took from the folk-singing farmer who, after three weeks, said: Forget it, Jack. You're a good shopkeeper, but you don't have the fingers for guitar. He resented not having the fingers for guitar or piano. Both sounds infiltrated his soul yet were denied access to his hands. He wondered who to blame.

When Tom pulled down the cover, he said: Your dad found it for me.

Andrew Muir? He hasn't a musical bone in his body.

Maybe not, but one of his Rotary friends asked him if he knew someone who wanted a piano and he asked me and I said yes and he got the bloke who delivers groceries to deliver it to me.

That night Andrew Muir took his son to the Rotary Club meeting in the Freemasons Hotel. Muir was nervous and smoked one cigarette after the other, as he had when he got back to the kibbutz settlement after being shot at by an infiltrator who slipped across the Jordan River planning a hit-and-run. Muir believed he had coped quite well with the inaccurate bullets and this suggested to him he would be solid and calm in a war zone. Then something inside disengaged, got tangled up with incompatible objects, organs and his nervous system lost control, his brain howled in sympathy and he pulled a smoke, smoked it to its butt, pulled another, and although that would have been enough on a normal day it wasn't, and as each one ended another kept appearing in his hand and six were ashes before five minutes.

He had been on his own in the pear orchard, about ten kilometres from the settlement, when he heard the first shot and ran to the end of the line of trees. When he hit the opening and showed himself, the man took aim. He fell flat a second before he heard the next crack and ran on his hands, knees and stomach in a way he would not have thought possible. He hid in long grass and lay still. He was sure he fell asleep because he woke with a jump when he heard the massive Romanian tractor charging through the orchard. He ran out. Yigal stopped. Muir climbed behind and the Romanian charged again.

There was an infiltrator, yelled Yigal.

He shot at me, yelled Muir.

He was a shit shot.

I'm glad.

We think some soldiers got him. Everyone inside the kibbutz now. Then we remembered you.

Thank you.

Don't mention it.

You got a smoke, Yigal?

When the president of the Genoralup Rotary Club, Arthur

Brockelhurst, introduced him, Muir kept his smoke in his hand as he walked to the front of the room. When he had finished, Brockelhurst said: Are they communists, those people, and doesn't that crush the individual person?

Let me tell you a story, said Muir, you remember that big fire out at Brookes' farm? They lost everything. I'll bet a lot of you gave stuff to help out. I know Dad gave a fridge and our best point twenty-two rifle. I was angry with him for that. He said to me: Listen, they have more need of this rifle out there on their isolated farm than we do in here, close to town. That's classic communism: from each according to his ability, to each according to his need. None of that Russian or Chinese totalitarian bullshit, which is about crushing the individual and making him subservient to the state, not even to the state, to Stalin and Mao. The kibbutz movement believes in the education and improvement of the individual because if the individual achieves, this will benefit the collective.

He let them think about that in silence and added: Now, you tell me, is Andrew Muir a communist?

The Rotarians laughed heartily.

They drove home in silence, but when they got out and walked to the front door, Andrew reached out and put his hand on Jack's shoulder.

You made some of those blokes think a bit, Jack, he said. Can't be a bad thing.

Muir didn't turn to look at his father for fear of him seeing the tears in his eyes.

There was nothing to do but work. It was why the kibbutzniks in the orchards, the kitchen, the chicken house and those who watched the volunteers, liked, or respected, the Australian Jack Muir – he worked. Give him a job, he went at it with a passion, a vigour, a kind of madness. Give him twenty minutes to do it, it was done in five. Give him a day, it was done in half.

He exhausted himself to sleep every night in his parents' house high on a hill in Genoralup, a town of peace and tranquillity, if you ignored the murder of that girl whose body was left dead in the creek behind the Kookaburra Café and the unrecorded incidents in the late eighteen hundreds of angry settlers murdering all inhabitants of two Noongar campsites on the outskirts of town.

There was nothing to do but work. He was preparing for his return to Israel, when he would take Neeva, she would take him, and they would seek a new life in another kibbutz away from her angry and traumatised parents. And Avram, who lingered somewhere, waiting, hoping. But not now, because Avram, at least, was in the army, at the front.

There was a war on, and Jack Muir was back on the kibbutz. He could see the soldiers coming over the hill from Jordan, wearing the distinctive square helmet. Not Arabs. Germans. He ran to the machinery yard and climbed on the massive Romanian tractor with the huge back wheels and the long nose. Yigal was there, yelling, but Muir could not hear.

I've got to save Neeva's mother, he yelled.

He rode the Romanian like a tank, stormed through the

German line, knocking them back into the death camp. Neeva's mother was waiting for him.

He woke sweating, yet relieved. He got out of bed and went to work.

He got a job in a shearing shed owned by a farmer friend of his father. He worked with the same zeal he had shown on the kibbutz. The shearers and his fellow shedhands sometimes made fun of his fervour.

What is it with you, Muir? Pete Jackson asked one day in smoko. Your brother's a bloody lawyer, isn't he? What are you doing fucking around in a shearing shed?

And the farmer, old Jim Williams, said to him one day: I always thought you were a lazy young bastard, Jack, but, I'll tell you what, you can bloody well work.

What made you think I was lazy, Jim?

I guess I didn't really know, just those stories I heard about you failing school, drinking and getting into trouble.

Muir upped his work rate, intensified his commitment, so much so old Jim took him aside and said: Ease up, young Jack, you're making the others look lazy. Not good for shed morale.

At night, after work, in his parents' house, he ate his meal in silence, showered, went to bed and cried until he slept.

His next job was in a pine plantation, full of young trees trying to make their way through the native shrubs and young marris attempting to retake their natural soil. Muir was given a knapsack with a tank full of chemicals and told to spray, and thus kill, all the plants that belonged there. He worked hard for two days, then sat and asked himself what he was doing, why he was doing it, and if it was the right thing to be doing. He decided he could not poison native plants so that a non-native, planted purely for profit, could prosper. He climbed on his borrowed motorbike and rode to the farmer's house.

The farmer was surprised to see him.

What is it, Jack? said Longstaff. I'm not paying you enough?

It's not that, he said, I can't do the work.

It's not that tiring, surely. I heard you were a good worker.

It's not right.

Not right? What the hell are you talking about?

To poison the natives so the pine trees can come on.

Right doesn't come into it. We're trying to make a living here. Me. You. The whole bloody town. What are you, a bloody communist now? I'd heard you'd gone a bit funny, but you still need money, even bloody communists need money.

I left all the equipment out there under the tarpaulin, Jack said. Thanks for the work. Don't worry about the money.

Now hang on a minute, don't you suck me into your communist bullshit. I'll give the bloody money to your dad when I see him next.

There were more shearing sheds, a cartage contractor, but the war raged and Muir was stuck in a small town with small minds and he could feel his own mind shrinking to fit.

Nothing was the same. Everything was the same. He couldn't hide. He thought the older men looked at him with disdain because they thought to themselves: We didn't kick the Ottomans out of Palestine so the bloody Arabs could have it. Why aren't you there?

Nobody understood. For most people, the war was a paper war, it was on television and radio. For Muir it was a place where he had lived and loved, a place that inhabited his inner, noisy self, and his imaginings were full of destroyed towns, villages, kibbutzim, and fields full of bomb craters, and dead people.

Neeva wrote that he should not return to Israel, that already one child of the kibbutz, a fighter bomber pilot, had died, shot down over Egypt. She was afraid, and afraid for Muir if he returned because she knew he would take risks and the war was not his war. Sometimes she went to the houses of others to sleep because of her fear, but she tried hard to sleep alone, to be strong.

He saw a note on the Freemasons Hotel window: DISHWASHER WANTED. All day he worked in a shed, or an orchard, and at night he wrapped himself in an apron and plunged his hands into steaming hot water.

It's a bit hot, isn't it? said the chef.

Hotter the better, said Muir.

Neeva's notes kept coming.

From Ein Dorot two men were killed and from Gavrot two men missing and we don't know about them anything.

He got a job in an apple-packing shed and worked so hard he broke a toe and didn't notice. When home with his parents, exhausted, bruised, sunburnt, he only left his room to eat. And wash dishes.

You haven't lost your knack, said his mother.

It keeps me sane, said Muir.

Each letter from Neeva mentioned Avram and his progress through a sad and depressing time.

It seems that Avram forgive everything about us, that I leave him for you, and he accept it like it is, because he said he is afraid from the hate. He also afraid people now start to hate the Arabs. From the village nearby, he has two Arab friends. They are Israeli Arab and also in the army. How can people hate them? he said.

Muir wrote back of his undying love and desire to return and she wrote to forget her, that Israel was not a place for him, that he should remember their love, to never forget it and try to find a new love and maybe their love would make his next love stronger.

Kincannup 2018

The Whalers Retreat Café and Restaurant sits one block back from the beach at Binalup. The long shoreline runs almost five kilometres in a wide glorious curve to Yakinup, the place of the long-necked turtle. In summer, Tony the owner cranks his coffee machine around sunrise and is ready for business by six o'clock. By the time we get there it is not unusual to find furniture stacked on the pavement for alfresco dining. While Tony brews his best we chip in and spread the tables and chairs ready for the rush of holiday-makers, city workers, retirees and occasional visiting celebrities.

You won't believe who was in here yesterday, says Tony.

Who?

Richard Roxburgh.

Who's Richard Roxburgh?

From *Rake*, that lawyer bloke on the ABC.

Whenever I hear a name that sounds like it could be Jewish, my mind wanders back to that time on the kibbutz and these days I fear for my friends bordering the Gaza strip, and those I once knew now trapped inside Gaza. No-one wants to live on a border between two parties in a constant state of war.

Tony and I were in my house on the slopes of Corndurup, the hill that rises above Binalup and the little cove that nestled in its corner of rocks, with jutting jetty and surrounding shark net. It was one of those crisp, still autumn days and we could see across the bay to the twin islands, once home to sealers who dragged

Noongar Menang women from onshore to keep as sex slaves. I had said the week before: Tony, you've been making me coffee ever since you took over this place. Come to my house and I'll make you *botz*.

And while you're at it, I'll rearrange your furniture, he said.

Over coffee, Tony announced that he thought he might be Jewish, because his mother was, but not his father.

According to the State of Israel and the Chief Rabbi, you are a Jew.

But what about me? I don't look, or feel like a Jew. And I don't want to go to Israel.

When I first walked the streets of Tel Aviv, I told him, the day after I arrived, I kept looking for the Jew. No-one looked like a Jew. You'd be fine there. People sometimes ask me if I'm Jewish. Look at me. I don't even look like Andrew Muir.

Who's he?

My father.

Tony sat back with his cup and let his eyes wander over the rooftops down to the bay.

I rubbed my face, messed with the coffee cups, settled and took my time to go on, because making *botz* was not an event I completed lightly. It was a ritual. I took the pot, filled it with rainwater, dropped in eight spoons of coconut sugar and eight heaped spoons of my favourite finely-ground called Lebanese Mix. I cracked eight cardamom seed pods with a pair of pliers, dropped the seeds into a marble bowl and crushed them with the marble pestle and then they too hit the pot. Once the mix was in, I stood over it all, managing the flame, waiting for a shift in surface tension. With first sight, off with the pot, let it settle, followed by two more waves across the flame for two more surface shifts. Then, and only then, was the *botz* ready. Almost. Because before drinking, it sits, to brew and settle.

You all right, Jack? asked Tony.

Sure, where was I?

You mentioned your father, Andrew.

Yeah, sorry, soon as I mentioned my father I heard his voice again.

Genoralup 1973

Jack Muir had no money, smoked dope, and clouds of despair were smothering him under a thick veil of depression. He tried not to read newspapers, refused to watch television but could not avoid the radio news. He knew the war in Israel was not going well and every night when he closed his eyes he could see Neeva crying.

Two miracles changed his life.

One evening, as he was heading towards the kitchen to wash dishes following the evening meal, his mother and father stopped him in the hallway. It was a memory he kept his entire life and even forty years later could still make him feel emotions so strong that, when telling others, he would have to sit down for fear of fainting.

We know you don't have much money, said his mother, but your father and I would like you to have this. You can use it to see a psychiatrist, to help with your grief or whatever it is that troubles you, or pay for a return ticket to Israel.

His mother was crying. His father stoic, solid, with a cheque in his hand.

I'm sorry, Jack said. You want to give me money?

His father held out the cheque.

Jack made a move forward with one hand pointing towards the kitchen.

The dishes, he said.

It's all right, Jack, said his father. We want you to have the money.

And then they all surprised themselves by reaching out and taking hold of each other, not in a hug, but a kind of hug, a hug by people who were not used to hugging, wanted desperately to hug but were not sure how to go about it. Then, just as quickly, they broke, all going in different directions – his mother upstairs to the main bedroom, his father outside to work on a machine, and Jack Muir headed for the kitchen sink.

Later, as he lay in bed, his eyes full of tears, his heart full of love and longing, he pondered what his mother had said.

What she said, really, he thought, was here is some money, get yourself sorted, psychologically, or go back to Israel, even if that means getting killed. What a mother you are, Glorvina Muir. Many mothers say such things, of course, or there would be fewer men off to war, but you, Glorvina, are not one of those mothers. You grew up with an abusive father who drank and had mistresses living on the family farm. You battled depression all your life and fussed over your own mother who talked to you as though you would never achieve adulthood. To stand in front of me and say such a thing must have torn you apart.

As long as they all lived, the cheque was never mentioned.

Two days later, the next miracle.

A letter arrived from Neeva with news of an even more surprising shift. Her mother, the Auschwitz survivor, had found the courage to seek reconciliation and offer the unimaginable. When Muir read her words, he wept so hard the stains never left the paper they were written on.

Jack, my mother has talked to me. And she surprised me. She asked if I would like to go and to see you. She said she didn't understand why it happened that they turned on you like they did and now they want to go with me, with my feeling. I hope your parents well.

Gavrot 1973

1

It was not the arrival I expected. Immigration was nervous, irritable. There was no-one working on my case, then two, then three. Not enough, so they called security. Security was nervous, irritable. That made three nervous, irritable men and one angry woman. Not enough, they called the airport police. The tall, rugged policeman said nothing, grabbed me, hustled me out of the area, up the stairs and into a holding cell.

Call Yigal at Kibbutz Gavrot, I yelled.

Shtok, said the man.

I was alone in the cell, not much of a cell, more a room with a grated door. They must have been short of real, or usual suspects. I was clearly harmless, an idealistic hippie socialist, and most of my clothes were standard kibbutz-issue blue.

Twenty minutes later, a good-looking young man in casual clothing, as though called from a nearby café, walked up to the cell door.

What is your name? he asked.

Jack Muir.

He held my passport in one hand.

Australian?

Yes.

Why are you here?

There's a war on.

Now is not the time for jokes, my friend.

All the young men and women from Kibbutz Gavrot are in the army or the air force. They are short of workers. I came to help. I grew up on a farm. I can do farm work.

Beseder. Okay. This man, Yigal, you know him?

He is my kibbutz father and in charge of the *mataim*, the orchards. We work together. We are a team. We give according to our ability and take very little.

Save your kibbutz propaganda. Tell me, why did you come to Israel with no return ticket and no money?

I didn't plan to return and on kibbutz who needs money?

Are you Jewish?

Does it matter?

Are you a brave man?

No. But I love my kibbutz, I love this country and I love a *sabra*.

A *sabra*? You must be a brave man. Or a crazy one.

Ken.

He smiled and I could see why, in his local café, he would attract attention.

I will call this Yigal. Wait here.

I took two bars in the cell door, shook them gently and said: I promise not to go anywhere.

Two hours later I was released and picked up by a member of Kibbutz Gavrot and taken to an apartment. Most kibbutzim owned city apartments for members who had to visit Tel Aviv on business, medical appointments, or brief shopping trips. I had not met the man before and he didn't speak English. I slept alone and the next day he drove me to the Tel Aviv Central Bus Station, a rabbit warren of roads and bus stops marked with iron railings that seemed to make it clear where passengers should line up. The passengers in the queue for the bus north ignored all signs and created their own queueing system. In the middle of the chaos that followed the arrival of the bus, I was hit on the back of the head by a woman who thought I should have fought harder to stop the family of eight who jumped the main queue. She also managed to reach across me and hit one of the family members, a young man wearing army boots but no uniform. He laughed at her. That was when she hit me.

Twenty-five kilometres out of the city, the family opened their lunch boxes and offered food to all the passengers down the back of the bus, including the violent young woman, and me. Both of us forgave, chose items, and ate.

As the bus headed north, young soldiers got on and off. Men and women. Even in uniforms, the determined young women with luscious hair were interesting, enticing, but I only had eyes for Neeva. At the last bus station before Gavrot I looked everywhere for Neeva, as though she knew I would be there and was waiting. She wasn't. And she wasn't on the kibbutz. She, like all those fulfilling their army and air force commitments, was at her post.

I went straight to work.

2

In the north, day and night, planes flew missions, artillery fired and troops moved. Although the major tank and ground troop battles for the Golan Heights had been fought, there was no sign of peace – unlike in the south, where Egypt and Israel had agreed on a ceasefire, although neither side kept its promise.

Yigal said he knew I would come back. He didn't hug me but took my hand and arm and pulled me towards him. On my first day back in the orchards, he asked: We know you can drive a tractor, but can you also shoot a pistol?

I worked in a bank, I said, as a teller. We had to do pistol training.

What for?

In case we were robbed.

So, the bank and the police said if someone comes to rob you, you can take a gun and shoot them?

It never happened in any branch I ever worked in.

Yigal took me to the armaments shed and showed me a Browning semi-automatic. It looked old and unkempt, as though discarded on a battlefield, forgotten and pummelled by tank tracks and truck tyres, then found and returned to its shed. It reminded me of the bank pistols that looked like World War II relics. They were always in the tellers' boxes, in Perth, country towns, and Papua New Guinea where part of me had wanted a bank robber to storm in, demand money, test me. Maybe it was the same part that had formed a belief that a man could never be truly a man until he had killed another man.

When you go to the orchard tonight, said Yigal, fire off a couple of rounds to make sure it works. And to scare off insurgents. Then you can finish spraying without interruption.

What about a holster?

There is no holster for this pistol. You will put it in your pants. This will make you very careful. Do you have children?

No.

Do you want children?

I do.

Well, you must be very, very careful, because if it goes off in your pants, you will not have children. Or the thing that makes them.

In Genoralup we sprayed the orchards when we had time, always during the day, and when the winds were light. Our equipment was old, third-hand and required constant maintenance. The hose nozzle was inefficient and liquids found their way over the sprayer standing on the trailer, the tractor driver and, sometimes, its intended target, the fruit trees. We wore ordinary clothes and, if it was hot, we bared our chests. We sprayed malathion, DDT and 245T, otherwise known as Agent Orange. The Agent Orange we sprayed on blackberry bushes because we were tired of hoeing, slashing and digging. They kept coming back. And we began to hate blackberry jam. We didn't know 245T was Agent Orange until the Vietnam War ended and all the horror was revealed. So much about so much we had no idea. My grandfather introduced the only innovation – an empty wheat bag cut all the way around, leaving one corner attached. Our heads went into the corner and the bag draped down like a cloak over our shoulders and backs. This was designed to keep our head and backs dry. The heavy hessian material was fine on a cool or cold day, but on hot days we discarded the bag for a hat and an old tea towel.

With the gun in my possession, Yigal showed me the airtight space outfit with helmet I had to wear. It was made with heavy-duty rubber, and my skin began to ooze sweat as soon as I climbed in.

The gun, Yigal, where do I put the gun?

It must go inside, he said. If you wear it outside it will get wet and if the bank robbers come it will not fire.

He did not hold his laughter as I unzipped, placed the gun in my pants, zipped back up and headed for the outer orchards.

It was a long, slow drive, accompanied by frequent stops to ensure the Browning safety catch had not slipped. With every stop I turned off the tractor and sat in the dark silence, listening for sounds I did not want to hear, of creeping men, armed and murderous. It was nothing like sitting in a jarrah forest with its soft cracks, rustling leaves and carolling magpies, where you could only see the next tree and a murderer could kill you before you heard him. But murderers did not lurk in jarrah forests, only birds and possums and stories hidden in places sacred to the First People.

The road out of the kibbutz ran along a ridge up high above the Yizrael Valley and there was enough light to see the horizon where Jordan began and the infiltrator who shot at me once started his journey.

It was around midnight. Not a breath of wind. I could hear artillery fire. A fierce battle raged over Mount Hermon and on high ground in the Golan Heights. The south was getting noisier with an increase in incidents between Israeli and Egyptian troops in the Sinai. As for the Lebanese and Jordanian borders, there were no battles, but an increase in incursions with subsequent terrorist attacks on Israeli communities.

I was afraid, not of infiltrators, or that a stray shell would find me in the orchard and smash me to gristle, blood and bone, but that the pistol in my pants would go off and blow my genitals to blood and flecks. Neeva would not want me then.

Inside the fence surrounding the outer orchards, I stopped, turned off the tractor and sat, again in silence. I could see the flashes and hear the crack and echo of artillery. I fired off one round, felt the kick, then fired another and waited for the sounds of running feet. Nothing. I was alone and aware that people were dying not far from where I was about to spray, smashed to pieces by direct hits, maybe maimed for life, or survived to pick up the broken members of units, platoons, or families. I had returned to save the kibbutz, to work while others fought. There were other volunteers, but they were mainly big-city Jews and Yigal said I was the only one he knew who had grown up with tractors and guns.

I started the tractor, drove to the designated orchard, lined up in the first row, and started the spraying machine behind me. It was then I regretted not having a camera, because this was equipment my father and grandfather should see. This was how to spray an orchard – one operator, body fully enclosed and protected, rotating spraying machine behind.

I completed two rows before I stopped to check the pistol.

3

Neeva came home on leave and our first meeting was awkward. We had exhausted so much love in our first months together and in our letter writing, it was strange to see each other in the flesh. And we waited until we got to her room before we hugged and tugged and rolled naked and glorious because, although her parents had given us permission, we thought it best to keep our affections private. And then there was Avram, her first boyfriend, the young soldier she met in high school on the kibbutz next door, the man she left for me, then I left, and I knew she had seen him again and she said she was finished with him but I wasn't sure. I met him once and I liked him. He was a tall, thin, shy man. He looked too sensitive to be in a war lugging a gun for killing. I could not find anger in his eyes, even though I thought if he was going to be angry with anyone, it would be me.

Have you seen Avram? I asked.

Yes, she said. He is a good and kind man.

You are finished with him?

I am finished with him, but I am not sure he is finished with me.

Neither am I.

In her youth, Neeva had been a gymnast and a dancer, and when I picked her up she rode me around the room and we bounced back and forth, sometimes I rode her, sometimes she me, and then we fell to her mattress on the floor for the final tangle which nearly broke my soul.

She was home long enough for us to go on a short trip with

Yigal and another couple, down into the Negev, where we walked along a stream and came upon a waterfall tumbling over smooth rocks, as though polished to impress tourists. We had let Yigal and the two New Zealanders go on ahead. We lingered as though knowing something, thinking something, and as soon as we came to the falling water, we knew what it was. It was a hot day and it made sense to remove our clothes before we hopped in the cold, fresh, cascading stream.

Don't drink, she said. The water might be bad.

I drank anyway, held my neck and faked my death. She wrestled with me, slapping water off my face. Then we ran in and out, chasing, dancing, laughing. It seemed to me the lovemaking of teenagers, wanting, but not quite ready, full of desire, but not yet sure how to complete the game until she forced herself on me.

I lost all fight, let her have me, in the way she wanted, unlike the first time we locked, when I was too eager and she sat up at the end of it all and said: Are you normally finished so fast?

I had told her then that I had been abstinent for over two years, that I had not wanted to have sex with another woman unless I loved her, that I was tired of casual sex tainted with nervous desire, and more than anything I wanted to love and be loved. She held me close and asked that we do it again after a quick shower and she taught me to hold and wait, to make sure she was with me, and I loved her so much I wanted to run to her parents' room and tell them I loved them too because they had forgiven me my non-Jewishness, allowed me to be with their daughter in the way of men and women in love and it must have taken so much courage and I would never forget.

That day in the Negev, as we lay in the sun, up against the rocks by the waterfall, she turned to me and said: You have learnt so much.

A student is only as good as his teacher, I said.

After she returned to the army and I was alone, there were old friends to catch up with. First was the Argentinian, Eliezer.

I found him in his room. He looked older, thinner and I could see his upper arm muscles were fading. He wore the standard kibbutz-issue blue short-sleeved shirt with accompanying long pants. His grey hair and moustache were both snowy white, but his blue eyes had not lost their sparkle.

How come you, I asked, an old Jew, have such blue eyes?

To be a Jew, Jack, all the women before me had to be a Jew, but who said anything about the men?

He laughed, and when he laughed there were no more wars. Just for a few seconds, and then there was one, because we could hear the planes fly overhead.

Not only that, *chaver*, the women only had to say they were Jews, or look like Jews. Who knew? And the *goyim* knew that life for a Jew was so miserable, so dangerous, if you said you were a Jew, you had to be a Jew, or you were *meshugge*.

Conversations with Eliezer always took place at the back of his house, with *botz*. He thought he could make coffee, but he made the worst Turkish coffee in the kibbutz. It didn't matter, I didn't go there for the coffee, but the enlightenment, the laughter, and the conversation.

I am an old man now, Jack, he said. Soon all this will be over and I am not sure my children and their children will want to keep living the socialist dream. Already we have lost three young people to the United States, the best example of the opposite to the kibbutz, full of the high priests of capitalism. The only way to continue, I believe, will be to open our community to idealists, like you, from anywhere and everywhere. We are not religious. And who is a Jew anyway? In fifty years, who will care if someone is a Jew or not a Jew?

Eliezer's family migrated to Argentina in the eighteenth century and he considered himself lucky compared to European

Jews because all he had to survive was the Argentinian dictator Perón.

I left Argentina because of Perón and all those Nazis he let in, he said. Like that monster Adolf Eichmann, the traffic controller, the man who organised the transportation of Jews to concentration camps. No-one was surprised because Perón was on the side of Hitler and Mussolini in the war. And now the bastard is back in power with his new wife as vice-president. Argentina is doomed.

Israel was not doomed. The tide would turn. I was back where I belonged, in the arms of my lover, in the *mataim*, with the apples, pears and peaches. At night I washed dishes when rostered and intimidated those rostered with me. When Neeva was away, I had to share a room, but my roommates kept their distance. They saw how the kibbutzniks treated me, that I was favoured, that I was almost one of them.

4

When we drove out to the outlying orchards during the day, I swapped the Browning semi-automatic for an M16. Yigal and I took turns riding shotgun for each other – one day he took the tractor and I rode shotgun, and on another he took the gun and I took the wheel. Yigal wasn't there all the time because he was in the army reserve and when called, he had to head to the hills for some sort of duty he would not explain. He was a legend with some members. In the Six-Day War of 1967 he had been a paratrooper and they dropped him over the Golan Heights and left him and his company to kill, expel or capture Syrians – once invaders, now invaded. He and I were the only two in the orchards the day he told me what had happened.

I am a founding member of this kibbutz, Jack, he said. My parents came from Austria to escape the evils of that country and its brother country, Germany. We were full of ideals and we wanted to be a country like no other country on earth. We Jews always felt oppressed and completely without freedom. We hated colonialism, totalitarianism and the rejection of those famous French words – liberty, equality, fraternity. Our new country was to be founded on real socialist values, and principles, according to the highest thinking of Marx and Engels. The last thing we wanted was to behave like one of the arrogant nations we came from. And now we are occupying other countries and suppressing their people and behaving in a way which seems against those values and principles. But what can we do? The Arabs want us dead and wiped from the

Middle East map. We will not accept this.

Yigal was tall, dark, with intense brown eyes that wandered below thick eyebrows. His afro-style hair would not have been out of place in a fashionable rock band, but he couldn't sing. I knew this because he tried to remember a Beatles song and it didn't matter how much he tried, it made no sense. He admitted his mother had forced him to join a choir when he was a boy in Vienna and he was expelled because the choirmaster said he was tone-deaf.

What do you say, Jack? About all this?

I'm Australian, Yigal. We share our land with no-one. Sure, we stole it from the Aborigines, but we are only one nation on the entire island continent.

And you will never share it, because I know about you Australians from the Jews who were here first and who never left. They tell of the great Australian army of men on horses and how they made the Ottomans run like frightened goats, bleating and shaking their heads.

Some of those men were great-uncles of mine.

So we must take two horses one day and ride down the valley to Jordan.

We never did, but we did take a four-wheel drive into the valley and shoot a renegade steer that had broken out of the beef cattle field. Gavrot did not have a large cattle herd, just enough to keep three cowboys busy. They asked Yigal to hunt the animal because he was renowned as a fine shot over distances. As it happened, Yigal was at the wheel when we saw the beast and it was me who shot him with five attempts from the M16.

You got him in the end, Jack, he said, but five was probably excessive.

Lucky they didn't all hit, I said, and so we can take what's left to the kitchen for the meat eaters.

Kincannup 2018

Under my house I have installed gymnastic rings. They are odd pieces of exercise equipment for an older man, but I have learnt that as we age it is important to have small aims, difficult, yet achievable. During a visit to my doctor after a bodysurfing injury, he suggested I attend a gym to engage in more weight-bearing exercises, to build up the muscles around the injury in my shoulder. I don't like gyms, never did, full of sweaty, puffing men in front of floor-to-ceiling mirrors, parading their egos and worshipping their physiques. The doctor said perhaps I could buy my own set of weights with barbell. On a visit to a local fitness equipment retailer I spotted the gymnastic rings and bought them. Not only do they take up less space than barbells, they are more challenging, due to the need to balance the entire body while lifting it through chin-ups, pull-ups and leg lifts. It's not easy, lifting and balancing, it puts a strain on every part of your body, forces all the bits to work together.

And that was what I told Tony when I saw him next.

With all that working out, Jack, he said, we're going to have to hold the ladies back.

The Whalers Retreat had just closed its doors and Tony and I sat inside behind the rear counter so customers wouldn't see us, assume he was still open and demand coffee.

Do you get it, Tony, the bit about all the bits working together? I said. That's the ring work, but it's a good metaphor for relationships, that it helps to think of all parties creating the whole, rather than existing as separate entities.

Tony's eyes were wandering. He didn't get it.

That comment you made the other day, I said, about women

being a mystery. It's funny, but I never really thought of women as separate, as others. I mean, I knew they were different, of course, and that they had something I wanted, and lusted after.

That's a relief, said Tony. I was pretty sure you were straight, but thanks for the confirmation.

There have always been women in my life and, if you think about it, I drink coffee here with as many women as men.

That's true, but you're not living with them. You don't have to find your way through daily life with them, the small things and the big things. You come in, they are here, you sit together. Sometimes you even buy each other coffee.

And sometimes we leave together, because sometimes they need to talk about one of those big things and the Whalers Retreat is a little too public for that kind of conversation.

You able to sort those things out for them?

Not usually. Mostly they just want an ear, someone, perhaps a man, to listen to them.

You should start charging.

He wasn't going to get it, Tony. He wasn't built to get it. In Kincannup I had as many female friends as male friends and I realised that for the first time in my life I had a gender balance in friendships. There had always been more men in my external life, but women had dominated my inner, intimate life; they were the people who consoled me, whose shoulders I cried on, who offered solace in time of pain. There has always been more of my mother in me than my father.

Two days later, when Tony came to my table in the Whalers Retreat with a coffee in his hand I said: Tony, have you ever thought of your wife as your best friend, someone you can share your entire life with, rather than an appendage, tacked on to you, a mysterious creature you will never understand?

No, Tony said.

Gavrot 1974

1

I met Neeva in Haifa. She was in the coastal city on a mission and took two days leave. I brought a bag of clothes from her room and we stayed overnight in a youth hostel. The next day, Neeva bought bread, cheese and tomatoes. Nothing more. Maybe a cucumber. Then we walked. We climbed Mount Carmel to see the Baha'i temple.

The Baha'i temple was an impressive yet simple construction, and in my memory it sat like an elaborate shed on top of a mound. I imagined my old childhood friend, Jesus, would have appreciated it. He might have said: Now that's more like it. Simple, not too pretentious, not like all those cathedrals and ridiculously imposing buildings you Christians have built in my name. My name? What a joke. I talked in the fields, on the sides of hills, by lakes and rivers and I didn't wear jewellery made of gold and silver, and I washed the feet of untouchables.

As we left, Neeva told me the last new ingredient Israel needed was another religious centre.

We on the kibbutz do not believe in God, she said. Any god. In this aspect we are existentialists.

Neeva was a strong walker and we wandered away from the suburbs, out onto a hill overlooking a magnificent valley. It was probably the scene of a great battle in antiquity. Such a place, with its high slopes and long flat plain, must have been an ideal battleground. I could imagine the hordes lined up against each other, charging, slashing, thrusting, clubbing.

And the aftermath – the dead, dying, limbless, headless, blood and innards, acres of them.

But when I turned, I did not see dead men, all I saw was Neeva and knew I loved her. I could not imagine a deeper or greater happiness. We sat, broke bread, cut tomatoes and cucumber and cheese and sucked in the peace, the quiet, the love.

The next day she got up and caught a bus back to her army camp in the south, I caught a bus back to the kibbutz and went out into the orchards with an M16 by my side.

I forget how long she was away but when I next saw her light on, although I had only just finished work, hadn't eaten and dripped with sweat and the stench of hard and filthy work, I knocked on her door and as soon as it opened we were at each other, in the shower before our clothes were off. Still wet, we danced naked around her room and, finally, collapsed in a heap on her bed.

You know now, she said.

Thanks to you, I said.

As I cried a muffled cry she held me and asked why.

I never thought I could, or would, I said, love anyone as much as I love you.

Shall we leave the kibbutz? she asked.

You want to leave the kibbutz?

This is my home and always will be but there are many people here with small minds and you don't know it because you don't know enough Hebrew and if you knew what they say about us being together you would want to leave.

But not yet. You can't. You haven't finished with the army.

I don't know if I can take another year of this stupid army. There is an agreement coming with Egypt and Syria, and when that is finished the army will go back to where it was before the war.

I was shocked that she could consider leaving her country when it needed her. Israel, homeland of the Jewish people, they migrated here before, during and after the Second World War. For two thousand years before Jews had wandered all seven continents, longing for the Holy Land, uttering the wish, ever since the fifteenth century, *Next year in Jerusalem*. And now she wants to leave? Her parents, both Holocaust survivors, how would they respond? They made their way to Israel through unspeakable horrors to a place of safety, where all Jews could live knowing all the haters were outside, somewhere else, in other countries.

Yet I also knew that the place you were born in, grew up in, was not always a perfect fit, because when she spoke about Gavrot, I thought of Genoralup, a town I loved, yet could not live in. It wasn't the place, the country, it was the people.

There was a time, right after my arrest for drunken and dangerous driving, following my dismantling of a bus shelter and a power pole, that some people in Genoralup said all kinds of things about me and some of them were true, but many were made up by folk who took great delight in spreading ill tales of the Muir boy who was not like the other boys. One day the pine plantation farmer walked into my father's office and said: You know, I hold your son up to my sons as an example of exactly what not to do in life.

Andrew Muir was a cautious man, in word and deed, but on that day, according to my mother, he stood his full height and said to the man: Get out. And take your arrogance, ignorance and hubris with you.

At the time it surprised me, knowing that Andrew Muir would, in the face of a critic, defend me. Even I did not deserve it. Maybe I had been missing something about the man who spawned me, yet never spurned me.

2

Neeva was nowhere to be seen. She was everywhere in my life. I went to her room, to smell her scent, wash with her soap, lie on her sheets. She was in my thoughts, dreams, reveries. She had not been home for three weeks. Something was wrong. She had met someone taller, stronger, smarter. My eyes wandered.

Two Danish women arrived at the kibbutz. They were blonde, strong-limbed, open. I filled a plate with salad, fetta cheese, egg and hummus, then sat with them.

We are together, one said.

Ken, I said.

You mean yes, right, Ken is not your name?

No.

But really, we are together, we are lovers.

I am very happy for both of you. My name is Jack. Tomorrow you will be working with me in the *mataim*, the orchards. Make sure you wear a hat.

We thought you were making a move.

Never, I told them, I have a boyfriend.

Uri arrived with long hair, long beard, large nose, small hands, harmonica and a thick lump of hash. His first day in the orchards, you could see he was looking for someone to befriend. He chose me, the third week of his short stay.

There was a knock on my door.

You want to smoke some hash? said Uri.

Sure.

Let's go up into that little grove of eucalypts.

How did you know they were eucalypts?

California is full of them.

One day they'll all go up in smoke.

Some already have.

They'll come back.

Some already have.

I liked Uri and liked him even more after we got stoned and he told me his story.

I shouldn't be here, he said. But I had to experience kibbutz. I'm Jewish, of course, but not a Zionist. This place, part of Kibbutz Artzi, the far-left movement, sits in my ideological framework, but they are still Zionists, still part of the Jewish state infrastructure. Did you know most kibbutzim were placed for strategic reasons, to secure the borders drawn up in 1949, or to counter Arab villages?

I think you better crush some more of that lump, I said. My head needs to lighten up.

When I smoke, my head goes the other way, said Uri. It gets heavier. I seem to dive into deep philosophic streams.

I hadn't noticed, I told him.

I reached up and took a leaf, crushed it in my fingers and put them to my nose. The strong eucalyptus oil took me back to Genoralup, in the virgin bush behind the house, hardly a sound, then a magpie in the distance. I returned the whistle.

What was that?

My favourite bird, magpie.

Have you been to that Arab village down the road?

No.

Were you told not to?

No-one ever said I shouldn't.

There will be reasons those people are still here, otherwise they would have been chased out like the others.

Who are you, Uri?

I am one of a small group of radical, anti-Zionist Jews who believe the only moral future for Israel is as a pluralistic society and a fully functioning democracy.

Israeli Arabs have a vote.

It's a sham.

How far are you prepared to go?

I'm going to roll one more joint, Jack, and tell you something you must never breathe to anyone, ever.

He broke another piece from the lump, crushed, ran it through the tobacco, rolled, licked, lit, and handed to me. He was an efficient and adept roller.

You have a skill, Uri.

I learnt well, in Lebanon. I shouldn't be here, Jack.

You said that.

For the past six months I have been working for Yasser Arafat's Al Fatah in Beirut.

Jesus, Uri, the PLO, why the fuck did you tell me that?

I didn't ask him what his work entailed. My head was heavy, not light. My fingers fluttered enough to make me hide them in my pockets. We sat in silence and smoked the joint to its butt. We stood, Uri pulled his harmonica and played a gentle tune as we walked back to our huts.

Uri was not there in the morning. Perhaps telling his secret weighed heavily on him. After two weeks I asked Offer, the new volunteer coordinator, if he had seen him go.

Uri? he asked. You mean the Jew with the harmonica? I heard about him. Only saw him once, eating an egg in the dining room. Soon after, he was gone.

He didn't sign in?

I told him to come to the office, but he didn't.

You have no idea where he's from then?

Klum, shum davar, none.

3

One of the volunteers said they thought they saw Neeva. After the evening meal I ran to her room. The lights were not on and Avram was sitting on her step, hugging his knees.

Avram?

Shalom, Jack.

You all right?

Who is, in this land full of hate?

He didn't stand, but I remembered he was about my height. His hair was thin and I suspected he would go bald. His fingers were long, narrow and I could see them dancing over piano keys.

Neeva doesn't hate you, Avram.

She once loved me. We were going to marry, have three children and live on my kibbutz. For ever. That's why she wants you.

What do you mean?

You can take her away. Save her from the life I offer, where you cannot choose for yourself and a committee must vote if you want a different kind of toothbrush.

It's not that bad, surely.

You know this war, it makes some people change. After the Six-Day War we thought we were invincible, that we could defeat any enemy, but now we are not sure and it has made much hatred. I can hear people on my kibbutz talking about forcing all Arabs, even Arab Israelis, to leave Israel, and going to the village close by and putting them in trucks or even killing them. It makes me disgusted.

Avram stood and I wanted to hold him. I didn't. I had stolen his girlfriend. He walked down the little track that wound its way to the dining room.

Have you seen Neeva? I called after him.

If you haven't and I haven't, I don't know who has.

Avram had every reason to hate me, I was worthy of it, but he seemed incapable, showed no sign. He was not a man for war, probably not a man for Israel, but he had nowhere else to go. His parents were from Poland and they would never return. This was their place, even if they didn't fit. I could leave whenever I wanted.

4

Twenty of them arrived on a bus, about fourteen women and six men, every one of them glorious to the eye. Arieh said they were stupid. I didn't care. I wanted to work with them, to behold them close.

Remember I told you about the Jews who like the Shah? Arieh said. Here they are. They will not work, cannot work. They live in houses with servants and their parents pamper them. They do not belong to gangs, they have minders who walk with them when they go shopping, not to protect them from the Muslims, but to carry their bags.

Look at them, Arieh, I said. They are beautiful, every one of them.

This beauty is skin-deep. When you get close you will see the makeup.

Offer, the volunteer coordinator, sent them into the *mataim* to help pick apples. Arieh was right, they were hopeless. The work was not hard, or exhausting – lift an arm, take an apple, twist upwards, pull gently, drop the arm, place the apple in a bucket. There were other volunteers from other cities picking and they picked at double the bucket rate.

You were right, Arieh, I said.

Of course.

They spend most of their time talking and laughing. What are they saying? Who are they laughing at?

They laugh at nothing. At boys. You. Me.

In what language?

You know nothing, Jack. It is the language of Persia, Farsi. Most of them cannot speak Hebrew. They are here for holidays, not because they are Zionists. If they leave Iran, they are more likely to go to the United States.

It is still hard to ignore their beauty.

Iranian people have a very strong sense of their place in history and that they were once a great empire. Jews have been there since Cyrus the Great released them from captivity in Babylon. That's almost three thousand years ago. Many of them are Iranian first, and Jews after. But this group, they are first for themselves.

Then came a kind of miracle – not really a miracle, but a wondrous encounter. One of the Iranians, quite possibly the most glorious of all to behold, sought me out during morning tea break. Most pickers sat in clumps around the Shed Quarters, as we had named it, but I was still collecting buckets. It was a hot day and my shirt was off and wrapped around my pants. I was not a big man, carried no fat, only skin, bone and muscle. I enjoyed working without a shirt and some days raced up and down rows clad only in boots and Speedos. The Middle Eastern sun was compassionate and allowed my skin to shift from its natural white pink to a soft brown.

As the wealthy Iranian walked towards me, I returned my shirt to my upper body.

There was no need for that, she said, in perfect English.

Your English is excellent, I said.

There are good reasons for this. One of them is Leonard Cohen.

You know Leonard Cohen?

Not in the biblical sense, but I know his work.

I asked myself, how often can a man fall in love and remain sane and true?

Unlike the others in the group, her makeup was gently and sparingly applied. Her eyes looked directly at mine and I felt her, not in the biblical sense, but in an intuitive, perhaps spiritual, sense. She put out her hand. I took it.

My name is Laleh. I am from Tehran. I am Jewish, of course, but not religious. But I think a lot about Buddhism and Zoroastrianism.

Did you want to ask me something? I have to collect these buckets, or the Israelis will shoot me.

They can be very rude and even brutal, according to some reports.

They expect the most from me. You have seen the way I work. It is who I am and who they are. We both respect work.

I heard you listened to Leonard sometimes and I wondered if I could join you?

You will be welcome. Let's meet after dinner.

As she walked back down the row, I refused to watch, dipped my head, grabbed a bucket, moved fast, faster again. Where was Neeva? Why wasn't she home? When she wasn't home, I needed protection from myself.

We met that night. I was very careful to make sure my friend Erella was with us, to chaperone, to make sure there was no biblical activity. I could have asked to borrow Erella's records and gramophone and instructed my roommates to disappear for two hours, but I felt the need to play safe, to protect myself from any chance of betrayal.

Erella was the kibbutz hippie. She didn't walk, she danced, everywhere. Although I was not fond of dresses, I sometimes imagined her in one, just to see the flow of the material as she danced her way through the kibbutz. And this bothered me, because I was against the dress, as it was symbolic of the patriarchal society I was attempting to escape. It clearly denoted the woman as vulnerable, weak, and, in a wind, brought out the worst in the worst of men.

In Erella's hut, there were three people, all in pants.

Leonard Cohen is not widely known in Iran, said Laleh, but I have all his albums. It started with an older cousin, who sometimes came to our house singing a song. It was 'Winter Lady'. I had no idea what the words meant but he sang it with such a quiet passion that I was entranced. When I asked him what it was, he refused to tell me, said it was not a song for a young girl. One day we visited his house when he was not at home and I sneaked into his room and found the record. The next day I went to the local record shop but they had never heard of him. From then on I went to every record shop in Tehran until I found the album. I didn't have much money but I got it and played it until my mother came into my room one day and took it from me.

As she spoke, Laleh moved her head and hands in a manner that reminded me of Arieh and I couldn't wait to tell him of my discovery – the intellectual Iranian Jew who listened to the songs of the poet philosopher Leonard Cohen.

After a week, said Laleh, my mother came back to me and apologised, saying that she too liked the music and the poetry and that we would have to go out and buy more. It became our secret. We never told my brothers or my father.

What if they sneak into your room while you are here? asked Erella.

They can if they want, but they will find nothing. My mother has them hidden in a place men never go.

What is this place? I asked.

Her underwear drawer.

You know when you laugh so hard you can't stop laughing and the laughter continues so long you forget why you are laughing but you keep on until your belly aches and your eyes are full of tears? Then we sat still and listened to 'Winter Lady', 'Suzanne' and all the songs on *Songs of Leonard Cohen* and when it was done we listened to all the songs on *Songs of Love and Hate* and

I knew I had been sensible and wise inviting Erella to join us because although I experienced a small desire to see them both naked and rolling with me, I loved them in deeper places too, and it was not possible because Erella had a boyfriend, a young man I liked and respected and if there was one person I was sure I would never betray it was a close friend.

All this occurred within ten days and on day eleven, they were gone. Laleh and I hugged before she left, in the privacy of Erella's room and, as they drove away, I realised I had not been near their toilet facility, but I did wash their dishes in the kitchen. I caught Laleh watching me one night as I sang 'Winter Lady' and I was sure I heard her hum along.

One week after they had gone and I was missing Laleh like a brother misses a sister, Zvi sent us on a trip to the Sea of Galilee as a present for the end of the harvest.

Our driver, Nissim, had the radio on and turned it up suddenly.

Sheket, quiet, he yelled. Listen.

The voice was loud and clear: Richard Milhouse Nixon's hold on the presidency of the United States took another blow yesterday when two former officials were convicted of a range of crimes. Gordon Liddy and James McCord were found guilty of conspiracy, burglary and bugging the Democratic Party's Watergate headquarters.

The entire bus rose as one, cheering, yelling, clapping.

The Shah will not like this, said Arieh, with a wide grin. Anything that upsets the Shah is *tov*, good, with me. Nixon has been to Iran twice, you know. The first visit was nineteen fifty-three, when he and the Pahlavi gang decided they could be best of friends. It was two months after the CIA and MI6 organised the coup d'état against Mossadegh, our prime minister. He went again two years ago, just after the Shah had his monster party to celebrate two thousand five hundred years of the Persian Empire. Maybe Tricky Dicky can build the Shitty Shah a house next to La Casa Pacifica, that hideout he has in California.

The Sea of Galilee was a favoured place for Jesus and his fishing friends. He once calmed a fierce storm for them, but it was hard to imagine violence on the placid lake. Apart from the view towards the Golan Heights, there wasn't much to look at and the water was warm, nothing like the fresh, invigorating and chilly waters of Binalup, deep south coast of my home state.

When the bus stopped in the car park, Arieh and I ran down to the shoreline. Arieh couldn't swim but paddled through the water like a dog in a pond.

They didn't give us swimming lessons in the ghetto, he said. I'm a Jew, maybe I can walk on it.

5

I was unsettled. Something in the air. Or wrong. Or not right. Neeva returned but was not the same. Where had she been? With Avram? Her parents? I didn't think so. Her mother now spoke to me when she met me on a path. Not really spoke, because her English was worse than my Hebrew, but acknowledged, said *boker tov*, greeted me as though I was worthy of a greeting. Every time I saw her I wanted to fall down before her and weep. Neeva's father nodded, looked like he might speak, then wouldn't. It was enough.

The kibbutz collective still held me in high regard. Not all of them, of course, but most of those working in the *mataim* and the *mitbach*, the kitchen. When Gavrot celebrated its twenty-five years of existence, volunteers were called for to work in the kitchen, to prepare food, to serve, to wash dishes. I was the first to raise a hand. The kibbutz secretary knew I would and apologised for not asking me in private.

All good, Yossi, I said. This is socialism, no? Now everyone can see that I give according to my ability.

Nachon, chaver, he said. And your needs, we don't have to worry about them, right?

The kitchen hands were allowed a break to watch the stage show. Neeva danced with a small group of young women in a sort of modern folk dance, with some acrobatics and moves depicting the early life of the kibbutz, featuring hard work, attacks from raiding Arab parties, British soldiers searching for stockpiled weapons, and the welcoming of new arrivals.

My hands were wet, my apron filthy, my mind on dishes, then it wandered and arrived on a Pacific island, naked Neeva dancing before me, plunging with me into the surf and wrestling in the sand.

I washed like a demon that night and, after throwing my apron aside, instead of joining Neeva in her room, I took two bottles of Goldstar beer and joined Arieh around a fire in the small eucalypt grove between the settlement and the peach orchard. It was the time Arieh's two friends were also there – Yousef and David. We were all close but I could not speak of Neeva to all three, only to Arieh. David had not long been called up for a tour of army duty and we were wishing him well and talking about his new stripes.

Only two stripes? said Arieh. It's *klum, shum davar*, nothing. You are an embarrassment to the brotherhood.

At least I have two, he said. But you, my friend, they still have you peeling potatoes.

Ken, but have you seen the potatoes? Such monsters, only an expert with a knife could take on such potatoes.

We drank, talked and laughed until the fire died and before we too faded into the coals we went to our huts and beds.

I woke in a daze, remembered Neeva, went to her room, but it was empty. Where was she? Who was she with? Why wasn't she waiting for me?

My position as a permanent member of the *mataim* was confirmed at a weekly meeting of the kibbutz. Yigal stood before the community and spoke for me.

There has never been, in the history of this community, a volunteer who has given more, he said. This man, an Australian man, carried an M16 to the orchards so that members of his age could go to the front and protect this Eretz Israel from invading forces. This man carried a pistol in his pants, endangering his own private parts because Chosta lost the holster. He did this every night for one week while spraying apple trees until the early hours in order to save on evaporation and loss of liquid due to wind. This man who, when in the orchards on his own, scared off an intruder who came over from the Jordanian border. He did this by means not fully understood by the security forces, but it was successful. He should not be treated as a volunteer. He should have all the rights of a member of the kibbutz, pending full acceptance by this gathering. I know some of you can say: But he is not Jewish. This is true, but this kibbutz movement is first and foremost about socialism and collectivism, first above all else, even Zionism.

There were mutterings when Yigal said *even Zionism*. A small group of older members yelled *lo nachon*, not true, and then others yelled at them. Yigal would not be silenced, but he waited for the yellers to exhaust themselves before he continued.

Let us be honest, he said, being Jewish has not always been of benefit to us and maybe now is the time to open our doors, our hearts, to all people of like minds. We are no longer, after all, tailors, moneylenders, antique dealers; we are farmers and warriors, and Jack Muir is a farmer and a warrior.

I had been allowed in to hear the speech and was asked to leave when they voted. It was unanimous – Jack Muir was accepted as a prospective member of Kibbutz Gavrot.

Then Neeva told me about the baby and everything changed.

Kincannup 2018

I hadn't seen my mother's cousin William Blakers since a family reunion a decade earlier and was surprised to find him standing over my table one morning at the Whalers Retreat.

He was a man about my height, solid build with piercing blue eyes. The kind of eyes that when aimed at you they made you think they could see something you couldn't. It was a rare man who gave me that sensation. There had been women in my life who made me feel uncomfortable, as though they knew me better than I ever could. Mother was one.

We hugged a long hug full of things unsaid and after we sat down there was an awkward moment until I stood again and said: I'll get you a coffee. Short mac traditional?

How did you know? he said.

Guessed.

As I stood in line to order coffee I looked back at William and wondered why he had showed up.

When William was young, said my mother, he showed much promise, dux of his school and a champion athlete, coming runner-up in the state one hundred yards dash, but after he came home from his tour of duty in Vietnam, he fell off his rail, left the state, and nobody heard from him for years. In the group with him at that family reunion were other cousins and he seemed distant but after someone quizzed me about Froukje and how we met in Israel, he looked up and as I moved away to get a drink, he followed me.

She was a good-looking young woman, Glorvina, said William.

It was an unusual opening comment but I could see he meant well and he was her first relative ever to mention her beauty to me.

She was, I replied. I heard much the same about you.

That I was a good-looking young woman?

We laughed as we both poured ginger beer into plastic cups.

You don't drink, I see, he said, but I'll bet you did.

Was William passing through Kincannup? Visiting other relatives? Needed to talk? Interesting family, the Blakers, not great talkers, closets jammed full of secrets and unkind rumours, mainly about the family's only ever member of state parliament.

He was in the Upper House, said Andrew Muir. Didn't do much. Must have got bored and, rumour has it, someone found him *in flagrante delicto* with the leader of the opposition. Needless to say he lost his next preselection battle. Typical, it's always sex that brings down the conservatives.

William looked up to see me holding two coffees and laughing.

What's funny? he asked.

Seeing you here for a start, I said, and I was just thinking of our famous uncle, the parliamentarian, the one no-one talks about. Did you ever meet him?

One Christmas lunch the family thought they should invite everyone, bring all the aunties and uncles together. It was a disaster. All the old feuds came up and Uncle Ted was a creep. I think he left with a bloody nose given to him by one of his sisters.

Andrew will enjoy that tale.

How is the old bugger?

He's an easier bugger to get along with than he was as a younger bugger. I saw him two days ago. He looks frail. It's not easy to watch, is it, the fading of the once mighty parent? And it's complicated. There were times I loved him so much I almost told him, and there were others when I wanted to punch him to the ground. You ever want to hit your father?

I did. Three times. He didn't get up.

It was then I realised I had never met William's father, only ever seen him and his mother, Aunt Harriet, from a distance,

130

at family gatherings. Another man lost, like Glorvina's father, expunged from the collective memory.

Mum was the youngest sister, William told me, and she married late and she married violence. I had to hit him. It was him, or me and Mum. I understand your problem with Andrew, you two are so different, but I always admired him. There was always something solid and kind about him. You know he helped Mum financially after she left Dad?

I couldn't answer. The Andrew Muir I hardly knew was dawning on me. He was strict and distant with young Jack Muir, yet at the same time warm and generous with others. Maybe both of us were blind to the truth of the other. He saw an unruly boy who had to be disciplined and I saw an unreachable, authoritarian figure.

Gavrot 1974

The volunteer community in time of war, Yigal told me, is always full of Jews from America. Not like in peacetime, when they are mainly European and Australian hippie travellers wanting to have a good time.

You have to be careful with the Americans, he said. They are not socialists like us. Some of them are religious and some are Jews who just want to fight, somebody, anybody.

He was right.

There were over thirty volunteers on the kibbutz, mostly American, a couple of South Americans, two English, a Scot, a Canadian and me. Only two of us were not Jewish, one Englishman and me. We made it clear to each other we were there to save Israel from the Arab hordes rushing over the borders to annihilate the Jewish claimants.

The noise from the north was quieting. There were not so many planes flying raids into Syria and less artillery fire. There was a ceasefire on the Syrian border and it seemed to be holding. Down south the Egyptian front broke out occasionally, yet retained its relative calm.

What to do? We went back to doing what we did before – work, smoke dope, drop quaaludes, which the Englishman called mandrax, play table tennis, argue, fight. And while I waited for Neeva, others were also seeking sexual partners and lobbying for supremacy of the volunteer community.

There were two big American men vying for leadership – James, a wiry Vietnam vet, and Arnold, a huge-limbed, Ivy League-educated doctor. They hated each other and they both wanted me on their side because I took no sides. I was Switzerland and they were France and Austria.

There were also two main groups on the kibbutz – the Israelis and the Argentinians. There were others, of course, small enclaves of Poles, Bulgarians, Americans, English, Algerians and South Africans. I heard one of the Argentinians say: In Argentina we were Jews and now we are here we are Argentinians.

In the dining room at night, it was not unusual to walk by a table and hear a language other than Hebrew – Spanish, Yiddish, and others made up of sounds I had never heard before. Speaking in your first language was not encouraged by the kibbutz founders and *sabras*, those born and raised in Israel; they frowned and snarled when they heard the foreign tongues. English, however, was exempted. There were obvious reasons. It was not the first language of the overwhelming majority of kibbutzniks, it was the most commonly spoken language among volunteers, and, more importantly, it was the primary language of Israel's best friend, the United States of America, the country with the world's largest Jewish population and from where vast sums were sent to enable the state to survive and flourish.

We were playing table tennis in the bomb shelter. The doctor was beating everyone. Until his shock loss, no-one more surprised than him, and he refused to give up the bat. No-one challenged him. The Vietnam vet was in his hut with his girlfriend.

I walked up to him and said: Arnold, you're a doctor, you're a good man, you're educated, now give me the bat.

Fuck off, Muir, he said.

There was something in his eyes when he spoke, a signal, a sign that he knew then that he had lost me, that I would never join his side. And I knew then that he was an old-fashioned bully, a man used to getting his way, to commanding, to being obeyed.

Give it to me, Arny.

He was not happy with the Arny call and walked away with intent, then turned and threw the bat at me, hitting me on the shoulder. I didn't move. Silence.

The bomb shelter was old, no longer in use for its original purpose. The new one was on the other side of the kibbutz, the Jordanian side, right beside the Holocaust memorial. It was an eerie thing, playing table tennis in a bomb shelter. As soon as you entered it, alone, the silence enveloped you and any sound you made seemed an abomination.

There was silence as the others waited to see what I would do. They were expectant. Some of them had seen me drive off to the orchards carrying the M16 and others knew I sometimes had a pistol in my room for the late-night spraying. I didn't have a gun with me. No-one carried a gun into the bomb shelter, not while we played table tennis.

Then the lights went out.

I knew where Arnold was sitting. I walked over to him in the darkness, lent down and said softly in his ear: I'm going up now, Arny boy. I will wait for you outside. Then, if you like, we will fight. You're a big man, but I will hurt you.

It was the only way to talk to a bully, direct, fearless, with fire in the eyes. He could not see my eyes but I was sure he could feel their heat. I walked out. He didn't follow. He, like all bullies, had no guts.

Jock the Scot and Chad the Canadian and I lived in the middle of a row of huts. Not really a row, more like one building with three separate rooms. We got on fine and shared our hash, peanuts and chocolate but not our girlfriends, mainly because they didn't have one to share and mine was the love of my life and the idea of sharing with anyone repulsed me, even though I had shared her with Avram during my first stay on Gavrot. There was, however, some partner-sharing going on in the volunteer community. And probably the kibbutz community. It was 1974 and the hippies were revolting.

Jock and Chad knew about marijuana and hashish but they had no idea about fire. After one hard day in the almond orchard I came home to find them screaming up against the back wall behind a raging fire bursting out of the upturned kerosene heater.

Jesus Christ, I yelled, you fucking idiots.

I grabbed a blanket, threw it over the flames, jumped on it, trampled, smothered and coughed. Through the smoke I could see the frightened and idiotic pair, staring, bewildered.

How did you know to do that? said Chad.

It was a fire, I said. It lives on oxygen. Cut off the oxygen and it dies. Same goes for you two fuckwits.

We all laughed and even after I stopped, they continued, right the way through the rolling of another joint.

Jock was a cunning bastard and eventually left after robbing our wallets and even though we tried to hate him, we couldn't, because he wrote a note saying he had to leave because his brain was exploding and although he loved us both we weren't enough and we had more money than him because he had bought the last two hash deals. Two months later we got a letter from Glasgow with ten Scottish pounds and another apology.

Jock had a place in my heart and always would because he was there with me, that day out of Haifa, when the US Navy delivered the latest F-16 fighter-bombers to the IDF, the Israel Defense Forces.

We were hitching out of town, following another brief attempt by Jock to find a life outside of the kibbutz that he could identify with. Jock was not made for kibbutz life and needed to escape at least once a month to buy something, anything, but mainly hash. Our lift dropped us on an open road and we were standing idle when we heard the roar. It started as a slow, dull, full and heavy sound, like a convoy of trucks on a long, straight, flat road in West Australia's wheat-growing country.

Soon the roar was everywhere and everything. We looked up to see a black swarm heading towards us, huge locusts on their way to consume all in their path. F-16s. Over the rise was clearly an Israeli air-force base and the bombers were flying in low before they landed. We didn't speak. Then, in the strange silence that came after their passing, I began to weep.

What the fuck is it, Jack? he asked.

I can feel the dead, Jock. Those planes are magnificent and awesome, and they will kill, hundreds, maybe thousands, with brutal efficiency.

No more words. When I looked at Jock, he too was sobbing. He might have been a cunning bastard and a thief, but he had a heart.

There was another place we often gathered called the Volunteer Playroom. It was an unused hut on the edge of the settlement and I was on my way there when Avi saw me near the toilet block and yelled out that Neeva was on the dining room phone asking for me. She had never called before. I ran.

She spoke quickly on the phone, saying she didn't have much time, that she had a report to file.

Are you okay? I asked.

Jack, she said, you have to know. I'm pregnant.

Silence. I felt a rush of joy and wanted to burst with it but held it back because her voice was empty of it, flat, emotionless.

Neeva, that's wonderful. When are you here? When are you due? How long have you known?

Jack, stop. I have to go. A few weeks. Six, seven. Please don't call back. I'm at work.

She hung up. I left the phone on my ear, waiting, wanting to call back, to be sure she said what I thought she said, that she was pregnant and that only I could be the father, not Avram. Something in her voice. I had said wonderful. She did not respond.

You finished with that telephone, Muir?

One of the American volunteers behind me. I hung up and turned to find my friend Caesar, reminding me that I had forgotten to bring him scraps from the kitchen. Caesar was a handsome mongrel with a bitter hatred of Thunder, an Alsatian owned by the economic secretary. If he turned up at my hut with a bloody face, I knew he'd been in Thunder's domain. The two ran the dog community and clashed over bitches and territory. On his own, Caesar was good company and looked at me as though he understood my mutterings. Outside the hut he was alert and suspicious.

I dug a few chicken bones out of the kitchen scraps bin, then let my legs find their own way to the Playroom where Chad and one of the South Americans had made what they called a nice cup of tea. As Chad handed me a cup, he promised an unusually high-high and said I might even get to a place I had never been before, or one that had not previously existed. He did not say what was in the mix. It did not taste nice. Some of the drinkers guessed it contained a mix of hash and fresh marijuana leaves picked from the plants at the side of the peach orchard well hidden among the tall grass. The seeds had been smuggled in by Harry, the Californian hippie. He said they were Colombian and all the other dedicated dope smokers made a noise in recognition.

Aarrrrr, they said. Colombian is where it's at. No dope finer.

I drank my tea fast. James had been there, then he wasn't. Arnold came late and when he came he was not alone. His side was with him. I drank again. Arnold looked at me with a hatred I knew and expected. I thought I would be fine. Another drink. I wasn't fine. Even my roommate, Chad, had taken on an evil tinge. Everyone seemed to flow to one side of the room, turn, and stare, Arnold at their centre. Did he know about Neeva? He had my pistol in his hand. One of his acolytes had the M16 I often fondled on the way to the outlying orchards of apple, pear and almond. Out there I was safe. I was from the bush, that bit of Australia where men knew how to live, work, love and play. That was why older Israelis regarded Australians highly, because we were the men on horses who chased the Ottoman Turks out of Palestine. No more fearful a charge than that led by the 10th Light Horse, the West Australian regiment that included five of my great-uncles, all on horses they bred themselves. It was the Australian and New Zealand Light Horse that paved the way for the Jewish homeland. But in that confined space of hot, toxic liquids and medieval warlords, I was lost. I had no sides.

The sky was swallowing the ceiling. The walls were pressing. The man with the M16 was advancing. Behind him, Arnold took aim. I ran. Found myself up a tree. Fell out of the tree. Ran. Ottoman Turks and Jewish doctors wanting me dead and I had no horse. No sides to call on. Alone.

I stumbled, fell, climbed another tree, vomited down the trunk, spotted a small building that reminded me of the toilet block, climbed downwards, slipped and fell the last five feet to the soft soil. I ran towards the shadow of a building. It was the unoccupied toilet. I fell inside, huddled over the bowl, vomited again, wiped, turned, sat. Voices in my mad head. Let me set you free. Who the fuck are you? Who the fuck are these people? Where's the artillery when you need it? You're in fucking Israel, where are the Jews? Jesus, my girlfriend is pregnant. I'm the father. She said. Not the other one. She's already two months. Must decide. What?

My brain was exploding. The others were out there, somewhere in the bushes, behind the huts, up the trees, looking for me, hunting me, meaning to murder me. Why? Maybe I was to blame for the pregnancy, but why the fuss? According to the Chief Rabbi of the State of Israel, the kid would be Jewish.

A knock on the toilet door.

You in there, Jack?

Silence.

Jack?

Silence.

After the door knocker left, the knocking continued in my head. There I was, a champion of the kibbutz, the man who saved the community from collapse by returning from the down-under country to toil and burn and watch over their daughters, one in particular – there I was, curled over a toilet bowl waiting to be shot, not by an Arab terrorist, a Palestinian expelled from his homeland, but by a highly educated Jewish American doctor in cahoots with Ottomans.

When I could see the light, I ventured out and found no-one. All the volunteers had left on an excursion to Jerusalem.

London 1974

It is still hard to believe how we got Neeva into Australia so quickly, and then how quickly everything turned against us. It was hard for her coming from a kibbutz culture, where work was everything and emotions were held tight and fast. When my mother greeted her, she did so with open arms, weeping face, cries of we will love you like a daughter and please accept this small cheque as a belated wedding present. Neeva tried hard to stay calm but later, in our room, she let loose.

How can Glorvina love me? she asked. She just met me. I'm not her daughter. We married so we could get the visa. She wears too much makeup. And all that crying, doesn't she know to control herself? When she put her arms around me, I wanted to shake her off.

Glorvina was yet to admit to her long history of depression and I had no way of explaining her to Neeva. And if I had, Neeva, raised in a children's house, away from her parents, could only have viewed this as weak and that would have been the end of any possible relationship between them. I needn't have worried, they never developed one and, when the marriage was long over, and I was long back in Western Australia, Glorvina never spoke of Neeva. Ever.

It was 1974, we were adrift in London and three weeks away from Gavrot when we decided to give ourselves a new life in Perth, a place I never liked, only ever tolerated, needed on my way to somewhere else. Neeva had no plans to return to the kibbutz and thought Perth was worth a try, given I had lived there before. We were also encouraged by the new left-leaning government in Canberra.

When we got to Australia House, we were ushered into a pokey little room with an immigration officer sitting behind what looked like an old school desk. The man wore glasses below a receding hairline and his eyes blinked as though not used to light. I thought of him as a harmless, meaningless bureaucrat getting ready to retire. He shook both our hands. His flesh was soft and pale. Neeva's eyes narrowed and her lips curled. She did not like him. I expected the worst. Then he surprised us.

Why don't you get married? he said.

What? I asked.

Why? Neeva said.

Neeva is an Israeli and getting a visa for her will take months. It would be a lot easier if you were married.

And then?

She is automatically an Australian citizen and no longer requires a visa.

How do we do it?

I suggest you go to Gretna Green, it's a small town over the Scottish border. They can marry you immediately. No residency qualifications. Then you come back here and you can be on your way in no time.

We had no desire to travel to Scotland. It was winter, snowing in the highlands and neither of us liked the cold.

What the hell, I said, let's get married. Doesn't mean we have to stay married. It's just for a visa, a piece of paper for the bureaucrats.

That was what I told her, but there were other reasons I kept to myself. Given how much and how deep we had loved, what we had given up for each other and what had happened between us, there was a large part of me that thought we owed each other a stronger, more formal and permanent commitment. And, I thought, marriage might save us.

We caught the train the next day. Neeva was happy to be on the move. I was happy because she was happy. We forgot about the fight we had had over my unwillingness to get angry with the waiter who brought me the wrong order in the little restaurant over the road from our bed and breakfast.

You should tell him to take it back, she said.

It doesn't matter, I said. I can eat it.

This is not what I mean. He made a mistake. He is a stupid man.

It intrigued me that a born-and-raised communist could exhibit such animosity towards the working class. She often scowled at bus conductors, movie ticket collectors, taxi drivers and shop attendants. In Israel, on the kibbutz, there had only ever been one class, but in England there were many and it seemed she hated the lowest the most.

Nineteen seventy-four was a big year for IRA bombers. In the middle of a movie, a siren went off and we had to evacuate the cinema. Neeva panicked and rushed headlong through the crowd, pushing and shoving and yelling behind her. The English remained calm and queued quietly for the exits. I wanted to join Neeva, to protect her and to escape the calm acceptance of the English. Inside my head a voice yelled: There's a bomb about to go off, run you idiot!

But something held me back. The good manners drilled into me at home and in boarding school? A dark desire to experience a bomb blast and be punished for past sins? My heart pumped vigorously as though attempting to break through my chest.

Outside, Neeva was scathing.

What is the matter with you? she said. You don't want to live?

We slept on the train and arrived in Glasgow late in the day. As soon as we climbed down from the carriage and the cold air smacked our faces, we regretted our decision, but we got married anyway, in Glasgow, because we learnt the Gretna Green rules had changed. With no witnesses available, we made friends with the storeman and the cleaning lady in the registry office and they provided their signatures. It meant staying in the city for a few days but the potato chips were the best ever and we visited every museum as though entranced, but all we could think of was getting on a plane to Australia.

It troubled me to think I was going back to a place that had been my home for five years in an expensive private boarding school and two miserable years working in a bank. And there was my new bride, my lover, a woman who almost bore us a child, and my mother, a grandchild. Glorvina would never know.

Perth 1975

1

Muir was working in the Perth Metropolitan Markets, the place where wholesalers met their customers, where men yelled at each other in foreign tongues, waved their hands at auctioneers and lost friends over the price of lettuce. It was Muir's job to stack crates, load crates, unload crates, sweep trading floors and pick up rotten fruit and vegetables discarded by Paulo, the inspector of quality. He took to the work possessed. It kept his mind off the past two years of trouble and turmoil and war. Almost.

At eight o'clock in the morning he signed off and caught a bus to the university. No-one sat next to him. He stank of rotting fruit and vegetables and sweat. There was never time to wash. In class, the others kept their distance. It might have been the smell, although many of them reeked of worse – cigarettes, booze, dope and general uncleanliness. But he didn't think so. He thought it might be what they saw in his eyes. When he looked at them, he tried not to compare them to the kibbutz volunteers and was pleased the university had a clean toilet policy and he didn't have to wash their dishes.

English Jim would laugh at me, he thought. Here I am at university, studying literature, philosophy and history. He thought I was an uncouth, Aussie colonial. Whenever I spoke at those meetings he sneered at me, dismissed me, never responded to anything I said, but continued his own train of argument, or waited until another spoke, so he could respond to something he thought sensible.

Muir was attending university because Australia had lurched

left and elected a prime minister called Gough Whitlam. Whitlam had turned the Australian education system on its ear. Muir was allowed in on the mature-age program. This meant people like Muir, who had failed high school, would be allowed in if they could prove they had the ability to cope, survive, even succeed.

Muir and Neeva were living in a tiny flat in West Perth, one open room including kitchen and sleeping space. It was close enough to the markets so that when Muir woke at 3 am, he could be stacking crates after a twenty-minute brisk walk. He took a day off and a bus to the Western Australian Institute of Technology. He was careful not to wake Neeva. She lay still, turned away from his side of the mattress. They had argued again the night before.

You said you hated Perth, she said.

I do.

Why don't we go to Melbourne? At least there are Jews there.

There are Jews here. I went to school with some.

Why don't you call them? Ask them to help me get work.

He understood. She was a kibbutznik and work defined who they were.

Let me see if I can get into this university, then I'll call someone.

You always say, but you never do.

When their love was deep, he had never felt her tongue cut hard and sharp, only soft and exploring the inside of his mouth and, every so often, along the shaft of his penis. The more vicious her tongue, the harder the fight to hold back the words that loitered on his: You didn't ask me about our child. I respected your right to final choice, but you didn't even ask.

The institute was, he had been told, a university in all but name and all its courses were standard, undergraduate degrees, masters and doctorates. He was excited. Until he saw the buildings.

The campus looked like it had been designed by an architect from the Soviet Union. He had seen photographs of apartment buildings and office blocks in Russia – great lumps of concrete, stacked on top of each other, with windows bashed out as afterthoughts. The English department was housed in the corner of a second floor at the end of a long straight corridor. He knocked on door 72, in building 402.

A heavily bearded man opened the office door.

Yes, he said.

I'm Jack Muir, he said.

So what? I'm supposed to know who you are?

I spoke to you yesterday about the mature-age program.

And?

You told me to come and see you.

That was yesterday? You're fucking keen. What makes you think you will succeed in this august institution?

Because I write and I think and I love history and they are all I have ever loved all my fucking life. So, am I wasting my fucking time here? Are you the wrong fuck to be talking to?

The hairy, loud and aggressive man had triggered Muir's fight, not his flight, because he wanted more than anything to go to university, to test himself, and to prove, to become the man he thought he could be if only he gave himself the chance.

The man responded in the way certain men do when challenged, with a kind of joy, as though saying: Well, thank goodness someone has stood up to me. I'm sick to death of steamrolling the meek and weak.

Here's what we will do, the man said. If you can talk your way into four units and you show you are up to it, then we will enrol you.

Thank you, Muir said. Then I have three to go.

How do you figure that?

Because you're going to let me into yours.

It didn't take him long, no more than ten days. He stood in

front of classes as they emptied, watched the lecturers walk out, how they walked out, how they spoke with students. He made his choices and waited outside their offices until they arrived, first thing in the morning, late in the day, it didn't matter, Muir was there, waiting. They all seemed to recognise him. Word must have got around about the fierce-eyed, long-haired, bearded man, waiting for them. You best let him in, they might have said, it's the only way to get him off your back. There was George the English novelist, Samantha the Indian literary academic, and Anthony the American. He was sure about all of them except the American, but he controlled one of the compulsory units and Muir wanted to get it over with.

Six weeks later, on his way home, or to the pub, or to visit a woman he was seeing on the side, the man from door 72 picked Muir up from the side of the road out of the university car park.

Muir was hoping for a lift that took him close to his flat. Neeva would be there. She would not be happy. Perth's rampant selfishness and greed did not suit her. It was a hot day and the sun burnt his sleeveless arms. It was what he noticed first when he returned – the Perth sun had no compassion and seared hard and nasty any exposed skin. In Israel he spent days in the fields with his upper body exposed and his skin turned brown and never a blistered red.

The wild and hairy academic opened his car door and said: You're still here.

You won't get rid of me now, said Muir.

You better come in tomorrow then and we'll make your enrolment official.

When the man let him out and Muir stood alone at the side of the street leading to his apartment, he wept as he walked. A new journey had begun. He could now apply for a student payment, leave his job with the rotting fruit and vegetables, help his wife find a job and sit next to people on public transport. And he would get a degree, like his brothers, like most of his friends from grammar school.

His parents were pleased, of course, but he refused to show them his marks, his sevens, eights, nines. He was not there to restore the good name of Muir. He was there because he had no choice, because he had thought of giving up, everything, even life, and the thought had forced him onto toilet seats as everything left him. He was losing weight, disappearing and, yet, inside, the fire to succeed kept him hot and focussed. He could not talk to anyone about his suicidal thoughts. Neeva and Andrew Muir would think him weak. Glorvina Muir would cry and faint. Tom in Genoralup was unavailable to him. But there were others he could share his residual hatred with, people who were scared of life, and he thought of them as friends. They were members of a Trotskyite group called Freedom Now. Muir and his closest confidant in the group, Brockman, spent days plotting to kill the premier of Western Australia, a man called Charles Court, the premier who introduced a law banning street gatherings of more than three people. He was an insult to democracy. Brockman was a tall, brooding man who, like Muir, had gone to an expensive private school, had failed, found himself digging ditches, hanging out with unionists, drinking with unionists, falling under the spell of a hard, left-wing core, and when that didn't satisfy, he enrolled in the university to study politics and philosophy. When that wasn't enough, he joined Freedom Now. The group met once a fortnight on campus, with no formal agenda, no minutes, no chair, or leader, just a motley group that raved and ranted and found ways of accusing each other of deviations from the Trotskyite line.

One day over a weak coffee, Brockman said: All they do is talk talk talk. No-one does anything. At least you have lived a socialist truth on the kibbutz. The others know fuck all about fuck all.

A lot of the kibbutzniks were Stalinists, said Muir. But after the Twentieth Congress of the Communist Party of the Soviet Union in 1956, when Khrushchev tipped the bucket on Stalin, most of them dropped him. My old kibbutz and others in the same political movement are still home to many Marxists.

Do they, like Trotsky, believe in continuous revolution?

As a movement they are still active in Israeli politics, don't forget that Moshe Dayan and David Ben-Gurion were both from kibbutzim.

They are hardly revolutionaries.

It's what happens when you get old, you mellow, you give up the fight, eat too much cake and slump in front of the telly, but on the kibbutz, there is only one telly and you have to watch it with one hundred and fifty others.

What can we do, Jack?

We could kill the premier.

They didn't and not long after, Brockman disappeared, and Muir took Neeva to meet some local Jews. When she arrived home, she was not happy.

I don't want to see them again, she said. Before I left the kibbutz, some of the Argentinians told me the diaspora Jews would disappoint. They were like your mother, all over me with false love, and their makeup and pretty things. Stupid people. They knew nothing about Israel, kibbutz, and I could see from their hands they did not know work.

He had wanted more than anything to prove himself at the university. After the Trotskyites, he joined the Student Guild and the English Students Association. When he spoke of socialism, the others listened. He was the first they had met who had lived the dream. He walked with his eyes furrowed and his head down. He only wanted to speak to those with the same level of intensity. Anyone else was inane, ignorant and had no idea what was going on. Anywhere.

One day, as he walked from a class to the university tavern, he stopped. There, in front of him, looking lost and disoriented, was Neeva. What the hell was she doing there? How did she get there? He stood still and then she saw him. And saw the look on his face.

Jack, she said. I had to see you.

Why?

I don't know why.

I'm going to a class.

He made no move to hold her, to offer her lunch, to ask if she would like a coffee. He felt threatened, spooked, stalked. How dare she come to his place of higher learning unannounced and freak him out?

How did you get here? he asked.

By bus.

Do you have enough money to get home?

Of course.

He led her to the bus stop and they waited in silence.

After she had gone, he sat on the campus grass with legs crossed, head dropped. She looks different, he thought. On the kibbutz, she had something of the Pacific Island princess about her, but here she seems to be shrinking, diminishing, no longer a princess, more a kitchen hand, which is what she was in her new job at the fast-food chicken place. He thought of her as weak and he knew she thought he had weakened too, lost the fire and determination he had shown on the kibbutz. It was as though, lacking a clear enemy, an external threat, they had turned on each other. Their weakened states fed off each other, in an ever-tightening circle of weakness. They were committed socialists living in a hotbed of capitalism and unable to cope with the demands on the individual. On the kibbutz, everything had been done for her. She didn't have to fill in tax forms, pay fees, keep financial records. Her life was managed for her by the kibbutz. In Perth, she was lost and frightened and he hated himself for thinking it a burden. And he, although better equipped, resented every demand made by the system and ranted against it.

Neeva hated everybody. She was learning to hate him. He could see it in her eyes and he had to fight off the desire for revenge, to punish her for what she had done. She had wanted so much to be rid of the army, she filled in the pregnancy form, the one that allowed her an honourable discharge, and then she arranged the abortion. Was there an abortion form, which might well have cancelled the previous form? Why are we together? he asked himself. Getting out of the army was not enough for her, then she wanted to leave the country? And me, he thought, so blinded by the guilt of the abortion, and the early rush of love, am I here to make sure we have a child that we keep, in order to honour the child we killed?

3

It all happened so quickly he thought he must have been asleep. He was sleeping a lot. Sleep was filling the major part of his day. Sleep was safe, secure, familiar and as soon as he woke, all he wished for was a return to sleep. But he stayed awake long enough to finish his first year at the institute. Every mark a distinction. He thought they should celebrate, so he took Neeva to dinner and a movie. Nothing went well. In the Italian restaurant, a waiter had winked at her.

Fuck him, she said. We leave.

They left.

The movie was called *Emmanuelle II*. Someone she met said it was a good movie. She became suspicious when a man sat in front of them wearing a raincoat. Ten minutes in, she said: That man is masturbating.

They left. Shame overwhelmed him. Why hadn't he asked around about the movie? Why hadn't he spotted the raincoat man?

When they got back to the flat, she went to bed and he fell asleep in a chair. The next morning, she made the announcement.

Maybe we are finished, Jack, she said. What I know for sure, is that I am finished with this country of yours. I am leaving.

Her last morning in Perth, they had vigorous and sweaty sex. Later, she sat on the end of the mattress and said: Jack, just because we can have great sex, this doesn't mean we should be together.

That hurt him, not because he smelt the bile on her lips, but because he knew the truth, that great sex did not make a great marriage. She, however, expected him to be hurt, to look hurt. He sat on the end of the bed hunched over like a man defeated.

He went with her to the airport where she boarded a plane for Athens and Tel Aviv. Back at the flat, he thought about his parents. Had he put them through enough? How could he tell them of this latest failure? He decided to say nothing, to keep his shame to himself. It was the shame that hurt most, not her leaving, that would, in the long term, bring relief.

He slept for two days, woke up and moved out into a cheap hotel in Northbridge, set small and ugly in that part of the city inhabited by pimps, prostitutes, gamblers and petty criminals, well away from the scene of his latest failure. He tried to get a summer job, although he didn't want a job but he thought it might take his mind off Neeva. He had chosen the hotel because it looked empty, and it was, and because it was off Roe Street, once the thriving heart of Perth's brothel community, now a collection of abandoned buildings, some occupied by the destitute, others boarded up by their owners.

The first morning he opened the wardrobe to get his clothes, he heard a scurrying noise, looked down and saw a million cockroaches, not the big ugly bush variety, but squat little things that reminded him of the tropical roaches from Papua New Guinea. He picked up his underpants and looked inside. They were full. He shook them once and another million fell out and scurried away. That was how he started each day, flicking his underpants to release the roaches.

During the day he walked into the city with his head down, his hair long and dishevelled, sometimes stopping to see a movie. It didn't matter what movie; he could never remember it after. There was a pub he stopped in and drank. It was en route to his hotel and close enough so he could make it back to his room if he got drunk.

Because he wore a beard and long hair, he always looked kindly on others of the same appearance, as though they were his people, as though they belonged to a club, like Rotary. No, not Rotary, an environmental organisation perhaps, like Greenpeace. Or a revolutionary organisation challenging the established order. Usually other bearded people smiled back at him, or nodded, or raised a hand in a half wave. But not always.

The man on the bike looked like one of them, but after Muir nodded, the man's mouth opened and let out a torrent.

Fuck off, he yelled. You fucking piece of shit, you think you're fucking smart, think you own this street, think you're smarter than anyone else, think only you know shit, well you're nothing but a nothing wanking piece of shit and with a great plague will the Lord smite thy people, and thy children, and thy wives, and all thy goods. And thou shalt have great sickness by disease of thy bowels, until thy bowels fall out by reason of the sickness day by day.

The man kept yelling what seemed to be Bible quotes, twisting his head back as he rode away, struggling to keep his balance. Long after Muir could no longer see him, he could hear his voice. Others on the street looked at Muir as though it was his fault, as though he had intimidated the rider, clearly a religious man, and was the source of the man's pain and anger.

The outburst upset Muir and he had to stop in the next pub and buy a rum and Coke to settle his nerves and ask himself questions.

Why did he yell at me? he asked. I was being friendly. But he saw something, but what? What did he say again? Think you're smarter than anyone else. Think only you know shit. And God is going to kill all my children? Well, too late for that.

He hung onto the man's rantings and went over them again and again, until he realised some of them sounded familiar and he knew he had heard them before – inside his own head. You have seen people looking smug, he thought, and entitled, and have wanted to yell such things in their faces. Yet you have kept your mouth shut. That man gave voice to his inner torment, his isolation, his rejection, pretty much how Muir was feeling but his upbringing held him back from yelling in the street. Muir wondered if the man had considered suicide.

Given the number of times I've been shot at, he thought, you'd think one of them, at least, could have aimed straight, saved me the trouble.

The memory did not help his mood and when he got back to his cockroach nest, he drank three bottles of warm beer and threw up in the basin. The last time he had thrown was on Gavrot, just after Neeva's mother had been to see him. He was sitting in his room down by the apricot-ripening hut when her mother knocked on the door to tell him the news he never wanted.

The operation is finished, she said. Neeva is okay.

He closed the door, turned and saw Caesar on his bed. Something snapped inside him and he launched himself at the dog, his cabin companion. He struck him on the snout. The dog whimpered, ran and crashed into the closed door. Muir ripped it open and kicked out at the dog as he ran out, slamming the door behind him, almost catching his scrambling back legs. It did nothing to stem the stench. There was something in the room, something more than the chemical odour from the apricot-ripening hut.

What the fuck are they using in there? he yelled.

His face melted, his soul died, his chest collapsed and his eyes flooded. The noise that came from his throat frightened him. He shook his head and wondered why he couldn't remember why he was so upset. Then it came. The baby. Dead.

I wanted the baby, he yelled.

He remembered how, when she had visited the kibbutz after the phone call, he had taken her and held her in happiness until he realised her own was lacking.

This is not good news, she said.

No?

We are not ready to be parents.

But we live on a kibbutz. It doesn't matter. The community will take care of the child. She will live in the children's house and we will work.

I do not want a child.

I should have argued, he thought, but I didn't, because it was her body carrying the unborn child and I wanted the child to live, to have a life, I also knew I did not want an abortion on my conscience.

She left me to my confused misery. They were not easy days. I kept to myself. Did not go to the coffee house after dinner. And, of course, there was always work.

Her next visit had followed quickly and her arrival with a happy face gave me hope.

This child was a blessing after all, she said.

You've decided to keep it?

You know how much I hate the army?

Yes.

It has allowed me an early discharge.

He grew fond of the cockroaches. It didn't matter how many dead bodies filled his dreams, the roaches were always full of life and vigour, and every morning he shook them from his pants and watched them celebrate their release.

He slept. He thought to call Glorvina. He slept. Even when awake, he felt as though he were sleeping.

Late in summer, Muir woke around midday, opened the wardrobe, reached for his unwashed underpants, flicked them. Nothing. The roaches had gone. At first, he felt lonely, abandoned, then he took it as a sign and booked a flight to Israel.

Gavrot 1976

I went back to Gavrot, with hope for the rekindling of dreams no longer dreamt. Neeva and I met and talked. We didn't say much, there were practical matters to conclude and a little money we had in an Australian bank account. We talked about reconciliation and did not dismiss it. Even her mother stopped me on a path.

Jack, she said, please, Neeva, will you be together?

Lo yodea, no idea, I said. Our love was so strong and then it seemed to go.

She took my hand and held it. Our eyes locked. We peered into each other and I could see a deep sadness and knew, was sure I knew, that she too had wanted the baby, who would have been a Jew, another child for Israel. I don't know how long we stood holding hands, but, even after the weeping began, we did not release our hold. She broke first, shaking her head in short sharp movements, before she released my hand, and walked away.

To the pain and longing and vast emptiness, I responded in the only way I knew – worked until my eyes bled in the *mataim* and washed dishes until my hands lost their skin.

Three weeks in, I was convinced Neeva believed my return to Gavrot was another sign of weakness. Neeva was working outside the kibbutz. On one visit home she would come to my room, we would go to hers, engage in robust, physical sex, and the next visit she would arrive and leave without notification. I would hear of her visit from others. The erratic relationship led me to Suzi.

Suzi, Canadian Christian, lithe of body, mind and soul. She was younger than me, in her late teens and because she seemed to have a great need of me, I let her take me. She told me I was all the things she sought in a man – handsome, strong, commanding, intelligent. I didn't believe her. I wanted to believe her. I let her believe I believed her. I almost convinced myself I believed her. When we were together, I made sure I looked all those things. I let her take me to bed, alone, then with others and later we entered a waterfall and even later she hid me under the back seat of a jeep and smuggled me into an exclusive Christian enclosure out of Jerusalem. She was adventurous, athletic, courageous and although I was sure I didn't love her, she excited me, fed my need to be loved and I no longer lingered in long sleeps.

Before she left Israel, Suzi took me south, where we camped naked on the beach somewhere between Eliat and Nuweiba, in Egypt. Such a glorious, naked time we had, running, diving, swimming, rolling in the sand. It seemed I had been there before but only in a dream. She was so full of vigour and enthusiasm and not a word about Jesus, or her parents, or their version of Christianity.

It had been a normal day in the tent. We slept. We woke. We made love. We ran naked along the shoreline, splashing, jumping, diving, wrestling. Then we heard voices. Up on the road, a bus. We dressed quickly as we watched people scramble down the bank to the water's edge. Neeva among them. It was a party of volunteers from Gavrot, with Neeva in charge. She let them go on ahead, as though she knew something. When they had all made their way to the beach, she looked up.

I had to look away, overwhelmed with shame, not that I had deceived her, we hadn't spoken for weeks, but because, although we both knew we were finished, we had not formally ended our relationship, our marriage. It seemed strange to me, the shame, because I had wanted to be a modern, hippie style of man who could have affairs at random and not concern myself with bureaucratic commitments, like a marriage certificate. Our encounter turned stranger still when I could see sadness in her eyes and I knew that she too had held hope, that perhaps in Israel we might have had another chance. Her hope, like mine, must have been faint, but there all the same, and I wondered if hers, like mine, had been born in a swirling pool of guilt, because of what we had done, what she had done, what I had not stopped from happening. For all that, I was unable to forget our love and our list of betrayals. I added Suzi to the list.

We stood still beside each other while others frolicked and Suzi ran up the beach.

This was not nice for me to see, said Neeva.

I had no answer, not one I could voice. Her family had suffered enough, they didn't need a disturbed Australian in their lives, one they had rejected, then given permission, who was betrayed by their daughter and now he was extracting revenge, or was lost, or behaving badly because that was inevitable. Had he been a bad man pretending to be good?

Neeva climbed back on the bus with a look that burned into my memory long after her eyes had left mine. It was a mangled look, mingled with hate, confusion and the memory of loss and love and I pondered if I could ever again love anyone who loved me as much, because their love would blind them to my faults, my flaws, my darkness. If they could not see me, they could not know me and, thus, I could not truly love them.

When Suzi came back, the shame must have dissolved some of me. She looked bewildered. After four days with little food, we made our way back to Eliat where we lived on top of a restaurant. During the day I washed dishes – pots, pans, cutlery, preparation implements for the chef. It was filthy, greasy work. I took to it in a manner that frightened the chef and he had to ask me to take it easy or he would die from exhaustion just watching me. Suzi waited on tables and at night we rolled, screamed and yelled as we made love. But it wasn't love. The darkness had come down and I drifted away from her youth, her innocence, her delusion.

On our last night before she rejoined her parents in Jerusalem, she said she thought her time had started but that she wanted to have sex once more. It was a strange coupling, somehow angry, punishing. We rolled off our sleeping bags, she on top, and continued tangling over the rough surface of the rooftop. When it was all over and we lay still in our sweat, we felt the wet, warm blood and assumed it was hers.

When I stood, she said: It's you.

What?

You're the one bleeding. Your back is cut.

It was years before that cut healed. It would seem closed but would open again and fester and I would apply iodine, mercurochrome, or whatever I had at the time. The scar, and the memory, stuck together.

Kibbutz Nir Zamit 1976

I left Gavrot. It was for the best, for Neeva, her mother, father, and those who no longer saw me as a builder, rather, a destroyer.

Down in Nir Zamit, another settlement in the Kibbutz Artzi movement, over the border from the Gaza strip, close to the Sinai, in the heat of the day and the cold of the night, I seemed to find a kind of peace. Strange, given the place was the setting for three nasty battles in the Great War. The West Australian 10th Light Horse fought in the area. In the regiment were great-uncles of mine and two young West Australian farmers, Ric Throssell and his brother Hugo, a Victoria Cross winner from Gallipoli. Ric lost his life in the second Gaza battle, somewhere between Nir Zamit and Beersheba. Hugo didn't have much of a life when he got home because in 1919 he announced to the world that he was a communist. Another of my great-uncles came home and said the same thing but he wasn't a VC winner, so no-one cared and the authorities didn't hound him for the rest of his days. As for me, all I did was tell the Genoralup Rotary Club that I might be one, and the only real consequence was a farmer insisted on paying me money for work completed so he wouldn't be tainted by a social philosophy he could not understand.

There was no hash, or secret plants, on Nir Zamit, not that I knew of, or had seen, and no-one offered me any. The kibbutzniks there were more ideologically sound and adhered closer to the guidelines as laid out by the more ideologically pure of the hard left of the kibbutz movement. It worked for me, because it was more disciplined, even rigid maybe, and we all knew where we were, what the rules were and how best to live in that place. The volunteers were a mixture but because the rules were held high, if anyone stepped out, they were quickly asked to leave.

Nir Zamit abutted Gaza and was about fifty kilometres from Beersheba, the scene of the first and, perhaps, the greatest Australian Light Horse triumph, when around eight hundred men of the 4th Light Horse Regiment took the town from the Ottoman Turks in a charge breathtaking in its audacity and courage. It was an important battle that changed the war in Palestine. It was the perfect place for a broken Australian, exhausted from my own battles, and alone again. Shame, confusion and guilt followed the breakdown of my marriage. Weariness often overcame me, exhaustion followed attacks of self-recrimination and the willingness to drag myself into a pit where I would wallow like a hippo in mud, only emerging to attract fleas and other torments. Sleep saved me, the sleep of the one afraid to wake.

On Nir Zamit, as before on Gavrot, I started at the bottom, and the bottom was picking mangoes.

Nissim drove us out to the orchards every day. He was an Israeli, born in Tel Aviv, and first visited the kibbutz with his city-based youth group. He went on to study engineering at Tel Aviv University, but could not disperse the seeds planted when he arrived in 1970 with a backpack containing his world and never left. After one week he invited me to sit up behind him on the mudguard and we talked our way out to the mangoes.

Why did you come, Nissim, to the kibbutz?

It was a way to live, he said, so true, I could not hide from it. I lived here for two years and then, on the weekly meeting in the dining room, the members voted me a member. I was very happy and when I got back to my room, I cried like a baby.

When I spoke to him I had to lean in from the wheel guard.

Do you ever use your engineering knowledge?

Of course. Here on the kibbutz we have many with degrees and my best friend, Amos, from Argentina, you have seen him collecting the garbage, he has PhD in philosophy from the Universidad de Buenos Aires. And you, *chaver*, even you have a degree and here you are picking mangoes.

Not yet, I haven't finished.

I wanted to tell him more, that I had run again, left after one year of being a university student, headed back to Israel following a wife who no longer loved me, or never did, I no longer knew. But I kept shtum, not wanting it known that I had married a *sabra*, that we had tried our luck in a hotbed of capitalism and our lives together had suffered events both of us wanted to forget, but never would. Eventually my secret would come out. Israel's population was only three and a half million and the kibbutz population less than ten percent of that and the Artzi component around half of the total kibbutz population and people from Gavrot would know people from Nir Zamit – and that, of course, is what happened. I knew it, but I wanted to establish myself before the dining room seethed with gossip of the reclusive Australian.

I did what I always did when I didn't want to talk about myself, I kept talking about everyone else.

What was Amos' thesis? I asked.

Something to do with existentialism. He studied all the French writers – Camus, Sartre, Malraux.

Maybe you can get us together over a *botz*?

It will be difficult. He doesn't speak English. That's why he keeps away from you volunteers. He is a little embarrassed about it but he should not be, because he speaks French, Italian, Spanish and, of course, Hebrew. And you, how many do you speak?

One.

You see, he has no reason for shame.

After two weeks I noticed a new American on the trailer. It was unusual for me to notice a new face, as my habit was to climb onto the cart, head down, body tensed, ready for the work, total focus on work. I knew the only way to a kibbutz heart was through work. Naturally, as soon as I arrived, I offered myself for regular night duty on the dishes. This surprised Rachel, the woman in charge of the volunteers, but she made a note and, soon enough, I became a kitchen regular at night, and sometimes during the day. If I had dishes during the day, I didn't leave them at night, continued working on until all were washed, rinsed, stacked. Following ten-hour stints at the sink, I wasn't much use in the dairy the next day. Then the executive of the dairy, after I had worked with them for two months, decided that I was one of them and could no longer be part of the volunteer kitchen roster for day duties. The only way the kitchen could have me during normal working hours was if I was nominated by the dairy as part of that section's commitment. Rachel insisted I was a volunteer and could be rostered as such. Shlomo, one of the dairy leaders, said I was more than a volunteer.

What is he then? said Rachel.

He is a professional dairy man, he said. He comes from a long line of dairy farmers and his expertise is essential for the improvements we are making in the dairy.

Not quite a volunteer, yet not yet a kibbutznik. A man in limbo. I knew the state well. Rachel rostered me on. Shlomo would not let me wash. The social secretary washed in my place and called a meeting. The meeting lasted two hours, during which Shlomo spoke of my past on Gavrot, my marriage to an Israeli citizen, my valuable innovations to the milking program and my commitment to the ideals and values of the kibbutz movement. A compromise was reached. Shlomo and I both washed dishes on the following Shabbat and from that day forth, I would only be rostered in the kitchen as a member of the dairy team. Shlomo barely touched a plate, not because he was lazy, but because I worked so hard and fast he could not get his hands on any and he could not keep his eyes off mine. I was rostered for dairy duty the following day, but he made me take the day off so I could join him on a trip to visit nearby Nabatean ruins. The very same Nabateans who once had a trading route through the region and who built the mighty city of Petra, carved into cliffs of stone, across the border in Jordan.

It is a tragedy, said Shlomo, that we cannot go to Petra. This is the scourge of nationalism. The people who live over there are our brothers, they came from Ishmael and we came from Isaac, both sons of Abraham. I know why I am here and how I came to be here, but I believe that this country should be for all of us, Jews, Arabs, whoever wants to live here.

When the American sat opposite me on our way to the mangoes, I took the opportunity to look him over. He was tall, reasonably well built, tired, slouching shoulders and eyes that seemed dull, lacking.

My name's Jack, I said.

Chuck, he said.

Strange name for an American.

Neither his eyes, nor his mouth, laughed. The Dutchman seated next to him laughed, but the American's face did not shift. And his hand was not firm, a reluctant hand, one that offered itself only out of necessity, as though forced and warned not to make an effort or there would be consequences.

Have you picked mangoes before? I asked.

Is it difficult?

Easier than an orange, but harder than an apple.

Again, no sign of life. We sat in silence until Nissim stopped the tractor inside the orchard. What an odd chap, I thought. He looked like most of his life had been taken out of him and all that was left was the shell sitting in front of me.

All that changed as soon as he and I teamed up and found ourselves working together on the same tree.

I didn't want to say in front of the others, he said, looking down on me from near the top of the ladder. But my real name is Jesus.

I'm sorry, I said, I didn't hear.

Jesus.

You're who?

Jesus.

The Son of God, that Jesus?

Yes.

No, you're not. I've read the Bible. He died and went home.

After rising from the dead.

So they say.

And I've done it again.

It was quite something, to be working alongside Jesus. I took my responsibilities seriously and kept his identity from the others, for fear they might laugh, or worse, tie him to a tree and stone him. Over the week we worked together, it was clear he was harmless. He had no plan. He could barely remember his old speeches.

Can you do the Sermon on the Mount? I asked him.

You're mocking me.

Only because I'm not sure you are Jesus and you don't seem to know why you've come back. Did your dad give you any specific instructions?

There are things I forgot to say, last time I was here.

Like what?

This is not the time or the place to say. I need to gather people near the Sea of Galilee.

You remember what happened last time, right?

What do you mean?

The Romans.

I'm not afraid of Catholics.

Well, there's them too, but also the Israelis, they won't like it, and all the kibbutzniks, they are atheists and only believe in work.

I asked him how long he would be staying in the desert and if it would be the traditional forty days and forty nights. His face went blank.

Nir Zamit is quite a way from where you hid out before, I said. This is not the same sort of desert and, let's be honest, given what they have done here, it's no longer a desert.

Blank.

You remember where you were before, right?

I felt sorry for him then, because I was mocking him, his lack of knowledge of Israel's geography and the travels of his previous self. I knew that Jesus had hung out in the Judean Desert, that bit of parched earth that included Masada and ran all the way down to the Dead Sea.

It came to me that I no longer had patience for people like me, who were suffering from depression or any other minor madness. I refused to avoid what I thought was a truth and hit myself most days with platitudes: The world is fucked. Life is unfair. It is what it is. Fuck off and get on with it. And I dedicated myself with a fanatical application to work. But Chuck was lazy. He picked at half my rate. He moved slowly, as though doped up to his forehead. Whenever we worked a tree together, I sent him up the ladder, out of my way, so I could work the entire lower perimeter.

Okay, Chuck, I said. You move on to the next tree and I'll finish the ladder work.

By the time I had finished up high, he had barely started around the base of the next tree.

This is all new to me, he said. Back home I was an engine driver in Wisconsin and it was there that the Lord visited me and told me who I was and gave me my mission.

Which is? I asked.

To let all Christians know that I have returned to save them, from themselves.

They aren't going to like that.

Why not?

You know how many types of Christians there are? You think they are going to agree with each other?

They have to. I am the Lord.

Have you been to Jerusalem?

Of course.

This time, not last time.

Not yet.

Every Easter they fight with brooms and sticks and whatever they can get their hands on – Catholics, Anglicans, Coptics, Russian Orthodox, Greek Orthodox. It's a madhouse.

He stopped what little work he was doing to tell me he had been delivered to the local mental asylum, right after he had announced to his railway co-workers of his new-found identity.

They kept me there for six months, he said. Every day they gave me needles and a psychiatrist came to talk to me. As soon as they released me, I booked a flight to Israel.

You booked a flight?

Yes.

Couldn't the old man just send you here? Get the archangel to fly you over?

Chuck was wearing me out. He said he was Jesus but he exhibited nothing of the man from my picture book Bible – tall, handsome, eloquent, able to convince people to follow him by simply looking into their eyes or saying something as simple as *Follow me*. Chuck was not a man I could talk to, explain that I had enough troubles of my own and did not need him revealing his as we attempted to empty a tree of its fruit. There was no doubt he was in trouble, but we all were, that was why we were there, and how would it be if we all responded to our troubles by pretending to be someone who was very dead and very important? All right if you were Gandhi, the Buddha, or Florence Nightingale, but what if you decided to be Genghis

Kahn, Rasputin, or Caligula? As a kid I wanted to be the Phantom, and some days I felt like punching Chuck in the side of his head and screaming: Shut the fuck up! You're not Jesus, you're Chuck, a train driver from Madison, you're lost and you'll never get found until you realise you are lost.

You stink, Chuck, I said one morning. When was the last time you took a shower?

That night he was in the communal showers, facing the corner, hiding. When he turned and walked to retrieve his towel, I saw.

Chuck, I said, there is something I must ask. Are you Jewish? To be Jesus, you got to be Jewish, one of the chosen, and, man, serious, you're carrying bits that should be missing. Like that bit on the end of your dick. It shouldn't be there.

Then he was gone. When I asked Nissim and Rachel, they said they had no idea – he was there one day and not the next.

Bugger him. Who did he think he was? Okay, he thought he was Jesus. With an American accent? What made him think he could be Jesus? He was a pathetic American gentile with a God complex who hadn't done his research and didn't know enough about Jesus, who he was, where he'd been and who his friends were. He was just another control-freak Yank who thought he owned the world. I never met an Australian who thought he was Jesus, or Joan of Arc. Something was rotten in the United States of America.

Had I pushed him out of the kibbutz? Did he leave because I taunted him? And why not? The arrogant goose never once asked about me, why I was there, why each morning my face was full of pain and self-indulgent misery. And why was my spirit so mean that I had to taunt him, a false Jesus who was nothing more than a railway worker from a poor and uneducated family in the middle of America where thought and self-reflection were not encouraged? My old boarding school with its false Christianity, brutality and unforgiving staff had left its mark. Anyone claiming to be Jesus in front of me, who had loved

Jesus, who felt he knew Jesus, was going to cop a heavy tongue laden with insults because my scars had not healed or even softened and my venom was nurtured among the privileged of a private school yard. Besides, he needed protection from himself, because if he really was Jesus, he should keep his mouth shut, because if the Romans found out they would take him again and do unto him what they had done before.

Later, when I told Nissim about him, he told me there was a ward in a Tel Aviv mental hospital full of men claiming to be Jesus. There was also a Jesus woman, but she was stuck in a ward with other women who mainly claimed to be Mary Magdalene. He had only been gone a week when I missed him.

Kincannup 2018

My friend Hansie is a psychiatrist and was once a South African. He would say he still is because he goes back every year, but I say he is more like us, whatever that means, than he is like them. Hansie is nothing like the fat Afrikaner cop I met in a Durban street not long after I disembarked; he is more like Etienne, the man I met on a film set in Johannesburg, the one who told me not to judge people by their accent, skin tone, or facial features. Hansie speaks Afrikaans, English, French, Xhosa – the language of Nelson Mandela – and Sesotho – the language of Lesotho and of Moshoeshoe, a Mandela-like leader who ruled the region in the middle eighteen hundreds. I know all this because Hansie told me over coffee. Our conversations roamed wide. We talked about me, him, Southern Africa, Israel, relationships, and Jung. With Hansie, many things were about Jung. Hansie trained in South Africa, then, of course, had to pass the strenuous Australian medical and psychiatric examinations.

Jung was the only psychotherapist who helped me understand the collective shadow, said Hansie. And that shadow was so rampant in the old South Africa. Jung helped relieve my collective shame, for being part of an ethnic group I never felt I belonged to, even though I shared in the delicious fruits of apartheid.

As is the way in a town like Kincannup, I met Hansie through Lester, a Noongar Menang friend who sometimes took Hansie fishing. They never told me where they went, it was a secret. Both would talk freely of their loves, their losses, battles with demons, authority and children, but never where they went fishing. For coffee we usually met at the Whalers Retreat, which

Lester claimed should be called Mamangup, or Place of the Whale. It was a joy to behold the two friends, one a wiry black man descended from an ancient people and the other a massive white man descended from a colonising people.

What is it with you colonisers? asked Lester of both of us. Why do you have to rename every place you come to? Wouldn't it be easier if you just said: Excuse me, what do you call this place?

I asked Hansie if Jung had anything to say about colonialism, given he had been to both India and Africa.

Jung said that what we in Europe call colonisation, including missionary work, the spreading of civilisation to the heathen people of the world, probably had another face more like a hawk or eagle, any bird of prey with cruel intent for a distant victim, even more akin to the face of a pirate or highwayman.

That works for me, said Lester.

It worked for me too. So many ships laden with plunder leaving our ports, even now. And we all benefit. Which is why, throughout my privileged life, I have had to give. It annoyed Froukje, at first, then she got used it.

That big cheque you got for that public relations job, she once asked, what happened to the money?

It was embarrassing, I said. The guilt I felt on that job. The only way I could ease it was to give most of it away, to not-for-profit groups who work with communities suffering because of that company.

Jesus, Jack, when are you going to learn to forgive yourself for making a living? You remember how you apologised to Neeva for your hatred? And those people in your life you thought you had upset in some way? Well, I think there's a name missing from that list of apologies.

Who?

Jack Muir.

Froukje and I had been living in Kincannup about ten years when I began to believe I had been blessed, with her, with all my new friends and many from the past. Two South Africans, Hansie and Etienne, particularly intrigued me. How was it that these two men, from whom I had learnt so much, could have been born among people who once ruled a nation with iron-clad, nasty fists and created a country based on the evil myth of race, with its accompanying assumptions of intelligence, morality and sophistication?

It is all about the shadow, Jack, said Hansie. The fanatics – the fundamentalists of religion and politics – deny their own shadow, their darkness. They suppress any subconscious thoughts of evil that arise and project them onto others. Germans, collectively, projected their shadow onto Jews. We Afrikaners projected our shadow onto everybody not us. When you fell into depressed states, you were in the grip of your shadow, your darkness, and often, when in denial, you projected onto others. You remember when you said you thought everyone around you was stupid?

Yes.

The shadow, Jack. Jung said even God had his shadow or he would not have created the serpent, sometimes referred to as representing Satan, and he would not have challenged Abraham to burn his son, or tested Job with such frightening unpleasantness and wiped out groups of people with fire, brimstone and floods. Whole countries do it. How many times have you heard America called the Great Satan? That's a collective projection of shadow.

I asked Hansie if I could book some sessions with him. He said no, there was no need.

Jack, we're doing it, he said, we're in a session.

What do you mean?

I'm a psychiatrist, but more than that I'm a psychotherapist, and the art of psychotherapy is the art of conversation and what are we doing? Conversing. All it's costing is coffee and cake.

Sounds like we're bloody communists. I do have one request, that you make me one of those Turkish coffees every so often.

Every so often turned into once a fortnight. Every Friday Hansie knocked on my door late in the afternoon. I put the pot on while he told me about his week, his family, his personal battles, then, over the coffee and cake, I ran through mine. One type of person played a consistent role in our discussions – narcissists. We decided they were everywhere. If we were in a café, we spotted them nearby, ran through high-profile people we could see on magazine covers scattered on tables, including sports men and women, politicians and entertainers.

It is possible, Jack, he said, that we are projecting, but I can excuse myself, given my first wife was a narcissist and I haven't quite got over how stupid I was to get caught in her web. She seduced me by telling me everything I had never heard before. At first, I thought it was because she was American and full of that trait many Americans have of being overly positive, even when they might wish a person dead. It's what I call the Have A Nice Day Syndrome.

Part of me was surprised and another part pleased, that I was not alone, that a psychiatrist – who had spent his life studying human behaviour, knew all the classifications, prognoses, diagnoses – could also make mistakes in his relationships and fall victim to a desperate need to be loved.

How did it happen, Hansie?

She said I was the best lover she had ever had, the best looking, most generous, kindest, most amazing man. Look at me – I'm overweight, got the smashed-in face of a man who played over a hundred games for the Transvaal rugby team and my ears look like burnt cauliflowers. I drank it all up like an overexcited puppy. She used the language of the seductive narcissist and she triggered my own narcissism. Friends warned me. I ignored them. I was, after all, a psychiatrist, trained to discern, to perceive, to know. Fell for it like the mullet that took the baited hooks Lester and I set last week.

There is something seductive about listening to the pain and weakness of others, people you admire, then reflecting on your own ability to keep above the fray, not get sucked in by the psychologically cunning, to realise your intellectual superiority. I didn't mention these thoughts to Hansie, because I was pretty sure they were characteristics of my personal version of narcissism.

What I did mention was my old muse, Kahlil Gibran, and quoted a few stanzas from his thoughts on marriage in *The Prophet*:

> *Give your hearts, but not into each other's keeping.*
> *For only the hand of Life can contain your hearts.*
> *And stand together yet not too near together:*
> *For the pillars of the temple stand apart,*
> *And the oak tree and the cypress grow not in each other's shadow.*

That works for us, now, doesn't it, said Hansie, with our current partners, our best friends?

In the nineteen seventies, I told Hansie, whenever I fell apart, I always consulted Gibran, along with Hermann Hesse.

Gibran was, by all accounts, a raving narcissist. Great writer, shitty family man, arch-manipulator, thought very highly of himself and probably had a messianic complex. He was also good mates with Jung. I wonder if Jung picked Gibran's shadow?

Hansie, who can we turn to?

Ourselves, Jack, you and me. Our partners. Lester. Friends we make in the Whalers Retreat.

He stopped talking to point at two men in suits sitting three tables away.

I'm not including those two bastards, he said, the psychopaths in suits, the city councillors who voted against my house extensions.

Kibbutz Nir Zamit 1977

1

Arieh was on a week-long visit to the kibbutz, to console me. He didn't need consoling. He had a new girlfriend. A New Yorker.

What happened to Norway? I asked.

I didn't see her yet, he said.

I got him a job in the dairy and we worked hard and well together, and he kept me laughing and living. Then the Italian arrived.

Arieh saw her first and said he heard in the showers the night before that one man, after seeing her, had cried alone in his room in the knowledge that he would never know her naked.

She might look at me, Jack, he said. But when she sees this scar down the side of my head she will turn to you.

There were no trees to climb on Zamit. When we finished work we climbed up the stacks of peanut hay, dug into the bails, found the forgotten peanuts, cracked, ate and talked.

You wait, Jack, she will come to the mangoes tomorrow.

There was a huge mango crop to pick and pickers were called in from all sections of the kibbutz. The dairy team said the mango team could have me for one week only.

She walked towards the trailer with a sway and an ease that had me dreaming of a film star in my movie memory whose name would not come to me. My eyes locked on her form, from the flowing hair tumbling down beside her wide brown eyes, the perfectly structured face, glowing skin with silky texture, past the small breasts, the neat waist and hips to the legs that knew walking and running. I felt faint and had to turn away and remind myself of where and who I was and what I had just been through but nothing was enough to erase her beauty. I looked again and could see she had seen me turn.

She picked mangoes slowly that first day and when I walked down her row it was with shirt off and muscles tensed. I did not look at her, ignored her, as though my work was too important, as though I was taken, committed, in love with another and she was nothing to me.

It was a good year for mangoes on Nir Zamit. The trees were heavily laden and Arieh and I were the work horses. We ran up and down rows all day picking up the full buckets and placing them on the trailer. I then climbed on the idling tractor and drove on to the next bucket cluster. During the breaks we lay flat on our backs while the other volunteers drank tea, ate biscuits and chatted.

Her name was Gina. One night after a hard day in the orchard Arieh and I climbed the swimming pool fence, dropped our clothes, jostled, wrestled, ran and dove into the glistening water. When we climbed out, Gina was there, staring, immobile, on the other side of the fence.

What you think? said Arieh. She thinks we are lovers?

She did. I knew this because one afternoon I confronted her and said: Is it you spreading the rumour that Arieh and I are having a homosexual affair?

Are you?

No.

I saw you wrestling naked.

We do that. Have you seen the movie *Women in Love*? Then you know sometimes men like to be naked with other men.

I think you should prove this, by taking me to your room, removing all your clothes, and wrestling naked with me.

We did, wrestle, gently, followed by awkward lovemaking. And yet there was love, a kind of love, because we wanted each other, knew something about each other, but could not find each other. After the sex we sat and talked and she told me about her life. For the next week we met after dinner and walked hand in hand around the fence surrounding the kibbutz settlement. Her early life had been full of promise. Her parents were wealthy, she went to the best schools, but she had always felt a longing for something other than that offered by her social class. At university she fell in love with a man who belonged to the Communist Party. The relationship did not end well. Like many of us in the volunteer community, she was on Nir Zamit to escape and hide. At the end of our walk, we kissed goodnight, hugged, and parted. There was no more sex, but a deeper knowing and a kind of spiritual sharing.

I said nothing to Arieh and he respected my silence. He knew, I knew that, and he knew that I knew he knew. After she had gone, we talked.

She was in pain, he said. You could see it through the beauty.

Not everyone, Arieh, I said. You could. I sensed it.

It is too late for us, but you should tell the people here to plant some trees you can climb. And when we meet here again, in thirty years, we will climb.

You think we will?

Meet? Or climb?

Both.

Of course. If we live that long.

2

After I had been on Nir Zamit for two months I called Neeva on Gavrot and told her where I was. We arranged to meet. It was not a happy event.

I walked through Gavrot with my head down. I didn't want to speak to anyone, not my kibbutz father Yigal, not Eliezer, Erella, no-one. As I walked to her room all I could feel was shame. I had failed my kibbutz, Neeva, her parents, my parents, everyone.

Why are you here? she asked, as soon as her front door was closed behind me.

When you left me, I said, I remembered how much we loved each other and I could not cope with how it all ended, that we promised so much and then you hated me because I failed you in so many ways I could not count them and by the next day I hated you too because of what you did and I wanted to tell you that if you had died I would not cry.

Neeva fell to the floor and lay there, curled up in the corner of her tiny kitchen. She began to sob, a silent, shuddering sob. I looked down, and that puzzled me because I was no longer beside her, but up high, near the ceiling. Below, I could see both of us, one broken and the other cold, hard, also broken, but unable to let the broken pieces fall out. The hard one turned, walked away and left.

It wasn't until the second bus, the one that aimed south towards Egypt, that the broken pieces fell away and I sobbed myself to sleep.

Three days later she called and asked if I would see her psychologist.

His room was in the north, out of Haifa, on a hill. He greeted me without warmth, sat behind his desk, took a pad and a pencil and poised as though I was about to say something important.

You are Australian? asked the psychologist.

Yes.

Why did you come here?

Because Neeva asked me.

I mean, why did you come to Israel?

I stood.

There is something wrong?

I came here to help you with Neeva, not for a security check.

Okay, then, to Neeva.

When I left his room, I hated him. He paid no attention to me, to my suffering. I was a vessel containing information and all he had to do was tip me to one side so it flowed out in the direction of his pen and pad. He wanted to know where we lived, how we lived, why I thought we separated and, of course, if I was Jewish.

Is not being Jewish an issue?

It's for my notes.

His eyes did not look at mine and I thought it was for more than his notes.

I came here before the war ended in seventy-three, to help on the kibbutz, to work, to carry a gun. For the kibbutz. Every night, artillery fire from the Golan Heights. I never slept. Even if I slept I woke as though I had never slept. This is because I am who I am. At that time, I was the only volunteer to have a gun. None of the others, mostly Jews, had guns. Does this answer you?

You are an angry man.

Angry? After all I did? Did she tell you what she did? Did she?

I have no memory of the bus back to Haifa, or of passing through that city. Somehow, eventually, I found the road back to Nir Zamit.

Long after I left Israel, and was again living in Perth, settled, working, with a family, I saw Gina's photograph in a newspaper. It shocked me. I had unwrapped the morning paper over breakfast, stood suddenly and left the table, claiming a sudden need of the toilet. She had been arrested, a suspected member of the Red Brigades, an Italian terrorist organisation, an offshoot of young radicals from the Italian Communist Party. I cried, because I understood her pain. When she had arrived on Zamit, she was recovering from an abortion. She made the decision to abort her pregnancy because her partner, also a member of the Young Communists, had abused her, hit her, accused her of attempting to trap him into marriage, of giving up the dream of a communist-led Italy.

We have no time for children, he had screamed. There is a revolution going on and you can't find the time to take contraceptives? You are worthless to me.

She could not allow herself to bring a child into a world surrounded by anger and hate.

She had arrived on the kibbutz, broken, lonely and confused. We needed each other. She was the first person I spoke to about Neeva's abortion and while walking around the kibbutz, clutching hands, we often cried.

The newspaper report made it clear that Gina's pain had not left her, only festered, nurtured by revolutionary propaganda and, finally, exploded into violent hatred and urban warfare. I knew this hatred and remembered well the Trotskyites of my early university days.

She had been charged with the murder of men, important,

high-profile men. It was not clear how many she had killed and I wondered about them: Had each one been the father of an unborn child, ripped from a lover's womb, with no further responsibility taken? Could I have saved Gina with my love, given her a child born of that love and made a life with her full of love, bereft of hate? Even as I asked the question, I knew our relationship had belonged to a time and a place and could not have occurred at any other time or in any other place. We were on a kibbutz, damaged by our past, misreading our love as sexual attraction and fumbling in the act. When she went, she took my copy of Kahlil Gibran's *The Prophet*. I was angry at first, then pleased, and hoped it would provide her with solace and guidance. Gibran will never know it, but I do – he and I both failed.

William Blakers ran a caravan park outside of Pinjarra. It was a sad place, full of broken vans, lives and discarded vehicles.

After reading about Gina, I needed to talk to someone and the only person I thought would understand was William.

He lived in the only house on the block. It wasn't much of a house, more a shack with a couple of vans tacked on the edges. He greeted me in bare feet, shorts, a longer beard than I remembered and a hearty hug.

You're the first cousin to visit, Jacky, he said. Sit down. Tell me a story. I'll make coffee.

I looked across at his sink. It was piled high with a single man's debris – dishes on cups on upside down pots, pots on pots, cups oozing unfinished drinks, plates under and over every other thing and among the lot ran a million ants.

William, I said, I love a sink challenge.

I knew you were insane, he said, but go for it.

I followed the trail to a loose skirting board. With a tea towel I slapped and killed, slapped and killed, up the side of the cupboard and onto the sink. There I ran the hot water tap and began rinsing ants from the items they cherished most. The rinsed I placed on the other side, stacked neatly among their fellow shapes. Once the ants were gone, I set about the washing in my customary manner – good scrub in steaming soapy water, rinse, then flick.

You know your work, Jack, he said, but you didn't come here because Glorvina once told you I needed looking after.

I told him Gina's story. All I knew. I told him about my love affair in Papua New Guinea. Finally, because he was family, because I was sure he would not judge me, I told him about Neeva. He sat quietly, listening with intent, fiddling with a tea towel as though he might get up and help with the drying. When I looked back with a handful of cutlery, he was hunched over and crying.

He wiped his face with the towel, slapped his face, first one cheek then the other, wiped his face again and spoke.

I know about this, the brutal end to the unwanted pregnancy, he said. I have been a party to it and now it sits heavy in me. At the time, circumstances deemed it necessary and I would never stand in the way of a woman who made such a decision. She's the one carrying the child. But I hate it all the same. All my adult life I have wanted to be a father, but I could never face it, didn't think I could trust myself. My father was a shit. Your mother's father was a shit. You have been blessed, Jack, Andrew Muir is a good man.

I finished the final dish, racked it, stood in front of him and waited. He rose slowly and we held each other, tight. And wept. No words. Until I sat in my car, readying to leave.

I never spoke to anyone like that before, Jack, he said. Thank you.

As I watched him waving in the rear-view mirror, I realised I was still crying, a sort of sniffing, dripping, affirming cry.

Kibbutz Nir Zamit 1977

She was tall, blonde, slim, with long hair she sometimes plaited and wore hanging in one piece, or two. I saw her first at the swimming pool and thought she was another northern European in search of a lazy time in the sun. Then we were rostered to wash dishes together.

Hello, I'm Jack, I said.

She was early, I liked that. Her fingers were long, narrow and when she pulled on the rubber gloves there was efficiency and purpose in her movements.

My name is Froukje, she said.

She looked me in the eye with a hint of defiance, as though she had heard stories about the wild Australian and was determined not to be dismissed. Her dishwashing technique, although lacking my pace, was precise, orderly, and her long fingers proved their commitment and stamina.

As we hung up our aprons, I made sure mine was next to hers.

I would like to wash with you again, I said.

You say that to all the girls?

I've never said it before, to anyone, man or woman, on this kibbutz, or any other kibbutz.

She smiled and something deep shifted in me.

We agreed, after knowing each other for a week, through talk, and one kiss, that she would return to her job in the village primary school in Friesland, resign, and join me later on Nir Zamit. It was a huge risk for her, and her parents opposed the decision. I had lived through parental opposition before and was sure they would change their minds, eventually. After she left, it was as though she took part of me with her. I stumbled, worked harder, asked for extra kitchen duties and wrote to her three times a week. I told no-one about our relationship. I wanted to tell Arieh, but he was on army reserve duty and unavailable.

I met her at Lod International Airport when she arrived back in Israel. She was nervous and almost immediately asked: Where will I be staying?

There are no vacant rooms, I said, but you can move in with me.

That's okay, but I must have my own bed.

I didn't know it then, but I discovered years later that her folk, the Frisians, were a proud and stubborn people. In their ancient cultural form, the Frisii were among the few Germanic tribes to halt the Roman advance north in the first century BC. They retained their independence when Rome ruled the known world and Froukje was not letting hers go in the State of Israel.

We stayed that first night in the kibbutz apartment in Tel Aviv. We were alone. She slept in one room and I in another. She told me her parents were worried about her, and her mother thought she was losing her. She was, of course, because we both knew that if we were going to live anywhere together, it would be Australia. Years later, she admitted that although she loved her mother deeply, she was driven to leave her village, her province, and had long dreamt she would live in another country.

The next day we caught a bus to the kibbutz. To the amusement of the other volunteers, we carried a single bed into my room.

The room was our home for four months of talking – learning about each other, how to live with each other. I was horny as hell but contained myself, wanting the relationship to last, knowing without knowing that whatever it was we were doing was right.

When people ask how we met, her story has always been different to mine.

He was part of the kibbutz, she says. He worked in the dairy and seemed to be a permanent member of the community. He never mixed with the international volunteers. The first time I saw him I asked who he was and they told me to keep away from him. He is aloof, angry, they said, about something. We don't know what.

When it is my turn, I have another offering.

I saw her at the swimming pool, I say, and was mesmerised by her long, shapely body. Later that night, I heard her talking in the coffee house and I enjoyed the sound of her voice. About a week later I found her sitting at the front of my hut and when I said hello, she looked me right in the eye and I thought she was going to stand up and slap me. Then one night we washed dishes together and that was when I knew that I wanted to know her and not to give in to any base desires.

Amsterdam 1977

After we left Nir Zamit, we flew into Amsterdam on separate flights. She flew in on her return ticket and I flew on a ticket I bought in Athens. The officials at Schiphol's immigration desk did not like my answers to their simple questions.

Do you have an onward ticket?

No.

Visa?

Didn't think I needed one.

Do you have money, traveller's cheques?

No.

Open your bag.

What they found did not please them: a typewriter, carbon paper, dictionary, two pairs of underpants, singlet, Speedos, one shirt, toothbrush, face cream, an old school exercise book, three pencils, half a towel, one pocketknife and one hunting knife, a new copy of Kahlil Gibran's *The Prophet* and a battered copy of Hermann Hesse's *Steppenwolf*.

My favourite books, I said. Don't go anywhere without them.

The three men did not look at me as they rummaged through my life. They stood over the bag and took turns to rummage. I thought they might fight over the rummaging.

I have been living on a kibbutz in Israel, I said. They paid us peanuts and I left them behind.

One of the men looked up and I thought he was going to laugh.

This is not funny, he said. You have arrived here with no money, no onward ticket and no visa. What do you want us to do?

My fiancée is waiting for me in the foyer. She is a Dutch

citizen. I am sure she will vouch for me.

What is her name?

Froukje van der Muelen.

They sent a tall and superbly built man to find Froukje, not yet my fiancée, because I was still married to Neeva. When she arrived, she tried to negotiate my release but failed. They allowed us to huddle in a corner of the room to say our goodbyes.

What will happen to me?

Your case will go before a judge. And they will let me know the outcome.

My case?

They said they are clamping down on illegal immigrants and you will have to spend a day or two in the airport jail. They said the conditions were quite nice, probably nicer than the kibbutz hut we lived in.

The room was long and narrow. The ceiling high and the only windows were just below full height. There was no chance we could see outside. My roommates were a Cape Verde Islander and an Egyptian, both arrested for illegal entry. The Cape Verde man was an eighteen-year-old boy, on his way to see his brother, a man with permanent residency in the Netherlands, but the boy had no money, no visa and no return ticket.

I came by boat to France and then caught a plane into Amsterdam, he said.

His English was good, his Dutch non-existent.

They will not even let my brother see me. He does not know I am here, but he knew I was coming. Tomorrow they put me on a plane back to Paris, I think, but they will not tell me.

The boy began to cry. The Egyptian went to him and put his arm around his shoulder.

Wait until you hear my story, he said. Then you will laugh.

They were both good-looking men. The boy was strongly

built and had the face of a film star. The Egyptian had an Omar Sharif face and moustache to match.

Unlike you two, Asim said, I have everything – a return ticket, ten thousand dollars in US dollars. But no visa. This, they have told me, is enough to send me home. Can I pay more? Of course. I have one of the most successful carpet businesses in Cairo. I am not a poor man. I made a mistake by not getting a visa and now they will punish me.

The door opened and two policemen entered.

You, Australian, one of them said. We have some food for you. Follow us.

They took me to a canteen and I ate an omelette. When I had finished, one of them said: You can stay here, if you like, and watch television for a while. There is no need to go back with the blacks.

I looked at the man and did not like what I saw, and asked to be returned to the company of my new friends.

Not one of us slept well that night. Asim woke every five hours to face Mecca and David woke himself up crying. By five in the morning, Asim and I made a pact to make the boy laugh before we were parted. We didn't have much luck until breakfast.

What is this? I said to the police guard.

Bread with *hagelslag*, he said. It's what we have for breakfast.

It's little strips of chocolate, said Asim.

When the guard left, Asim said to David: Look, David, this is what they made out of the last Cape Verde Islander.

David laughed so hard with such a need to laugh that he could not stop and had to leave for the attached toilet. Unlike the kibbutz, to get to the Dutch toilet we did not have to stumble through the night, along an uneven path, kicking aside fallen branches, with extra care not to drop the candle.

Around midday I was released into the care and custody of my pretend fiancée. She had heard from the court. The magistrate posted bail of four thousand guilders with the provision that I report once a week to the local police station in Leeuwarden. The money was provided by her grandfather who removed it from an old mattress in his garden shed.

An hour before I left the cell, Asim asked me a favour.

What I did not tell the police, he said, was that I was meeting my girlfriend here. She knew I was coming but she does not know I am here because if I told them, I knew they would not let me call her. Can you call her when you are released and tell her I am safe?

The police drove me back to the airport where I was to wait for Froukje and her father. It was an agonising three hours and not until the last minute did I call Asim's girlfriend. What if I had Asim all wrong and he was a member of an international terrorist organisation and a call would set off a train of tragedies? I ate another omelette. I drank four coffees. The toilet and I became intimate. No, I argued, Asim was a good man and I had to make the call.

Hello, my name is Jack Muir. Is this Rachel?

Yes.

I have been in the airport lockup for illegal immigrants. I spent last night with Asim, your boyfriend.

Is he all right? Will they send him home?

He is fine, in good humour and yes, they will send him back to Cairo.

Did he tell you about us?

No, just asked me to call you.

Did he say where I am from?

No.

I am Israeli.

What?

We met in Paris and fell in love. We have been seeing each other for ten years now, but never in Cairo or Tel Aviv, of course. Who in those countries would understand our love? I have been blessed with a certain kind of mother and she knows, but she is alone in the family. My father would deny I was his daughter.

I went back to the deserted toilet where I could weep aloud and shake as though with fever. Then the weeping turned to laughter with the memory of Asim's face full of cheek and good humour.

It was good to meet you, Jack, Asim told me before I left the cell. My father used to tell stories of the Australian and New Zealand soldiers in World War I. They burnt half of Cairo because they were angry about thieves and prostitutes and how much they had to pay for them. He would laugh when he told this because he thought they must have been very stupid men. But then they went and pushed the Ottoman Turks out of the Sinai and Palestine and he still thought they were stupid but they were also great warriors. Thank you, Jack, for being a funny and kind man.

We hugged, Asim and me, and me and David. There were tears in our eyes.

Froukje's father hated me as soon as he saw me and nothing changed for the rest of his life. It wasn't that I was a communist, a convicted criminal, or married to someone else, it was simply that, in his view, I enticed his daughter to a country as far away as he could imagine.

Perth 1978

Jack Muir was back in Perth and back in his degree course at the institute. He was as happy as a man could expect given he'd gone through a relationship collapse, the tail end of a war, a couple of beatings, car accidents and another period of depression. His family was happy to see him and expected him to settle, finish his degree and start a stellar career in journalism. They were also keen to meet his new partner, the Frisian, as he called her. She was delayed because of a visa issue, and that her Australian partner was married to another woman was of no assistance. She would eventually arrive on a three-month tourist visa. Muir was happy his parents were happy, and although short on skills necessary for living in a rampant capitalist society, he was prepared to do his best.

He spent a lot of time on the street, walking, waiting for busses, hitchhiking and he was, once again, faced with what he thought were among the most stupid people on earth. Even his old friend in Genoralup, Tom, seemed stupid and completely unaware of world affairs.

Yes, I heard Nixon had resigned, said Tom, and I know we've got some pseudo-fascist running this country but I have no idea who's in charge of the Soviet Union, or what's going on in Nicaragua, Venezuela, Nigeria, or the Belgian Congo. I came down here for a simple life, Jack. You said once that was why you left the family business, but it seems to me all you've done is pile complication on complication.

Jack was again reminded of his old kibbutz friend, Eliezer, from Gavrot. It wasn't that he and Tom looked alike, they didn't, or sounded similar, they didn't, it was that every so often they said something deep and worthy of further thought.

Eliezer said to him one night in the *moadon*: Jack, if ever you think that most people you know are stupid, then maybe it is time to think that you are the stupid one.

Perth felt like a place designed to torment him with memories he had tried so hard not to keep. Memories of old school experiences that he now realised had probably scarred him for life in ways that he needed to work through, probably with a psychotherapist, probably Jungian, or Freudian, or both. He wasn't sure about the differences but Sylvia, an American psychologist he had worked with on Nir Zamit, had assured him that either one would do him good.

Why are you here? he had asked her.

He had finished his early-morning shift inside the rotary dairy platform and was bringing her a cup of Turkish coffee as she fed the calves colostrum, the first milk from the cows after delivery. He always thought it a shame the calves didn't get to suck on their mother's teats but that was the way it was in the kibbutz dairy, all hustle and bustle and driven by the need for income to keep the community solvent. Muir thought it strange to be working in a dairy on the edge of a desert, close to the border with Gaza and almost as close to Egypt. In Genoralup, the dairy farms were nestled in lush pasture and gentle rolling hills. Milk was a major product for Nir Zamit, along with oranges, peanuts, grapefruit, mangoes and plastic from the chemical plant on the periphery of the settlement. And there were no bulls in the dairy, not like Uncle Bob's farm up the road from the Muir family orchards. There his uncle managed the cows, his coterie of eager bulls, and the newborn calves got to suck on their mothers until fat enough for sale.

I am here, said Sylvia, like all of us, because this is a time in our lives when we don't seem to fit the place we grew up in. The Israeli Jews are here because they have no place left to go. The Arabs are here because they have always been here. You and I are here for now, but eventually we will return home. You will, won't you, go home to Australia?

Probably. It's hard to tell, because when I'm here I want to be there and when I'm there I want to be here. What the hell is that about?

Sometimes the best place to see a place is from another place.

When Muir arrived in Perth, no-one met him at the airport. He had not told them he was coming. He felt that if they knew, they would prepare for the worst, expect another wife they could not like, or love, or perhaps he'd be drunk, like when he'd arrived home from Papua New Guinea, heavy in the thick of depression and denial. His father's sad face among the waiting crowd had never left him. Jack and Andrew Muir saw each other at the same time. Andrew's eyes closed, his head dropped, then shook from side to side. Glorvina stood silently beside him, gently weeping. He couldn't see the tears until he stood before her but he knew they would be there before he left the plane.

Now he caught a taxi to his younger brother's apartment. It was on the south side of the city, right in the heart of the suburbs. His brother had only recently started studying economics at university and Muir wondered how they would get on – the economist and the socialist. He need not have worried; Bill was open, tolerant, funny, very different from their older brother. Muir wondered how he got to be like that.

His brother was often out late, and this left Muir alone to ponder his life, his loves. He thought a lot about the men in his life, Eliezer, Shlomo, Yitzhak and Haim from Nir Zamit, the wise men who filled the roles that perhaps were once occupied by godfathers and godmothers, or uncles and aunties.

Yitzhak was an example of how to get on following tragedy. He had been a tank commander in the Sinai and was in the forefront of the charge to push back the Egyptians. The push took a heavy toll and a direct hit smashed Yitzhak's tank and killed everyone but him. He took it hard and wallowed for a period, but, like any dedicated and true socialist, he reminded himself that the collective was much stronger and much more important than any individual, picked himself up, studied, and took control of the kibbutz chemical factory and turned it into an important export earner for Israel.

Haim, like Neeva, was the child of Holocaust survivors. His parents were dead by the time Muir met him but his scars were clear and present.

He is a *sabra*, said Shlomo. He grew up on the kibbutz and spent his childhood with his group in the children's houses. This makes it difficult to understand how much of him is about his parents' war and how much about his war. What we know, is that the Yom Kippur War changed him. He came home not the same man who went. He is the only soldier on this kibbutz who enjoys war. We don't know what happened to his parents, but we do know they went through something terrible. Maybe his mother was raped, and his father humiliated in the same way. He went into his war with this on his shoulder and what he saw, what happened, all went to make him what he is – a man crazy for killing.

One afternoon, as Muir left the dairy, he heard machine-gun fire. On instinct he dropped to the ground.

It's okay, my friend, said Shlomo, it's Haim. He is killing a diseased calf.

Muir walked down the line of buildings and saw Haim, Uzi submachine gun at his waist, peppering an animal hanging in a eucalyptus tree. The animal's head had disappeared and Haim was laughing. Maniacal, hysterical, mad.

As Muir passed, Haim stopped, said: *Shalom*, Muir. You want calf for dinner?

Muir attempted a smile, failed, and walked on as Haim returned to dismantling the animal, pumping shell after shell into the lifeless body.

When questioned later, Shlomo said: Jack, this man has suffered enough. He has a need to kill, so we provide him the opportunity. If we didn't, we cannot say what he would do. He also kills all stray dogs, cats, horses, anything.

Shlomo was the uncle, the godfather, the older brother Muir never had, yet wanted. Shlomo read wide, the works of Albert Camus, Jean-Paul Sartre, Hermann Hesse, Dostoevsky, even George Johnston, the Australian writer who lived on the Greek Island of Hydra with another Muir muse, Leonard Cohen.

How did you get to George Johnston? Muir asked Shlomo.

He was recommended to me by an Israeli historian as a writer who had covered much of the Second World War. This war interested me, of course, because at the end of it, the State of Israel was created and I wondered about this Australian because your people made it possible by helping push out the Ottoman Turks.

Some old soldiers back home think it was all the Australian and New Zealand Light Horse and that the British were bloody hopeless.

You can find that opinion here too, but no-one wins a war on their own. And no-one causes it on their own.

And so it was in a marriage. Muir knew this and took some credit for the collapse of his when he faced the Australian judge, alone, in his divorce proceedings.

We were both to blame, your honour. We were the wrong people in the wrong time.

He and Neeva had married in Glasgow, then divorced in Perth. Muir did it all himself, with the help of new divorce laws introduced by Gough Whitlam, the reforming zealot for the Australian Labor Party. All Muir had to do was show proof that they had not lived together for one year. He had made a previous attempt in Israel and had given up when he discovered that an application had to be made to the Supreme Court, requesting that the state recognise their marriage so that it could annul it.

Marriages between Jews and non-Jews were not recognised by Israel.

With the divorce complete, he was ready. Almost. Where is Froukje? He asked himself every day. Why isn't she here already?

He needed a job, so that when Froukje arrived he would have enough money for them to find a place of their own. He found one at the Perth Entertainment Centre. Every morning he rose before his brother, dressed, walked to the bus stop and took a bus into the city where he wrestled an industrial vacuum cleaner for two hours before heading back to where he came from, to wash and head off to classes. The place was owned by a television station and was a hotbed of distraction and capitalist propaganda. He hated it, hated himself for working there, but he needed the money.

Perth 1988

1

Muir was talking to himself again. Hearing voices, sounds. Artillery? Asking questions: Let me set you free. Who the fuck are you? Who the fuck are these people? You're in Perth? And you live in a fucking suburb? What the fuck are you doing here? You hate the place. You're a dead man. Where are the blacks, the Jews, Arabs, Iranians, the people of your dreams? You left home, then you came home, for this shit? You have a wife? You love her? He thought he did. He knew she was his best friend, but sometimes it was not enough and he had to get in his car and drive away, south, Yallingup, sleep on the back seat, eat shit, drink shit, then, when he was pretty sure he was nothing, a waste of space, he would drive home and fall into Froukje's arms. She went to work, washed, cleaned, cared for their son.

Something was wrong. He no longer made sense. His mind a thrashing machine. All the good work he had done over the years to sort himself out, to settle, to be free of the demons, had amounted to nothing. Some nights he went out, stayed late, drank, smoked marijuana, hash, talked nonsense for hours, drove home, fell asleep on the settee. That was not the worst of it. Their son, already four years old, looked up to Muir. Thought his dad was the greatest, funniest, smartest, ever. First only to Andrew Muir, also funny, smart and clever in ways denied Jack, like an ability to make a small train out of wood, or fix a broken battery-powered crane. Muir could sense the danger in his son's admiration. Throughout his life,

Jack had turned on people who looked up to him. This was his biggest test. He could not turn against his son, betray the boy born of his seed.

When Froukje fell pregnant, Muir was ecstatic. He could not have been happier. Yet even then, in the middle of ecstasy, he felt the darkness looming and when it fell over him, enveloped him, bound and gagged him, pummelled him, the drunkenness intensified and his brain screamed for mercy. Mercy was busy. What if the boy was born with a severe defect, one that could be traced to Muir's lifestyle, his drug and alcohol abuse? His rampant and random sexual past? He lived in a mad fear for the last three months of the pregnancy and the first three after the boy's birth. He could not shake it, even when the doctors pronounced the baby healthy in every way. It was not enough. Doctors made mistakes. Some medical issues did not reveal themselves until a child had lived for years. And what if the boy was born with deficiencies that only showed up if he caught an unrelated illness? It was as though Muir tried to will the things that he dreaded most.

There were many old men in his memory and one kept coming to him, not Neeva's father, or Eliezer, but Moishe, a man who spoke no English, only Yiddish, Russian, German, Polish and Hebrew. He spoke all those languages because he lived in most of those places. Moishe, Yigal told him, was an inspiration to all kibbutzniks.

This man fought for the Bolsheviks in the Russian Revolution, said Yigal. After the revolution with the chaos and the madness there were random pogroms against Jews, mainly carried out by anti-communist forces who were blaming Jews for all their troubles.

Moishe ran away to Poland and joined the Polish army to fight against the Russian Army when it invaded in 1939. He was caught, put in a prison camp, made to work in a factory making bullets, and after an attempt to escape was about to be executed when Germany invaded Russia. They needed him in the factory then, but he escaped to Italy, hid for the remainder of the war and fought with the resistance. This man survived many horrors and you can see in his face that life has made him work hard and here he is, with us.

There were days when the memory of Moishe helped Muir overcome himself and there were days when he forgot the man who walked his way from Russia to Italy and crossed the Mediterranean in a leaky boat to Palestine. On those days Muir sank into his own morass.

Froukje stood by, watching, caring, waiting.

It was not easy for him to see her watching. He couldn't talk. There was too much going on, so much to condemn himself for. He drank. He smoked. He hardly slept. He became manic. One night he would talk for hours about a life he imagined he had led, a political system he believed he had demolished, lives he had saved with a hunting knife and a fierce eye, terrorists he had defeated with a Browning semi-automatic, and the next night he was nothing, a heap in a corner, silent.

2

It was late. Muir was at a music concert featuring a legendary Australian rock band. His ears hurt. He was with his friend Brett Jones. They had not seen each other for years, not since Jones waved him goodbye as he left on the *Fairstar* for South Africa in 1972.

You're pissed, Muir, said Jones.

So what, Muir said. In the morning I'll be sober, but you'll still be an ugly bastard.

And that's how it went, all night, two old friends heckling each other, holding each other, and as they left the concert venue, Jones said he would drive Muir home.

But it's my fucking car, said Muir.

And it's my fucking life.

How will you get home if you drive me home?

I left my car at your place. Remember?

When they arrived at Muir's house, Jones removed the key and refused to give it to him.

I'm taking you inside, he said, but before we go in, I want to show you something.

What?

Not now, tomorrow morning. Can you get an hour off work?

What you got in mind?

You'll see.

The week before, Muir had come home after work and entered, almost immediately, into a shouting, heckling, insulting argument with Froukje. His son had cried and clung to his mother in fear.

You don't listen, she screamed.

What is there to listen to? he yelled. You don't make any sense.

It had started when she complained about him not coming home straight after work, that he took liberties with her willingness to comply with what she called an Australian way. This inflamed him, because he didn't think of himself as embracing an Australian way. He thought he was above it, beyond it, a man of the world. He hated her for saying it at the same time he realised its truth. He began to cry, yet still he spat venom and accused her of crimes against men and he even, once again, suggested she might be better off back where she had come from, that northern European province where people were so bloody neat and tidy and in control and totally fucking anal. All this did was intensify his self-loathing because he knew she was the best friend he had ever had and that without her his life was a meaningless confusion.

He turned and ran, as he had done so often in his life, and as he ran he asked himself when he would stop running and this made him run harder and he missed the opening to his private room at the back of the house, the one with all the books on philosophy and psychology that he showed to visitors who thought he must be an intellectual and he liked the idea even though he knew he was no more than a lost boy trying to find ground he thought he had been on before but was beginning to realise he had never even seen.

He fell into the doorjamb and the jarrah cut his forehead and soon his face was warm with blood. He took an old t-shirt from a chair, held it to his face and poured port into an empty Vegemite jar. The jar went to his mouth and the port disappeared. He poured another. It too disappeared. He fell into the chair that gave up the old t-shirt.

He had no idea how long he sat sobbing, but one thought suggested hours, while another only minutes. Then his son entered. He looked at the dejected figure, turned to the half-full jar on the bookshelf, picked it up and put it in his father's hand.

Here, Papa, he said, drink this, it will make you feel better.

This boy is my son, Muir thought, I am his father. Yet here, now, after the verbal violence that took place on the other side of the house, he is offering advice, solace, taking on a role suggesting a higher level of maturity than this man, me, the pathetic example of what it is to be a man.

In that moment, he realised that his life only showed signs of maturity, of wisdom, of growth, and that what his son was looking at was a pretend, puffed-up man. He took the jar, put it aside, took his son and held him.

I am sorry, Eli, he said. I will become a better father. I promise you, because what I want more than anything in the world is that when you look at me, you see a solid example of what it is to be a man. I thought I was. I was wrong. You have shown me. Thank you.

The boy sat still in his father's arms, not understanding what his father was saying, or confessing, yet lulled by the tone of his father's voice, and when Muir had finished talking he looked down to see his son asleep.

At ten thirty in the morning, Brett Jones picked up Jack Muir and took him to an Alcoholics Anonymous meeting. As he walked down the flight of stairs to the underground bunker that was really a basement, he heard a voice.

I was in Vietnam, said the man. People died. I was sprayed with Agent Orange. People tried to kill me. I hear artillery fire when I am in crowded spaces and the voices crush in on me. My only response has been to drink, get drunk, lie in my own vomit and blame everybody I ever knew, or who I thought poisoned my life.

He knew the voice belonged to another man, but it seemed to be coming from inside his own head, and it seemed to know

Muir, his life, his misery, confusion and darkness.

By the last step of the long flight down, Jack Muir was weeping. Brett Jones put an arm around his friend's shoulder. Muir never drank, or smoked, again.

Perth 2003

It's a curious thing, he thought, here I am in a place I never liked, living a full life, almost a success, almost a failure, not quite one or the other. A son at university studying architecture after becoming dux of his high school, and Froukje finally making Australia home. He realised at a certain point, he wasn't sure when, that he had never wanted to be a journalist. He did not have the analytical skills, the patience for research and desire to destroy a life. Often when interviewing a subject he should have torn to pieces, he could sense incompetence, deceit, but, alongside, often pain, suffering, fragility, trauma, all the elements he recognised in himself. Looking back, he wondered how often he had transferred those elements to the subject, or the subject had played him.

And then he saw her again.

She was at a writers festival event. He could not remember who the writer was, or what he or she had written, all he remembered was seeing her there, three rows in front of him. He knew it was her. He saw her walk to her seat, face down, negotiating people's knees. He couldn't see her face, but he knew her body, her walk, the way she moved her shoulders.

They first met in his second year of university. He walked into the class and the only seat available was next to her. He took it. He didn't take her. He wanted to. She was from Sri Lanka, newly arrived, and smelt of saffron. He didn't know what saffron smelt like but that was the word that came to him as she washed over him, exotic, erotic, enticing. In week two he asked her to join him for coffee. They talked of Hermann Hesse's *Siddhartha* and how much it had influenced their lives. Then they moved on to

Steppenwolf, then the songs of Leonard Cohen.

We seem to have so much in common, he said.

But what does it mean to our lives? she asked.

It was four coffee weeks later that he told her he was married. She didn't seem surprised.

What does this mean to our lives? she asked.

I'm not sure, he said.

But he was sure. He knew he wanted to ask her to his room, to remove all her clothes, so they could tangle up their nakedness in their philosophic platitudes.

I am sure, he said.

I can see you are, she said.

She invited him to her house, to meet her family. Her parents dressed in traditional clothing and her two brothers dressed like students and with voices that would not have been out of place on ABC Radio.

You are in a class with Asheni? her mother asked.

Yes, he said.

And you have been helping her with her essays?

Muir nodded and knew they could be together because she was prepared to lie to her parents. And he realised how close he was to another betrayal.

When the writer finished talking, and the audience left the auditorium, they met in the foyer. They hugged, as though they had been lovers once, and he realised his love for her was the same as his love for Gina, the urban terrorist, although he and Asheni had not removed their clothes to discover friendship.

It was close and, given his past, Muir put it down to a crack in the wall of his behaviour and a Leonard Cohen line came to him. Was it the light that got through cracks in the dark, or the other way? Muir couldn't remember.

When he got home from the writers festival he told Froukje

the story from beginning to recent end and they laughed together as best friends do when they share failings, weaknesses and secrets long held. Then they lay in each other's arms and he asked her why she stayed with him during those years he drank, smoked and displayed all the elements of mental instability.

I loved you, she said. I trusted you. I was sure you would pass through it all and come back to us.

Kibbutz Nir Zamit 2016

Some of my ancestors arrived in Kincannup in the middle eighteen hundreds. When they got off the ship they may have been greeted by an old Noongar man trying to sell them artefacts. They may have been rude to him, dismissed him. I have no idea. No such stories have been passed down. What I do know is that many of the descendants of those Noongar Menang people became close friends. These relationships strengthened my sense of place, of belonging, of knowing. We also know that some of our early relatives had children with Noongars, even married them. In this new world it is spoken about openly. And for the first time in my life, since I came to Kincannup, I did not feel like a visitor, someone passing through. Kincannup felt right, where I belonged, where I felt more me than any other previous me.

And it was from this place, where I felt I belonged, that I chose to go back.

I flew into Israel from London. In silence. The man next to me tried to engage, but my answers were monosyllabic, lacking inviting tones, and he gave up. I knew what would happen as soon I saw the land and I did – I cried.

Everything was different. The airport arrival lounge had doubled in size and the customs and immigration desks had multiplied. Probably built to accommodate the Russian onslaught that began in the late 1980s. I expected to be held up at one or both desks. I had been to other countries since I left Israel, including Indonesia, a predominantly Muslim country, but here there were no delays.

You have been to Israel before? asked one official.

Ken.

Arr, you speak *Ivrit*?

Lo, not really, I'm just good with accents.

Once through all the gates, I could see Yigal, my kibbutz father, in the distance. He looked the same, although a lot older. He was in his eighties, the afro hair had gone, indeed most of his hair had gone, but the face and the eyes were as I remembered them. I didn't expect him to recognise me, because the long-haired hippie was now a clean-shaven, short-haired, reasonably well-dressed Westerner. But he did, came straight for me, hugged me, insisted we sit and drink *botz*. Turkish coffee was our glue. Before we got in his car and headed north, we had to share coffee, metaphorically break bread, open our hearts, minds, bring each other up to date.

Well, *chaver*, he said, what a journey. You are now retired?

Not yet, but close.

And me, the kibbutznik, the strong socialist, the man who took back the Golan Heights, I now have a restaurant in Tel Aviv and pay my workers shit money.

There is a mood you take with you when you meet old alcoholic or drug-addict friends, that compels you to speak the truth, however brutal, and I felt it was the same with old socialists.

And me, Yigal, this old socialist, I live in a two-storey house on a hill, I own shares in large corporations that fleece populations in many countries and when I work, I charge exorbitant sums. What have we become?

There is still a part of me who is the kibbutznik, said Yigal, and I only left because of the new people who wanted to change everything and now we are not a kibbutz anymore, but a private company. I didn't want to be a part of that. If there was to be change, I thought it better to change everything and leave.

When people ask what happened to the idealist Jack Muir,

I tell them it is impossible to be a socialist where I live, but I still hold the ideals and call myself a romantic socialist.

One hour later, Yigal drove me to his home, a two-level house north of Tel Aviv. He made more *botz* and then I surprised him with my gifts.

What have you done? he asked.

We worked the *mataim*, Yigal, you and me. I ate your apples. I wanted you to eat mine. They come from a cousin's farm.

I handed him two large, yellow Granny Smith apples, ripe from a tree, and two Pink Ladies. He took one of each in his hands, got up, retrieved two knives, and we sat, peeling, slicing, eating, the juice dripping down our chins.

These, he said, are apples.

You know, of course, that the Granny Smith is an Australian apple, as is the Pink Lady.

So many gifts to the world, from such a young country.

Australia is not a young country, Yigal, far from it. When you consider that the Noongar Menang people, the people who first inhabited the place where I now live, Kincannup, have descendants going back sixty thousand years. Israel is ancient. Been around since before Babylon, before the Persian Empire of Cyrus the Great. But you know all those plants we saw on our way to your house, the Australian plants you've got alongside the road, and the eucalypts, you know why we still have them? Because while so-called civilisations, all over Africa, the Middle East, Europe, even South America, were fighting, burning, pillaging, destroying, everything, Aboriginal people were living peacefully, apart from the occasional skirmish with near neighbours, caring for country.

Over the years many Australians came to Gavrot, Jack, and they always said the Aborigines were a primitive people.

Who are those Australians, Yigal? I want their names and addresses.

There we were, two old friends, drinking *botz*, and me on

another history rant, one the regulars at the Whalers Retreat at Binalup were used to. But not Yigal. The look on his face told me he could see the new, old man Jack Muir and I wondered if he was quietly comparing him to the young one.

You remember when that great Roman civilisation laid siege to Jerusalem? I told him. The future emperor, Titus, had to import timber from Macedonia because there was nothing left in Judea, all consumed in their mad efforts to build more weapons of mass destruction. And when they got home with all the loot they stole, they couldn't decide what to do with it and then it came to them – let's build an entertainment centre. When I visited Rome with Froukje, I woke early on the first morning and walked to the Colosseum. The only people in sight, apart from me, were a woman setting up her fast-food van, and a gladiator. As I walked around the monument, I began to weep. It surprised me and then I remembered – the Colosseum was built on the bodies of dead Jews.

Jack, the world is full of huge structures in history made possible by the dead.

Too true, and while Babylonians, Romans, Persians, Greeks, Egyptians, Parthians, were laying waste over three continents, Noongars and other Aboriginal nations were caring for their country, and that is why I live in a biodiversity hotspot and why the healthiest bees on the planet live where the Noongar live.

Noongar? Is this the Australian word for Aboriginal?

What a lot of people, most people, don't know, is that when the English invaders arrived, there were over five hundred different language groups. It was like all other continents on earth, populated with many nations speaking different languages, having different cultures.

Why didn't you tell me all this before, when we were on Gavrot?

I've always had Noongar friends, but we never spoke before. It was too hard, for them, for me. They kept their Noongar stories to themselves and I only ever felt guilt when I visited those towns with reserves.

Reserves?

This was a place, a fenced-off area, where many towns forced them to live.

Ah, said Yigal. We European Jews know about such places.

We talked until the sun rose between the houses. Yigal and his wife had bought their house in a new area, not far from what was once an Arab village. The development was well advanced, but the northern side contained remnants of three-storey buildings that once housed families of two, or three, generations.

We told other stories we had never shared when I was on Gavrot, when Israel was ruled by a kinder government, a government that condemned apartheid.

The change began after the Six-Day War, said Yigal, but you and I have talked about this before. Let me tell you a good story. I am now part of a group that mentors young Arabs and Jews. There are five of us. Two of them are psychologists and the others are like me, people who have lived and are near the end of their lives. They are troubled *yeladim*, kids, and we do what we can to help, but, most important, we get them together.

How is it going?

It is not easy work. They are not children of the kibbutz and grew up in poor areas, with some poverty and a lot of hate.

You have hope?

If I had no hope, I would not do this work. You think if you have twenty kids, you just want to change one or two, maybe three. If you get more, you cry and can't believe it.

The Arabs, are they Israeli citizens?

Nachon, of course. This is one of the great tragedies of this country, that many of our Jews have turned against our Arabs and many of our Arabs have turned against our Jews. We should think of ourselves as brothers and sisters in the same land.

We sat silent for some time before I said: I want to see Neeva.

Is that wise? he said.

Maybe not, but I have to. It is like this work you do, it must be done.

It was arranged. We met in a restaurant, not Yigal's, one not far from her work. I arrived early. She came late. She walked the walk I knew and she showed signs of her mythical Pacific Island heritage. She looked older. We both did. She was nervous. We both were.

Why are you here? she asked.

I came to apologise.

For what?

For loving you so much. For betraying that love. For all the things we did, I did, did not, to ourselves, to each other. And for the hate.

I remember you as a weak man.

You didn't know me, what was going on with me, because we never spoke of such things, because of my weakness and because I thought it would make you think I was even weaker.

She stared at me as though I was a stranger. I was.

But the lasting memory I have is of the love. Thank you.

She moved as though she might hug me. It would have come as a surprise, because kibbutzniks were not known for their signs of affection. But she didn't hug and that was the moment I chose to hand her a gift, a scarf made by Froukje.

We did things, we said things, I said, we were both weak, but we should not forget the love. It was real.

And the hate?

Of course, but you know what fills my memories? The love.

She looked down in thought, held the thought, fumbled in her handbag and removed what must have been her house keys.

They could not have been her car keys, because I knew she never learnt to drive. She fiddled with the bunch, removed a small item, and held it out.

This is the dove of peace. It was made after the assassination of Yitzhak Rabin. For the memory of him.

I held the small, smooth, metal dove in my open hand and could feel the tears arrive.

Please, take it. And thank your wife for the scarf. It is beautiful, and I will wear it.

We looked at each other, not quite knowing how to part. I made the first move, took her shoulders and kissed one cheek, then the other, in the way of Europeans.

In Friesland, I said, they kiss three times.

She smiled and we kissed again. I held out my hand for hers. She gave it. We held, and looked at each other and I knew she, like me, would never forget the love.

Your mother, is she still …?

No, she has gone. And my father too. And your parents?

They are struggling, said Neeva. I think I too will soon be an orphan.

Although the two mothers never met, I wished they had – both survivors who found the courage to honour love.

The bus dropped me at Nir Zamit's front gate where Shlomo was waiting. We shook hands and I pulled him into me for a side-only hug. He did not resist. The rest of the morning we worked in the dairy with the new herringbone milking system, while the old rotary dairy lay idle, abandoned, broken, collapsing. I asked him if later I could wash dishes but he said those days were long gone and all the dishwashing was fully automated.

Even the pots and pans? I asked.

Jack, he said, you and the dishes caused me much trouble when you were here. But now, before anything, lunch.

The dining room was as I remembered it, except for the till. Shlomo stopped, pulled a card, punched in a number, and swiped. The dining room was now a restaurant.

Did I ever buy you lunch before?

Never.

We live in a new world, Jack.

I didn't need to ask him how he felt, I could see it in his eyes. Shlomo was a socialist. He had arrived on Nir Zamit full of zeal and it had been taken from him. Not all. Most.

Tell me, Shlomo, those men who came over from Gaza, your Arab brothers and sisters, where are they now, now the border has closed?

What did I tell you, Jack, family is everything. We don't let them go. Every week the kibbutz pays them money, for their families, for their lives. There is a small group of us who made this happen. One thing the economic lunatics have not taken from us is the general community meeting, okay, not every week, like the old days, but every month. It was voted that we give them money, remember them as family. And every day one of us calls them: Hello, Mustapha, you all right? Your family? What do you need? We are living a tragedy, but we don't forget our brothers and sisters.

I remembered the last time I saw Mustapha. He came over for the twenty-fifth anniversary of the kibbutz. He was a softly spoken man and his English was worse than my Hebrew, but there was something about him I liked, the way he sat down next to me, with respect and a quiet dignity. I learnt through Shlomo that although he had spent his entire life working in construction, he was also a published poet.

This so-called Second Intifada, said Shlomo, I call it the Palestinian War of Independence. The Palestinians just want what we wanted, Jack, a country to call their own. How can we deny them? And now to you, Mr Muir, because you are also our brother, we have a plan. You have four days left in Israel, right?

Good, this means we have enough time to go for a camping and walking trip.

There were five of us in the party. Shlomo and Rachel from Nir Zamit, and their two friends from a nearby *moshav*, a farming cooperative where all the farmers in the community pooled their resources. We rose at dawn, loaded a four-wheel drive and headed north, up past Gavrot, right up to the Lebanese border, and we walked through Crusader ruins, visited ancient Roman forts, and got lost in a valley full of thistles and oleander. Oleanders back home were an awkward, ugly tree, but in that valley they were things of beauty, growing in tight hedge-like clusters and forming long tunnels amidst their interwoven branches. Then a miracle.

Perhaps the most beautiful young woman I had ever seen appeared in front of me, out of an oleander tunnel.

Hello, she said.

And the second, also the most beautiful young woman I had ever seen, said the same. And the next, and so on until all sixteen were among us and each one as beautiful as the one before. They strode down the narrow path, greeted us we stood aside to let them through, as we struggled with our backpacks, marvelled at their smiles that held the universe and their voices that tumbled out in musical rhapsodies. They were Ethiopian Jews on a school hike.

I had to stop. Shlomo had to stop. The others stopped.

Jack, he said, breathe. In out in out. You know, every classy restaurant in Israel now has an Ethiopian on staff. You cannot get customers without them. There is some resistance, of course, and we must work hard on those resisters to have them understand that Jews come from everywhere and look like everyone. It will take time and the Russian Jews are not helping.

Shortly after, our group decided to split up, because we

realised we were lost. I went one way, the way I believed in, Shlomo went his way, and the others went their ways. It was not a sensible arrangement, but we all believed in ourselves, that we knew the best way back to the car park. The rough direction, we all agreed on, but how to get there varied. My way began well and I made good progress, but it soon turned into a thistle-thicket nightmare. I was ready. I put my head down, well covered with the thick leather hat I bought from a tourist store at the base of Uluru, and charged.

I arrived first into the car park, dripping sweat and blood. The sweat came from everywhere and the blood from all the bits not well covered – arms, legs and neck. Shlomo arrived just after me, but not the others, because they had found a longer way free of thistles.

You see this man, said Shlomo, he only knows the hard way.

And then we hugged a bloody sweaty hug that has never left me.

Kincannup 2016

1

Our Kincannup house has a long and steep flight of stairs. Stairs are not sensible in the house of an aging couple, but we keep them, and the house, because we know the movement up and down is good for us, our legs, our willingness to keep challenging ourselves, not to give in to the flab and complacency of old age.

It was good to return, asked Froukje, to see her again?

It was, I said. Thank you.

Before I left, I had not been sure, but Froukje insisted I meet Neeva and reconcile. I dug around my bag and showed her the dove of peace.

That is special. You must put it on your car key ring.

You think I should?

Israel is where we met, it inhabits our souls, and every day you go to your car you can think peace. If we all did that it might make a difference.

Froukje and I were romantic socialists when we met on Nir Zamit and we still are. Nothing pleases me more than when she comes home to reveal she has given money to a friend in need, or a stranger. Or gone out of her way to take an injured friend shopping. Or to do the shopping for her and drive the goods twenty-five kilometres out of town. Her sense of community runs deep and her kindness she wears in the open.

There was an old saying once, long passed over, that if you were young and not a socialist, you had no heart, and if you were old and not a capitalist, you had no sense. We have accumulated enough capital to live comfortably, and enough to give to those less fortunate, less able, less endowed, less privileged, less lucky.

There are two beggars in this town I keep an eye out for. One is a Noongar man with a smile, a sense of humour and quick wit. Last time I met him, he asked if he could borrow a couple of dollars.

No, I said. A couple is not enough.

I handed him ten.

You, brother, he said, will be repaid for your generosity. Not by me, but by the Lord God above.

Then he laughed a laugh that ran across his face and all over mine. He is never drunk, or drugged, but clearly battling demons that won't leave him, yet cannot dismantle his humour.

The other beggar is an aggressive chap who stops me in the street with a smoke in his hand, demanding five dollars. The first time we met I gave him five, then I saw him at an ATM withdrawing funds. I see him often, and never without a cigarette in his hand. I save all my money for my Noongar brother.

2

There was a rocket attack from Gaza on Sderot, a southern Israeli city. The military responded with dozens of strikes against Hamas targets deep in Gaza. Whenever such violence erupts, I cry for all the people I know on both sides of the three-hundred-metre buffer zone between Israel and Gaza. Shlomo and his co-workers in the dairy as they run to the bomb shelter, and Mustapha and his family, crouching low in their houses, trying to stay calm, or hiding in basements, both groups worrying about the safety of their friends on the other side and probably condemning the actions of those claiming to act on their behalf.

Here in Kincannup, I have secular Jewish friends who don't tell anyone they are Jewish and who have never been to Israel. My journey fascinates them. I have Muslim Indonesian friends, Catholic Filipino friends and English Anglican friends. We all live not far from each other in ways that different ethnic, cultural and religious groups once lived side by side in Damascus, Isfahan, Beirut and Jerusalem. Noongar elders regularly welcome us at public events and offer new insights into the history, geography and habits of this land. In the rephrased words of Woody Guthrie:

This land is your land, this land is my land
From the Kalgan River to the Mistaken Island
From the jarrah forest, to the Leeuwin Current waters
This land was made for you and me

I have invited all my old friends from all those troubled lands to join me here, in this place of peace and goodwill, but most of them cannot because of restrictive immigration rules and regulations. Old friends from Israel have had their visas rejected, no reasons given.

A Palestinian friend and her family managed to get in before the shutters came down. Her parents had fled East Jerusalem in 1967 as the Israelis stormed into territory not granted in 1948. The family headed for Amman, Jordan, moved to Cairo and kept moving and settled in London. But that was not far enough from their troubles and memories and so, they thought, which city is the most remote city on the planet, where we will know no-one, no-one will find us and we can make a life that is so different from our previous lives that they will seem like dreams? Her father read a story about Australia, and Perth was mentioned as a city of note because there was no city on any other continent so far from the next city. We're going to Perth, he told them.

Once a year this friend visits Kincannup and we sit in the Whalers Retreat and laugh and drop our faces at the latest news and she never asks if I've ever been to Gaza and I never say I haven't because she knows I haven't and that I have no need to go and I have no need to visit a refugee camp because I had been to Soweto in 1972, when Nelson Mandela was safely locked up on Robben Island and apartheid was at its height and I don't need to go to more museums that display the highest level of depravity, brutality and inhumanity of the species, because I have been to Yad Vashem, the Holocaust museum in Jerusalem, to the Genocide Museum in Yerevan, Armenia, to the Ebrat Museum of torture in Tehran and the Hiroshima Peace Memorial Park. There is only so much misery a person should take in.

There was another place I once visited, as the young Jack Muir, the boy. It was 1967, two years out of high school. We were parked next to the entrance of the Department of Native

Welfare reserve in Pingelly. Young Jack and his friends were waiting for a man who said he would sell them a bottle of whisky. It was late, long after the local pub had closed, and they were underage. They thought he was a white man and he may well have been, but when he directed them out to the reserve they got suspicious and only gave him five dollars and told him he would get the other five when he returned with the whisky. He promised he would.

I might even bring back young Joy, he said. She likes white boys.

Young Muir felt a rush of anticipation and disgust, all at once. They never saw the man again. Relief. Morality intact. For then. It didn't last long.

Young Muir never entered a Noongar reserve, and old Muir was relieved he hadn't because he knew it was immoral and evil to enclose entire families behind a fence and allow representatives of authority to enter at will and take children. Or outsiders the freedom to take advantage of their disadvantage.

From my old kibbutz, I could see the fence that held in Gazans and I knew that everything that entered, or left, was controlled by the two abutting powers, Israel and Egypt. Whenever I thought of Egypt and Israel, I remembered Asim, the Egyptian I shared a prison cell with in Amsterdam and his girlfriend, Rachel, the Israeli.

I am old now, but I find myself returning to socialism, not the socialism of the totalitarian states, Stalin's USSR, Mao's China, Ceausescu's Romania, Tito's Yugoslavia, but the socialism of the kibbutz, where everyone gave according to their ability and received according to their need. Where no member could own a television set unless it was available to every other member. And nothing happened until it had been argued about, in the weekly community meeting, in the field, dairy, factory, over meals, coffee, on paths, in bedrooms and on tractors, in cars, busses and even through walls as members abluted in community toilet blocks.

If it wasn't for kibbutzniks, their toughness, resilience, ability to live on very little, to fight hard and long, then there may never have been an Israel. They have always been a small percentage of the Israeli population, but their contributions have always surpassed expectations. Just think of the warriors David Ben-Gurion, Moshe Dayan and the writer Amos Oz. Among those who visited, like the young Jack Muir, were comedians Jerry Seinfeld and Sacha Baron Cohen, actors Debra Winger and Bob Hoskins, and singers Alanis Morissette and Simon Le Bon.

Roger Simpson is a friend of mine. He is a committed member of the Australian Labor Party and constantly refers to left and right factions.

I don't know how you can use such terms, Roger, I said.

There's no real left in the Labor Party. It's all right, just different shades, but the shades are so close you need a colour consultant to pick them.

That's just what I am, Jack, a colour consultant.

We were in our favourite café in Binalup. Every morning Simpson and I rise early and head for the beach, whatever the conditions – wind direction, temperature, rainfall. We arrive about the same time, greet each other and our co-plungers, remove our dry clothes and run into the slightly warm, cold, or bloody cold, Southern Ocean. It's an interesting contradiction, the Southern Ocean, victim of two currents, one warm and the other cold. They meet just offshore and we swimmers never know which will be in control of the water we enter.

This place of the honourable and ancient Noongar Menang was once a thriving whaling town, thus the name, Whalers Retreat. The last whale was harpooned and dragged into the whaling station in 1978 and opinions still vary on the industry's demise. Some say it was all about economics because the world had stopped buying cosmetics with whale oil. But not Roger Simpson.

Bloody Greenpeace closed it down, Simpson says. If the government had had guts we'd still be hunting because there's more whales out here now than ever.

Simpson is, of course, for the working man. He has to be, it's an essential component of his political dogma.

All those poor buggers put out of work, he said. It was all right for the owners, the rich pricks, they walked off with pockets bulging and their guts falling out of their pants.

What did the Labor Party do, Roger, when it was in power last time, to address the ever-widening gap between the rich and the poor?

I know what you're going to say next, but it's too late, Jack. Socialism got a bad rap under the communists.

Simpson will never know true socialism. For him it will

only ever be a story told by Jack Muir. Socialism was one of the drivers that took young Jack to Israel. Even if he did not realise it then, it was where he needed to be to set him on the path towards the old Jack, me. Young Jack wanted to live on a kibbutz. The religious symbols of his Christian youth were of no interest to him. He didn't want to be in Bethlehem at Christmas. And Nazareth and Jerusalem were only of interest because they were places of conflict between the West Bank Palestinians and the Israelis.

That first day I wandered the streets of Tel Aviv looking for the kibbutz office, before I had met Neeva, Gina, or Froukje, in my hand I held a note a South African Jew had written on a piece of paper. The streets were hot, busy, unfriendly. I asked for directions twice, from young people, one with a submachine gun over his shoulder. He sent me down a street that I turned back up after receiving new directions from a young woman with flaming eyes. I walked, and walked, one way then another. Eventually my eyes met those of a bent old man with a walking stick. He reminded me of my grandfather. He stopped when he saw me and I stopped with him. He looked like he had survived everything. I imagined him in a concentration camp.

Where are you going, young man? he asked.

I am looking for a kibbutz office, I said.

Eyze kibbutz?

I'm sorry?

Which kibbutz office?

I handed him the note. He glared at me.

Are you a true socialist? he asked.

I think I am.

Well then, you don't want this kibbutz office. This office is *kharra*, the people there know shit about socialism. You want this office. This is the office for a socialist. This office is from the Mapam, true socialists, not the Mapai, the pretenders.

I had no idea what he was talking about, but I never forgot

his introduction to kibbutz politics, or the contrast between his tortured body and the fire and life in his eyes. He pulled out a pen and wrote on the back of the paper. I watched him walk away, not wanting him to. I never saw him again. He was right. He sent me to the perfect office, to Kibbutz Artzi, a hotbed of socialist activity, argument and philosophical conflict that was going to change my life.

Iran 2017

I wasn't ready for the tears, as the plane landed at Shiraz International Airport. The man sitting next to me was busy with his nerves and didn't notice my wet eyes. He was an Australian on a visit to his family home and, he told me, always broke out in cold sweats for take-offs and landings. He wasn't worried about his reception at the immigration desk, as his family were not Baha'i, Sunni or any other group that might be questioned, but simple businesspeople with a long history of international trade.

I asked him why it was that the Baha'is were singled out for particularly brutal treatment.

Their founder broke away from Shia Islam, he said. It's the same thing, why Sunnis hate Shias – they broke away. Why Jews hated the first Christians – they broke away. Why Catholics hated the first Protestants. It's a human thing. It's why I hate that bloke who once worked for me and went down the road and set up in competition.

You're not religious?

Not me, mate, and Iran needs people like me. I'm one of those who does business – we keep our mouths shut and we don't make trouble. But if you were to ask me why I left, it is because I have three daughters. I have nothing more to add, except to say that they are very happy and one is already in university studying international law.

I had travelled to Iran in search of Arieh, not to see him, because he was dead, but to know something about the place he came from.

I soon discovered Shiraz was a city of poets, where you might meet an illiterate man who could recite entire books by Hafez, the most renowned of all the renowned.

I woke early on the first morning and walked the main street up towards the Karim Khan Citadel, built in the Zand dynasty that ruled Iran briefly in the seventeen hundreds. It was already hot and there was a distinct smell of cats' piss. I tried to find other smells, but the cats dominated.

On my way back to the hotel two young women walked past and one said: Good morning, sir.

Sobh bekheyr, I replied.

She continued to converse with her companion in English.

What do you think, she asked, is he English, or Iranian?

I'm not sure, said the other.

They laughed as I stepped onto the road, still glancing back at their open, joyous and laughing faces under hijabs hardly covering their hair. When I got to the island in the middle of the road I neglected to look in the direction of the oncoming traffic behind me. I heard the car too late and its left side mirror clipped my jacket, and left me standing, marvelling at my life. The driver heard something, looked quickly behind him, waved, and drove on. He didn't stop, get out and yell and scream and lunge at me, simply offered a friendly wave. I looked again for the young women but they had hurried on and left me and my knees to shake alone.

Arieh, I said aloud, first day in Iran and I almost joined you.

Later that day I visited the tomb of Hafez and saw budgerigars on the arms of men, poised above boxes of cards, waiting for money to change hands, so they could peck from the boxes, at random, Hafez solutions to love problems. In 1959, I travelled north to the Pilbara with my parents and marvelled as thousands of budgerigars painted the sky green, yellow and black in great flocks that seemed to bodysurf the sky. I couldn't watch the captured, clipped birds as, on command, they picked a quote from a box. I couldn't imagine the wine-drinking, freedom-loving Hafez filling his garden with birds clipped and controlled. Once inside the walled garden my nostrils were relieved with smells from the cypresses and flowers around Hafez's tomb.

Arieh wasn't dead when I saw him last, on Kibbutz Nir Zamit, when he visited while on leave from the army. He looked tired, exhausted. I worried about him. He was in a despondent mood. A heavy mood did not suit him, given his face already carried a natural weightiness. We didn't wrestle naked and probably our time for that had passed anyway. We were older, both of us had loved and lost, and so instead we walked and talked.

Don't worry about me, Jack, he said. Don't forget I am a Jew from Iran. We had to fight many to survive. First, we survived Nebuchadnezzar, then Cyrus saved us from slavery, only to suffer, like all Iranians, from the enslaving by Greeks, Mongols, Turks, Russians, British, even Americans. If I can defeat all of them, what is the Israel Defense Force to me? You know how many Iranian Jews there are in the IDF?

A lot, I said.

A lot? One. Me. Where are the others? Did they buy their way out? Did they come to get away from the Shah and leave to get away from the IDF?

There must be more.

Of course there are more, but where are they? Are they all chefs, because, you know, there is no food on this earth better than Iranian food? You've met my mother. You have tasted her food.

One weekend in 1974, we had travelled together from Gavrot to Haifa and met his mother, who had probably worked the entire week preparing the sumptuous meal with hard-boiled eggs, lamb, three kinds of rice with vegetables I couldn't name. She was a tiny, quiet, yet flustered woman, who seemed to want to hide from any hint of conversation. There were three of us

230

in the weekend party – Arieh, Yousef from Turkey, and David from Argentina. We were an interesting mix. Yousef wanted to be a conductor and composer and David a photographer. Arieh wasn't sure. He had expended so much energy living and fighting, he found it hard to settle on the idea of a profession. After our meal we explored the Haifa night-life and came home early because we failed to find it.

I was the only non-Jew, but we were brothers. They had all arrived on Gavrot in a party of workers from Tel Aviv, city folk sent out to help pick apples. Arieh was the only one to stay. Yousef had the best command of English and when he spoke he waved his hands in front of us, conducting our responses and we swayed, rose and shrank in unison. He was a visionary.

My people may well have emanated, said Yousef, in the immediate sense, from Turkey, but we are, in essence, from everywhere, and have inhabited every place, except, I do believe, that vast southern continent from which comes our glorious brother Jack. And now, take a peek at all of us. Can you tell me, in all truth, that we look the same, like the stereotypical Jew? No, my brothers, we all look more like the people from the places we have come. David looks Argentinian. Arieh looks Iranian. And I, we cannot escape this fact, look like a bloody Turk.

When Yousef spoke we expected to be spellbound and to laugh. Every year the internet has existed, I have loaded search engines and attempted to find him, to discover him leading a highly regarded Bulgarian orchestra, or to read of the latest composition by the famous composer who once worked on a kibbutz.

Late in my year on Nir Zamit, David surprised me as I left the dairy after an afternoon shift. We hugged and he took me to a tree, which we didn't climb, because he couldn't, but it was there he wanted to tell me about Arieh.

He died under a train, Jack, he said. He was on reservist duty and his platoon was on a patrol near that railway line running close to Jordan. The troop carrier they were in attempted to cross the line before the train but it blew a tyre and the train smashed into them. Only one death and it had to be our brother. All those people he survived to make it to here and then one shitty little tyre blows and he is killed by a train.

And that's why I went to Iran, to pay homage to a brother.

It was no longer a country run by a royal dictator, but one run by a religious dictator. The more I learnt, the more I thought of Rome. The Ayatollah reminded me of Augustus, the way he manipulated the system, clearing out the senate, packing it with his own appointments and having elections for various official positions that seemed to hold power, yet all the power resided in Augustus, his wife Livia, and his small group of advisers and confidants, including the great general, Agrippa. Augustus also had his Praetorian Guard and thugs who would intimidate opposition, maybe do away with them. The Supreme Leader of Iran had his Revolutionary Guards and the Basij and no-one got into parliament, or to be prime minister, without the approval of the Council of Elders and the Supreme Leader.

But there are always exceptions and I met one at the airport, the Revolutionary Guard in the pillbox at the end of the immigration queue. I was in a long queue and his queue was shorter, so I stepped over the barrier rope and joined his line. As I did so I felt a hand on my shoulder from someone behind me. I turned. It was my Australian Iranian friend from the plane.

Don't intimidate the guards, he said. They can do what they like with you.

I looked up to see the guard smiling and waving me on. When I got to face him in his box, he looked at my passport and said: Australian. Good.

And you, I said, Iranian, good.

He laughed then, stamped quickly and ushered me through.

In Iran I saw many men who looked like Arieh and when I nodded at them all, not one said: What are you looking at? They politely nodded back, those with beards, those without. Even the women nodded and smiled. Some stopped me and asked where I was from and when I said Australia they smiled and said Australia was a good country. When I asked where they were from they laughed and said, Iran, of course.

It was the friendliest country I had ever visited and made all the stories I had heard and read seem no more than a stack of lies made up to denigrate an entire people. It made me think of the lies made up to denigrate, humiliate and to subjugate Jewish people, Arieh's other people, in their long and bitter struggle to find a place to be safe.

Back in Shiraz International Airport and this time the Revolutionary Guard on duty at the security checkpoint was not laughing, was not pleasant, and frisked me in a way that made me question his motives. He ran his hands all over me, up into my crotch, where he stayed too long, moved down my legs and up again to linger and squeeze my left pocket before running his index finger and thumb across to the front of my pants, where he searched for my penis, found it, and gave it a firm pinch. I took the advice of my travel agent, said nothing, did nothing, until I walked away, then turned back midstride and said: Thank you, very thorough.

I had a clear plan for Tehran. Once settled in my boutique hotel, off Asad Abadi Street, I sought out a café for fine coffee and conversation. Not far down one street and across another, I found the Lamiz Café, favoured, I discovered, by filmmakers, poets, novelists and professionals with artistic temperaments. Like Vahid, a lawyer, who really wanted to make movies. And Morteza, a doctor who wrote poetry.

It was there I met Siavash, an engineer, who found time to

audition for bit parts in Iranian movies and, occasionally, secure a role. We met one morning when he asked where I was from, why I was in Iran, and what I intended to do with my time.

Mr Jack Muir, he said, it would be my pleasure if you would allow me to take leave from my work and be your tour guide.

You serious? I asked.

Is the Ayatollah a Muslim? he said.

That night I had a dream set in Lamiz Café. A movie was being shot in the café. Siavash was the love interest and when I walked in I was somehow absorbed into the film and the leading lady took a fancy to me. Siavash didn't seem to mind at all and when I asked him how he felt about her interest in me he said: It's only a movie, *dadash*. Eventually you will walk out, go home, and everything will return to normal.

What's normal? I asked.

Exactly.

There's a scene shift and I'm sitting with the leading lady. Her name is Lakshmi. She looks at me with eyes that gleam, entice and suggest. I can smell her but cannot recall the smell yet know it so well I can remember the danger it portends and her lips are parted for tasting.

He doesn't get it, she says. Her silky voice floats around the room and somehow finds its way to my ears.

Who?

Siavash. He doesn't understand that this is real, not a movie, and that I love you and want to be with you.

When I entered Lamiz Café the next day, Siavash was not there and I found myself looking at all the women in the hope I would find Lakshmi. She was not there and I was glad of it because I remembered I was happily married to my best friend and I missed her.

I got a message from Siavash to say that he couldn't join me, because something had come up and he would meet me the next day. After coffee and a chat with a finance broker who really wanted to be a sculptor, I went looking for CD shops in memory of Laleh and Leonard Cohen. Not only was he there, there were also CDs by a famous Iranian folk singer doing Leonard covers. There was no sign of Laleh.

Tehran's streets were full of women wearing hijabs, some completely covering their hair, most just off the forehead, some halfway across the skull and some clinging, as though on a cliff edge, as though their existence depended on the clinging, to the back of the head. And I saw three who had clearly abandoned any head covering.

The heat was searing my own head. I looked around. There was barely a man in a hat. Did the heat on the cranium add to the fervour of the religiously hot-headed? The hijab that fell over the ears and the neck made sense. I took my fibre towel from my backpack, removed my narrow-brimmed hat, put the towel over my head and replaced the hat. This protected my ears and my neck and worked, as I walked, as a cooling device.

I found an antique shop run by a Jewish family. I had entered on a whim having been told that many of the antique dealers in Iran were Jewish. When approached by the man from behind the counter, I asked him if he was Jewish.

I am, he said.

Have you ever been to Israel?

Yes.

Why don't you live there?

The man looked like many of the men in the street outside his shop, except for the kippa he wore on his head, under a hat, which he removed to reveal the evidence. He was short, stocky, with a long, neat beard. If I had seen him outside, without the kippa, I would not have said: There's a Jew. I remembered that first day in Tel Aviv, when I wandered the streets looking for the Jew. I saw redheads, blonds, people who looked Middle Eastern,

African, Indian, Chinese. And, every so often, someone who looked like the stereotype. This man looked Iranian.

Why would I live in Israel? he asked. I am Iranian. This is my country. My people have been here for three thousand years. Israel is good for those European Jews and others who have suffered from anti-Jewish attitudes, but I am a free man here. As free as those people in the street you came from. As free as the Supreme Leader will allow. I could leave tomorrow, and many Jews have already left. We are now down to maybe twenty thousand, from somewhere near two hundred thousand. Why did they leave? Many were frightened after the Islamic Revolution and many were Zionists. Some bad things happened, yes, but I will never leave.

Have you ever heard of a man called Arieh Sadieh? He was my best friend when I lived in Israel. He left Iran in the early nineteen seventies.

The name I have heard, but I did not know that man. Is he here, or is he there?

He was killed. He told me he lived in a poor part of Tehran. There was another name that I remember from my time in Israel. Her name was Laleh but I don't know her family name.

We Jews are in every country, even now, even some countries that do not want us. Here in Iran, we have a better life than a Sunni Muslim, because they are Arab, and we are Jew, and our religion is one of the two oldest religions, along with Zoroastrianism. As for Laleh, well, it is a Persian name and means tulip, the flower. You know this plant? But I might ask you if you know an Australian called Tom?

Have you ever felt insulted, or been attacked for being a Jew?

Sometimes such things happen, but you must remember, the largest group in Iran is Persian, and Persians think of themselves as among the world's most civilised and sophisticated of peoples. The real Persian is proud of his sophistication, his education and his place in history.

What about the anti-Israeli rhetoric?

This can upset, but it depends. When I see *Death to Israel* on a wall, I don't like it, but if there are protests about what Israel does in Gaza, then I protest too, because I am Iranian, and I don't like to see such brutality. Iranians don't hate Jews, they hate the government of Israel. They don't hate Judaism, they don't like Zionism. And they can tell the difference. Also, we don't hate Americans, we hate the government of the United States. And like all Iranians, we don't hate other Iranians, but everybody hates the government. Okay, not everybody, not the Revolutionary Guards and not the Basij, and most clerics.

He bent down under the counter and came back with a bottle of clear liquid.

If we are going to keep talking, he said, I better pour us a vodka.

Is it wise to drink alcohol in the middle of Tehran?

I thought the old man's head would explode, so loud was his laugh.

This is Iran, he said, a civilised country. If you are Muslim of course, for you it is forbidden, but not for me, or any Jew, or Christians. We can have alcohol in our own places.

Mamnoon. Thank you. But I don't drink alcohol.

No alcohol? You must be a lucky man with a good life free of all suffering. I congratulate you.

The old man was warm and generous and reminded me of another old Jew, one who wore his *kippah* for all to see, who gave me a book in a Johannesburg backstreet. I had been wandering, aimless, looking for something, I didn't know what. Then I saw the bookshop, almost hidden in a clutter of shopfronts laden with old furniture, second-hand clothes and bric-a-brac. I entered and made my way down stacked shelves and had to move my head in all directions to read titles. On one shelf I found Herman Hesse's *Steppenwolf*, took it out and discovered another beside it that seemed out of place. I took them both to the old man behind the front desk.

I found this in the wrong section, I said.

He looked at it. Turned it over.

Jew Süss, he said. Have you heard of this book? Do you want it?

It is a hardcover and I found it stuck in among paperbacks. What does the title mean?

It means Sweet Jew. And are you buying the Herman Hesse, *Steppenwolf*?

Yes.

Okay, so you can have this one, free of charge.

You serious?

Of course. Do I look like a joker?

Thank you very much.

There was laughter in his eyes.

This, he said, is a great story of greed and power and triumph over evil. That you have found it on the wrong shelf means it was meant for you.

I shook his hand and left the shop with hope.

As I left the Tehran shop, I noted there was a major difference between Israel and Iran that the antique dealer and I had failed to mention – Iranians had always been the majority in twentieth-century Iran, whereas Jews had not long been the dominant group in Israel.

Siavash eventually made contact and took me to a traditional restaurant for lunch. It was full of schoolgirls wearing uniforms and hijabs and behaving in ways you would expect – giggling, pointing, squealing. Three of them kept looking at me. I smiled. They came to our table.

What country are you from? asked the tallest of the three.

Australia. And what country are you from?

Iran.

The room erupted with laughter, Siavash led the way, closely followed by the girls and a man sitting close by with two crutches leaning up against the wall behind him. As the laughter faded, the music took over. The musicians sat on a raised platform above the tables and played a song that must have been distinctly Iranian but sounded like a fusion of Middle Eastern, Greek, Indian, with traces of Africa. I couldn't sit still. The girls couldn't sit still. The man with crutches was unable to control his head, gently rocking to the rhythm. He left before us and as he passed our table he stopped and spoke perfect English.

You sir, he said, I enjoyed your jokes and your dancing. We need more like you to visit us.

He held out his hand and as I took his I looked down.

You remember the eight-year war between Iran and Iraq? he said. When the West supported Saddam Hussein? I was in the Revolutionary Guards, in the frontline. I was young and brave and mad. Now I am old and frightened and still mad.

He said it all with no hint of bitterness and the smiles did not leave our mouths and I stood up as he leant in and insisted we touch cheeks. But he hadn't finished.

No doubt you have heard of Hafez, he said. But have you heard of a man who was perhaps even a greater poet, Saadi Shirazi? Let me give you a taste.

Human beings are members of a whole,
In creation of one essence and soul.
If one member is afflicted with pain,
Other members uneasy will remain.
If you have no sympathy for human pain,
The name of human you cannot retain.

As Siavash and I walked through markets, down alleyways and into small cafés selling Turkish coffee, the broken old warrior's words lingered and a part of me felt less than whole, because Arieh was not with me.

Arieh, brother, I said under my breath, your line lived long and strong for all of human history, until you, but even then, you lived on, in the memory of others. In these streets, cafés, places where five choices of rice dish are not enough, where sohan, baklava, almonds, dried figs and walnuts vie for space on wide tables, alongside a multitude of other delicacies of your youth. All these things are piled high and enjoyed by your brother, Jack Muir, born Australian, owned by the world. And here, in this place, one of civilisation's cradles, I feel guilt, for nowhere have so many people come to me unannounced and offered food, hospitality, conversation. There has been no yelling, no rejection, striking, beating of this battered and aging body, nothing to suggest anything other than a civilised society based on respect and human kindness. Newspapers and television stations tell other stories and many of them, of course, must be true – but is it not the same for all countries? Is not Israel itself a mixture of wondrous glory, beauty, kindness and love and, alongside, unimaginable brutality, death, destruction and separation of peoples based on religion, ethnicity, economic wealth and skin colour?

That night I went to Siavash's house for dinner.

In the party around the large round table were Siavash's wife, his son and daughter and his immediate neighbour and his wife. And Siavash's mother. When I saw her, I wanted to cry out loud and had great difficulty maintaining composure. Standing before me was Arieh's mother – tiny, quiet, easily flustered and wanting to hide from any hint of conversation. The dinner started late and ended very late. Among the dishes were boiled eggs, three concoctions of rice and a fried trout. I ate well and long and answered all questions asked: Why are you here in Iran? Is it true that you lived in Israel? Why does Australia lock up refugees?

When it was time to leave, I held his mother's hand for too long, but both of us, although feeling awkward, refused to let go.

It was 2.30 in the morning when Siavash dropped me back at my hotel. He said the others would stay on longer.

This is how we eat in Iran, he said. And we sleep in the next day.

Your mother, Siavash, I said, she reminded me of Arieh's mother. It was why I had to stand up and wash some dishes. I hope I did not offend you.

It was funny, Jack, no-one visits another person's house in Iran and washes dishes.

She was so much like that old Jewish woman in Haifa, the mother of my best friend. They could be sisters.

Maybe they were. My mother grew up in the time of the Shah, she longs for the Shah. She carries deep pain from what happened after and she never talks. We know nothing of her own family.

I slept well that night, part of me believing I had found a relative of Arieh's and that I had closed a circle.

Kincannup 2018

1

Tony's new kitchen hand at the Whalers Retreat, a backpacker from Lithuania, had absconded with the till and ten bottles of wine.

Dammit, Tony, I said. How much did he get?

Just the till, Jack, he said. There was nothing in it. I'd emptied it before I went home. The thieving bugger got here early this morning and ripped it out, probably took it out bush to smash. He'll have a laugh when he finds the contents.

How did he get in?

I gave him a key three days ago. Was starting to trust him.

I pulled on the apron, gathered up early-morning cups and plates after the swimmers, loaded up the dishwasher and set to on the pots, pans, and large plates. In no time I was in the zone.

A tap on my shoulder brought me back. It was Roger Simpson, the theoretical socialist.

What about a coffee when you're done here? he said. Some of that stuff you call *botz*?

When I'm done here, Simmo, I'm sitting down over there. Tony can make us both a coffee, that's all the payment I'll get anyway.

You bloody commos, you never learn, do you?

The plates kept coming. It was a busy morning. A bus load of tourists arrived from Perth. They clustered around the counter in twos and threes, attempting to form a queue, forming, disbanding, reforming, finally settling into what looked like a family at a jumble sale.

Tony, I yelled, send Simmo in, he can stack the dishwasher while I keep ahead of the old people.

It was a glorious morning for washing dishes – the plates kept sliding, the cups tumbling and the cutlery clattering. After the jumble sale left, the baby boomers headed home for a nap and the working folk were back in their pigeonholes, we sat down for coffee and a small breakfast. I had my usual, poached eggs on toast, and Simpson loaded up with fried eggs and bacon.

Tony, said Simpson, given how hard we worked, I reckon you could ignore your bloody capitalist profit motive for a change and throw in some cake.

You blokes, said the laughing capitalist, wouldn't know how to spell hard work.

Israel lives in our memories; it will be on our lips when we say goodbye. But it is no longer the place it was, all those years ago. The place where Froukje and I met once had a chemical factory producing plastics and shade cloth and exported its products to Europe. That same factory is now owned by a Tel Aviv private equity firm and it employs workers who live on the kibbutz, thus breaking one of the basic tenets of socialism: that there be no exploitation of many, for the profit of a few. And that other kibbutz, where I met my first love, Neeva, and where I learnt about forgiveness and later forgot what I'd learnt, that place has been privatised and is no longer a kibbutz, more a kind of townhouse development where individuals own houses but common ground is run by the body corporate and where the dining room is a restaurant and the laundry is owned by a bloke from Haifa.

The socialist experiment is over and the political parties of the left, like their colleagues in most modern democracies, have become shadows and only inhabit stories told by aging baby boomers with beards and memories. Israel is not alone, as there are other countries that have lurched to the political right and suffered a sharp decline in a humanitarian spirit, like our own, the fair-go country. Who would have thought Australia would toss refugee women and children into detention camps, scarring them for the rest of their days? Do Froukje and I still believe in the right of Israel to exist? Of course. It has as much right as any country. All countries are contrivances, with boundaries, in many cases, drawn inappropriately, arbitrarily, and by officials from other countries with agendas not aligned with the best interests of those enclosed by the new boundaries. Many nations are shams. Syria was a sham. Iraq, Lebanon, Armenia, Georgia, all on the list of countries suffering ongoing trauma and turmoil because of boundaries drawn by others. Then, of course, there are those who were not considered in those drawings: Kurds, Palestinians, Azeris, Ossetians, Assyrians, Baluchis.

Georgia, up high in the Caucasus, just north of Armenia, is a popular tourist destination for Israelis, as I discovered when I visited after my trip to Iran. Georgians also share a dilemma with Palestinians – how to maintain agreed borders. A tour guide told me that most weeks Russian forces shift the border and most mornings when Georgians wake up, the Russians have taken a little more. Similar events occur in Palestine's West Bank. The locals might wake up one morning and find a new Israeli settlement on their doorstep. And Arab citizens of Israel might come home at night and find their homes have been demolished by Israeli authorities to make way for a new business centre, a museum celebrating Israeli architecture, or a children's playground.

Many Middle Eastern boundaries are blamed on a famous duo – Sykes and Picot. I don't know much about the Frenchman Picot, but Sykes was a classic English explorer. His father was a baron and his mother a lost and lonely drunk. Sykes grew up travelling the Middle East, first as a privileged son and, later, as a colonial wanderer, always with an entourage of attendants, including a small troop of soldiers. He was born to rule, to imagine the world as a place to be carved up between major European powers. He fought in the Boer War, and among his heroes he counted the narcissistic, manic-depressive Emperor Napoleon.

And me, Jack Muir, what am I? Surely, I am also a contrivance, a made-up man, cobbled together from bits and pieces, borrowed, left over from the lives of others, made-up in the moment to suit that very moment. In the beginning, I was an angry, poisoned boy in a boarding school, then a drunken sex addict in a colonial outpost, and a drug-addled hippie in a police state, followed by an idealistic lover in a country once admired by many and now increasingly isolated. One thought, ever present, each and every day as I plunge into the cold waters of the Southern Ocean, and I do, in all weathers, is that Jack Muir, this *Homo sapiens* speck in the history of humanity, is even less than an atom in the history of the universe.

Genoralup 2018

1

We were on a houseboat with Andrew Muir, our father, who was dying. Glorvina had already left us. We always thought she would go first. It is usually the case with the very old – one goes and the other follows soon after. In her last ten years she battled angina and kidney failure and then, finally, admitted her battle with depression. One week before she died, she had been admitted to hospital for a check on all her failures and, almost as soon as she arrived, she began to deteriorate rapidly.

When I arrived in her room she had a visitor, an old family friend, and as soon as we were alone she said: You know, Jack, every night before I fall asleep, I pray to God that I won't wake up in the morning.

Well, I said, he's not listening.

There's something I have to tell you, Jack. You know you asked me sometimes if I was depressed, well, I was, but I never wanted to admit it, because I didn't think it would help you to know. I remember the first time. I was twelve. My parents sent me to stay with an uncle in Kincannup.

Is that why you never visited us after we moved there? I said.

It was a very bad time in my life. My father seemed to hate my mother and we were frightened of him. Did I ever tell you that when I was carrying you, he chased my mother off the family farm?

You didn't, but she did.

I stayed with Uncle Amos, on his dairy farm. He was such a lovely man but very damaged from the war. He was in France, in the artillery I think, and he came home with shell shock. It was a gloomy house and Patricia, my first cousin, was away at boarding school, so I was alone with a traumatised old man and his frightened wife.

Glorvina had been a beautiful young woman and whenever she spoke from deep places, near, close to, or from her core, she softened, grew somehow stronger through the painful revelations, and her beauty shone through and my love for her caused me to shudder.

You all right, dear? she said.

I couldn't answer. And then she shocked me.

I wasn't much of a mother, was I?

It was one of those glorious and painful moments when a person you have known from the beginning of your time opens their heart and soul and all you can do is hold them and thank them for honouring the relationship. She could only admit such pain to me, not Thomas, or Bill. Thomas would have argued with her, dismissed her submission and mounted a defence. Bill would have sat silent beside her, perhaps held her hand. Not Jack, the wild one, the crazy boy who battled his own demons, he knew where it came from and that it required acceptance, acknowledgement. We sat still, staring at each other.

Mum, I said. Thank you. Now I am going to tell you what you did really well, because I think we'll find it's quite a long list.

Like what?

You made the best cakes in Genoralup.

She smiled. I continued.

No-one made a better shortbread biscuit. Ironing. Not a match in town. Later, when you got a woman in to do the ironing, as soon as she left, you had to do it again.

She was laughing then.

And, here's an important truth, you loved deep, deep, deep, and your loyalty was unsurpassed. As my list of misdemeanours mounted, you never once rejected me, you never once denied I was your son and once when I was sick with depression you gave me money so I could go somewhere I probably shouldn't have and you know what kind of a mother that is? That's a mother with deep understanding, courage and love.

She sat up high in the bed and we hugged in a way we had never hugged. She had never been comfortable with the hug and only ever greeted her sons with a peck on the lips. It was when I came home after that first trip to Israel that she forgot the peck and held me.

Only the nurse bustling into the room with her clipboard made Glorvina break her hold.

When she sighed her final breath, I remembered Neeva's mother, another survivor of great courage and love. Together they altered the course of my life.

Glorvina had woken an hour before that last sigh, and the smile she showed then stayed with her as she left.

The three brothers, their wives, partner and children, were all there in the room and after we had walked by, kissed her forehead and stood in a cluster, holding hands and shoulders, Froukje said: In my family, when someone dies, all the men leave the room and the women wash and dress the body.

The men left. The women, led by Froukje, did their work and what fine work it was, because when we returned Glorvina held firm her smile and her beauty.

Andrew Muir was never going to last long. He'd lost his lifelong companion. He did his best but he didn't seem able to focus on anything, to find an interest, a hobby. He was a man in charge all his adult life and after Glorvina had gone, he had nothing left to run, no-one to care for, to order about, to chastise, or to explain complex issues to.

We were on a houseboat with him – Thomas, the oldest, me, and Bill, our younger brother. Dad had an advanced melanoma eating into his liver, lungs and brain. We decided to take him away, fishing, because we had never, all the men of the family, been fishing together. With our separate families left behind, we could be men together in a way we had never been. It was for the best, our partners did not always get along. Thomas had married a woman who was clearly a narcissist. He was a good man, Thomas, and he understood the law, technically, but emotions confused him and he lacked an ability, or willingness, to self-reflect. For his partner he chose a woman who did not require emotional maturity in a man. It was not her fault; she carried a narcissistic wound for which there was probably no cure.

His became a life of importance, prestige, tradition. He arrived at his goals early on – partnership in the well-established law firm, marriage to a woman who loved the social whirl, three children at expensive private schools. My life, it seemed to me, had barely begun and I remained aware of the ongoing journey of self-discovery and a need to determine my greater purpose.

The youngest, Bill, was even stranger to me. He never married. He occasionally turned up to family gatherings with a female friend and we would feign excitement but held no hope. He had a new partner as our father faded. She was a private person and gave nothing of herself, so we knew nothing of her. Froukje said she reminded her of an old lady she once met in a café overrun by women from the Country Women's Association. Froukje was there to help out her friend, the café owner, who was short-staffed.

But, I said, she's not that old.

Maybe not, said Froukje. Perhaps life has been too much for her and she is worn out before her time.

What is Bill doing with her then?

He lives alone. Men are not good on their own.

The trip down the river was Thomas' idea and Bill and I agreed immediately. Thomas didn't think it through the way I did, and when I asked him he said: I just thought it would be nice.

No underlying agenda? I asked.

Like what?

To bring the family closer together, bang our heads and reopen old scars, or heal festering sores?

You haven't changed, have you, Jack? Still digging for deeper meanings. You should have been a barrister. You would have been excellent in a courtroom.

Glorvina had wanted me to study law, believed the skills I had lent themselves to it, the analysis of issues, the pitch battles in the courtroom, and she thought I had a thick skin because I seemed to go off and do things without considering the consequences. But she was wrong. Consequences sat heavy in me. I did, however, enjoy a good argument, especially if it finished with both parties recognising the validity of the opposing position. It was like old friends who fought a good fight, would pummel each other to submission, get up, laugh, hug, forgive, and move on. I took a Jungian view in argument. Andrew said to me, not long before his melanoma diagnosis: You were a cantankerous, argumentative boy.

No I wasn't, I said.

Yes you were.

No I wasn't.

Yes you …

Hang on, when you and I argued, what was your objective?

To have you agree with me. That is the purpose of an argument.

It was never mine, Dad. All I ever wanted was for you to accept who I was, that I might hold a different view, sometimes, perhaps, even agreeing with you, but from a different perspective.

He needed to ponder that suggestion and settled back deeper into the chair he had not long got up from. It was one of those chairs popular with older men, with a footrest that moved forward when the occupier pushed back. He sat leaning forward, not quite ready to rise, or to fall back, then lifted his head and stared at me.

You and I both lived in a country at war, he said. We never talked about that, did we? I'm sorry.

To watch a man you have known all your life as a strong, firm man soften before you, then apologise, in particular for an occurrence, event, or slight perceived on reflection, is a moment to savour, and cherish. He opened before me, but I held back from him. I did not tell him about South Africa, the drug dealers, the drug binges, and I did not mention his first grandchild, the one never born, aborted. I saw the baby in a dream once, dead on a sink, thrown there after torn from his mother's womb, as though waiting to be washed and put in a dish rack among plates, cups and cutlery. I took him, shed tears over his face and blew in his mouth, worked full of fear and desperation to give him life. His mother stood watching me and did nothing to help. I woke with anger, wondering about the image and where it had come from and remembered I once visited the Kincannup Whaling Station and saw a humpback whale embryo dead on a table.

I sometimes pondered Neeva and her decision to abort. It seemed odd to me that I had never asked her for a definitive answer. The army she hated released her, there was no need to abort. Abortions had not been uncommon among Jewish settlers before 1949, there was so much pressure on them to build communities, and the state. And among some American collectives readying themselves to migrate to Palestine, pregnancies were forbidden. But once the nation was born and kibbutzim were settled, babies were welcomed.

War changed us both, Dad, I said. You came home in 1946 and started a family. I came home in 1977 and gave myself some time before starting a family. You gave yourself no time to recover. And I think I'm still recovering.

He lifted himself out of the chair with difficulty and walked towards me, slowly, as though considering his next move.

You want a hug?

I'm not good at it, Jack.

We hugged the hug of the quick and the living. He went back to his chair and I moved into the kitchen. It had become clear to me that as my parents moved through their final weeks, it seemed important for them to reveal long-held secrets. I wondered if I would need that time, later, with my own son.

2

The houseboat was on the Blackwood River, the river of our childhood, of our dreams. The river that taught us to swim, to fish and beside which Andrew Muir once broke off a balga stick and beat me so hard my upper thigh bled. He didn't beat Bill, ever, and he only ever beat Thomas with a light stick. There was something about me that brought out the fire in the man. Perhaps it was because we were so different, he a man of precision, of numbers, plans, capital, collateral and me a man of dreams, reveries, seeking adventure, both physical and spiritual.

The night before we drove out of Genoralup for our male farewells, something happened in his head and, once on the road, he began talking gibberish. Bill stopped his car and I said: Dad, you all right?

Of course I am, he said, with some irritation. What makes you think I'm not?

You want to do this trip?

It was the father I knew well: impatient, annoyed with any sign of incompetence, in himself, anyone around him, or of a loss of control. This was the dad he had been for most of my life, but not the dad he had been for the last eight years, the softer, more reflective dad. The old dad had come back and was sitting beside me, haranguing, challenging.

What's the matter with you boys? he said. Get on with it.

We learnt later from his doctor that his brain had suffered a small stroke and this affected his speech. He seemed better on the boat, but we kept a keen eye on him. On the first night he got us all together around the galley table and said he wanted to talk about his will.

Now look, he said, you three will split it equally.

I put my hand to my mouth and held my breath. He said three? Who is he talking about? What three? Bill and Thomas already owned the business, having bought him out ten years ago. They ran the business from a distance, as directors, and had a long-term manager in place.

When he finished, I left the cabin and climbed up the stairs to the deck and burst into tears. Bill followed.

What's the matter, Jack? he asked.

He said three, I said. I think he meant me.

Who else would he mean?

But you guys own the business, and the house and farm are long gone.

Jack, you know nothing. When was the last time you had a discussion with a member of the family about financial matters?

When Mum handed me that cheque to fly back to Israel.

I didn't know about that.

You know nothing, Bill.

Dad has always had shares in the business and there is more than one house. You'll be able to clear that mortgage of yours and pay off all those old drug debts and court fines.

My body convulsed as my brother consoled me and all the words I never uttered in my father's presence came to me, flooded me, and never left me: After everything you were and were not for me, I still loved you.

He is dead now and yet I hear his voice and I don't think it will ever leave, because it is the voice of that other side of me, the side not fully developed. He was a man it might help me to be more like, a man of reason, sensibility, equilibrium, a careful man. In our last eight years together we grew close, he told me secrets he could never tell another, some I could never tell another, and some I could.

When I was in the air force, I was court-martialled, he said.

You?

For being drunk and disorderly. We had gone into Alice Springs on R&R. It wasn't long since we'd been bombed in Darwin, by the Japanese, so we were a bit haywire. A mate and I ran from the bombs and dived into a lake. For some reason we thought we'd be safer in there. We watched the bombs drop. One dropped on a bloody dunny Johnny Wilson had only just left and he joined us in the lake at a speed that would have made Jesse Owens blush. Anyway, in Alice we bought a dozen beers then headed into the bush. When we'd downed all the grog, we went back to buy more and got into a fight with a mob of blokes from the army. They thought we'd be a pushover but we got stuck into them and the fight finished up out in the street and when the cops came, they arrested the lot of us and because I had a couple of stripes, I got court-martialled. The bastards ripped the stripes right off me.

He sat back, as if he'd run out of words. But he hadn't, he was gathering energy for the next instalment.

There's something you need to know, he said. You remember how your grandfather peppered his stories with Noongar words? Did he tell you about Nookum and Yabbi? They were his best mates as he grew up in the 1890s. Noongar boys. Hardly spoke any English. How do you think he spoke to them?

What are you telling me, Dad?

Your grandfather spoke Noongar.

Fuck, Dad.

Jack, I have a few regrets, and this is another one, that I didn't learn Noongar, that you didn't, that the language didn't live on and we developed a different relationship with Noongars and other Aboriginal people. You know how much I love Froukje?

The goose ran hard. I could hear its feet pounding and feel my eyes preparing for a waterfall.

Her language, Frisian, she said there aren't many native speakers left and I see how much it means to her, to who she is. Dad didn't teach me, and Nookum and Yabbi's mob were pretty much wiped out with the Spanish Flu, then he died, so who could I speak Noongar to? At least when he was young he had his Noongar mates, his Uncle Thomas Muir and his old friend John Bletchynden. I love listening to Froukje when she talks on the phone to her family. Don't let her stop.

Nothing warmed me more than sitting with the man who spawned me, listening to the stories he had kept all his life, had not even told a mate, because he was supposed to be an important, upstanding man, of integrity, of honour, beyond reproach, a justice of the peace, and one who had to pass judgement on the bad behaviour of others. His own softness, regret and bad behaviour could never be known. Unlike his wayward son, whose bad behaviour was sometimes splashed on the front page of a newspaper.

I made him laugh one day when he said: You know, Jack, that son of yours is a much nicer boy than you were at his age.

Of course, Dad, I said, that's because he's got much nicer parents.

He knew that he and Mum started badly, married in 1946, right after the horrors of their war, at a time of economic hardship, when she was in a depressed state and the family was hiding from the shame of her father's affairs. They took some of their frustrations out on their first two sons. I realised their coming good took a lifetime and when I added up the years it took me to come good, there was not a lot of space between the two numbers.

Not long before my father's melanoma grabbed, I stood washing dishes in the sink of his house that faced the Indian Ocean out of Bunbury. They bought it for their retirement. We never understood why. They never liked Bunbury, a drab, dull town that was a halfway place between the bush and Perth.

Why here, Dad? I asked as I rinsed, shook and stacked. You don't surf, swim, you don't even walk along the beach. You no longer fish.

He leant down to take a tea towel from a drawer and, as he stood up, he put an arm around my shoulders.

I've often asked myself the same, Jack, he said. And I think you will understand the answer, because I've got a little bit of you in me. I think it's because I like looking at the ocean. From our front room, I can see all the way to everywhere.

Acknowledgements

This novel was written in Noongar Menang Boodja, a place that sustains me through its elders, past and present, its landscape and arts community.

This is the third book in a series about Jack Muir's journey to manhood. I have worked on all three with Georgia Richter. The relationship has been full of meaning, hard work and joy. Georgia has been everything I could have wished for in an editor.

Unlike earlier works, this book only had three early readers – the exuberant yet serious and funny author Brooke Davis, my lost-then-found cousin Jai Friend, and the handsome yet humble Nigel Brennan.

Nothing is ever written without help and so I must thank the much honoured Great Southern writer Dianne Wolfer for her Windy Harbour retreat and her encouragement and friendship. The Southern Salties, my early-morning, all-year swimming companions, for their cheek, their conversation and occasional coffee shouts – we swim all year round, and most mornings gather at Bay Merchants, at Binalup (Middleton Beach), for a laugh, a ruckus and a hot cocoa. And one Noongar man of the world, Kim Scott, for offering a piece of advice I accepted and kept: Jon, keep your mouth shut until the novel is done.

Then there are my Noongar Menang spiritual brothers and sisters. In my time in Menang Boodja, these people have shared insights, friendship and a deep love of place and community.

For his assistance with Hebrew words in the novel, Gadi Barak, and an Australian of South African heritage, Piet Claassen, for his conversation, insight and love of Turkish coffee. Thanks also to Naama Grey-Smith for her fine proofing and honed insight.

There are three women in the dedication of this novel. All of them made decisions that changed my life and one of them – Grietje – is still with me.

The quote from Louis Aragon on p.68 is from *Auschwitz Testimonies, 1945–1986*, Primo Levi, Polity Books, 2018. The quote from Kahlil Gibran on p.175 is from *The Prophet*, Heinemann, London, 1971. The poem of Saadi Shirazi on p.239 decorates the entrance of the United Nations Organization building in New York.

The writing of this book received early assistance, in 2014, from the Department of Local Government, Sport and Cultural Industries.

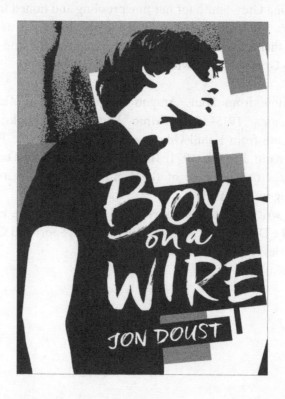

Dedicated to all those boys who carried their scars into manhood, *Boy on a Wire* is about an underdog who bites back. Sent to boarding school at a young age, Jack Muir has to decide who he is going to be. Will he roll over or bare his teeth at the bullies, the bullied and the boarding school system? Jack gets by with a quick wit and humour – but not everyone is so lucky. This novel depicts alienation and the beginnings of depression with poignancy and humour.

'*... a writer with a distinctive voice and an uncanny ability to capture the bewilderment and burgeoning anger of a boy struggling to remain true to himself while navigating the hypocritical system he finds himself trapped in ... If you know an angry teenager, give this to him.*' The Age

and at all good bookstores

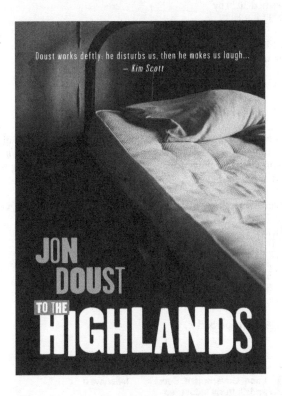

It is 1968. All around the world people are marching, protesting, fighting for freedom and free love. Jack Muir arrives in the islands fresh out of Grammar School: a failure, a virgin, and a reluctant employee of The Colonial Bank of Australia. Life in the islands is raw, sensuous, real. Here, the white man takes what he wants. But the veneer of whiteness is flimsy, and brutality never far from the surface. 'To be free, you must set free.' So says George Kanluna, future leader of the islands. Yet there is a world of difference between freedom and those things you unleash in others – and in yourself.

'There is a relentless rawness to this book that make its moments of tenderness hit their mark even more keenly.' Books+Publishing

First published 2020 by
FREMANTLE PRESS
25 Quarry Street, Fremantle WA 6160
(PO Box 158, North Fremantle WA 6159)
www.fremantlepress.com.au

Cover image Kolderal, 'Man watching sunset above desert landscape', Getty Images.
Printed by McPherson's Printing, Victoria, Australia.
Return Ticket

A catalogue record for this
book is available from the
National Library of Australia

9781925816396 (paperback)

Department of
**Local Government, Sport
and Cultural Industries**

Fremantle Press is supported by the State Government through the Department of
Local Government, Sport and Cultural Industries.

**Australia
Council
for the Arts**

Australian Government

Publication of this title was assisted by the Commonwealth Government through
the Australia Council, its arts funding and advisory body.

MIX
Paper from
responsible sources
FSC® C001695